A Nightcreature Novel

USA TODAY BESTSELLING AUTHOR

THUNDER MOON

Desire will take them by storm.

Don't Miss These
Other Novels From
Bestselling Author
Lori Handeland

HIDDEN MOON
RISING MOON
MIDNIGHT MOON
CRESCENT MOON
DARK MOON
HUNTER'S MOON
BLUE MOON

Available from
St. Martin's Paperbacks

...And turn to the back
of this book for an exclusive
excerpt from

ANY GIVEN DOOMSDAY

Coming soon from
St. Martin's Paperbacks

OUTSTANDING PRAISE FOR LORI HANDELAND

RISING MOON

"Eerie atmospherics and dark passion intertwine, making this a truly gripping and suspenseful read."
—Romantic Times BOOKreviews

"What makes the latest in her Nightcreature series stand out is how Handeland paints such a vivid portrait of the Big Easy and its inhabitants. The city itself is a character, not unlike its real-life counterpart . . . her gift to skillfully repel and attract commands the reader's attention to the very end and will lure genre readers enamored of paranormal romance or mysteries."
—Booklist

"Phenomenal . . . the story, characters and dialogue, and descriptive setting are perfect."
—Romance Reader at Heart

"Keeps you guessing until the very end . . . I was awed."
—Fallen Angel Reviews

"A great plot, wonderful characters, and a setting to die for. You gotta pick this one up."   *—Fresh Fiction*

"Mmm . . . mmm . . . mmm! Get ready for the ride of your life . . . an intriguing eye-opener . . . Twists and turns, secrets and shadows, captivating characters, a well-written, well-developed plot, and a romance."
—Romance Reviews Today

"*Rising Moon* is suspenseful, passionate, and edgy, but it's also a true feel-good read with a message of hope and redemption."
—Eternal Night Reviews

MORE . . .

CRESCENT MOON

"Strong heroines are a hallmark of Handeland's enormously popular werewolf series, and Diana is no exception. *Crescent Moon* delivers plenty of creepy danger and sensual thrills, which makes it a most satisfying treat."

—*Romantic Times BOOKreviews*

"Handeland knows how to keep her novels fresh and scary, while keeping the heroes some of the best . . . pretty much perfect." —*Romance Reader at Heart*

"An enchanting and romantic love story . . . compelling characters and a gripping plot . . . This captivating tale is wrought with mystery, mayhem, and an electrifying passion hot enough to singe your fingers." —*Romance Junkies*

"Enticing, provocative, and danger-filled."

—*Romance Reviews Today*

"Will appeal to readers on the most primal level. It effectively centers on the dark side of life, the forbidden temptations."

—*Curled Up With a Good Book*

DARK MOON

"A riveting continuation to Handeland's werewolf series . . . Handeland has once again delivered a remarkable werewolf tale that is a superb addition to the genre. Fans of this genre won't want to miss out on this paranormal treat."

—*Fallen Angel Reviews*

"The end is a surprising, yet satisfying, conclusion to this series . . . another terrific story."   —*Fresh Fiction*

"The characters are intriguing and the romance is sexy and fun while at times heart-wrenching. The action is well-written and thrilling, especially at the end . . . *Dark Moon* is another powerful tale with a strong heroine who is sure to please readers and a hero who is worth fighting for. Handeland has proven with this trilogy that she has a bright future in the paranormal genre."
                                        —*Romance Readers Connection*

"Elise is Handeland's most appealing heroine yet . . . this tense, banter-filled tale provides a few hours of solid entertainment."
                                        —*Publishers Weekly*

"Smart and often amusing dialogue, brisk pacing, plenty of action, and a generous helping of 'spookiness' add just the right tone . . . an engaging and enjoyable paranormal romance."
                                        —*BookLoons*

"A fantastic tale starring two strong likable protagonists . . . action-packed . . . a howling success."
                                        —*Midwest Book Review*

"Handeland writes some of the most fascinating, creepy, and macabre stories I have ever read . . . exciting plot twists . . . new revelations, more emotional themes, and spiritual awakenings are prevalent here."   —*Romance Reader at Heart*

ST. MARTIN'S PAPERBACKS TITLES
BY LORI HANDELAND

Hidden Moon

Rising Moon

Midnight Moon

Crescent Moon

Dark Moon

Hunter's Moon

Blue Moon

THUNDER MOON

LORI HANDELAND

St. Martin's Paperbacks

This is a work of fiction. All of the characters, organizations, and events portrayed in this novel are either products of the author's imagination or are used fictitiously.

THUNDER MOON

Copyright © 2008 by Lori Handeland.
Excerpt from *Any Given Doomsday* copyright @ 2008 by Lori Handeland.

ISBN: 0-312-94918-9
EAN: 978-0-312-94918-1

Printed in the United States of America

St. Martin's Paperbacks edition / January 2008

St. Martin's Paperbacks are published by St. Martin's Press, 175 Fifth Avenue, New York, NY 10010.

10 9 8 7 6 5 4 3 2 1

ACKNOWLEDGMENTS

Grateful thanks to:

The guys who run a very funny Web site called "4q.cc".
They graciously gave me permission to use some of their Chuck Norris jokes in this book. Check it out at:
http://4q.cc

Peggy Hendricks, who was so helpful in providing information about the technicalities of dying. Bet you never thought working in that funeral home would come in so handy—for me.

The usual suspects: My editor, Jen Enderlin, and all the people at St. Martin's who make it such a great place to work—Anne Marie Tallberg, Matthew Shear, Sara Goodman.

THUNDER
MOON

1

A STORM BENEATH the Thunder Moon is both rare and powerful. My grandmother believed that on that night magic happens. She neglected to mention that magic could kill.

Mid-July in northern Georgia was an air conditioner salesman's wet dream. In theory, the creek behind my home should have been balmy. In practice, it wasn't.

Nevertheless, I dropped my robe and waded in; then I lifted my face to the full Thunder Moon and chanted the words my *e-li-si*, my great-grandmother, had taught me.

"I stand beneath the moon and feel the power. I will possess the lightning and drink of the rain. The thunder is your song and mine."

I wasn't sure what the chant was for, but it was the only one I remembered completely, so I said those words every time I came here. The repetition calmed me. The memories of my great-grandmother were some of the few good memories I had.

According to her, a chant spoken in English was

worthless. Only one spoken in Cherokee would work. Unfortunately, she'd died before she could teach me more than a smattering of the language. I'd always meant to learn more, but I'd never found the time.

She'd left me all her books, her notes—what she called her medicine. But I couldn't read any of the papers she'd gathered into a grade school binder, so they accumulated dust in the false bottom of my father's desk.

I'd loved her deeply, and I mourned her every day. I missed her so badly sometimes a great black cloud of depression settled over me that was very hard to shake.

"Someday," I whispered to the night. "Someday I'll know all those secrets."

Lightning flashed, closer than it should be. The moon still shone, though clouds now skated across its surface. Thunder rumbled, a great gray beast, shaking the hills that surrounded me.

The Blue Ridge Mountains had always been home. I could never desert them. The mountains didn't lie, they didn't cheat or steal, and, most important, they never left. The mountains would always be there.

They were as much a part of me as my midnight hair, my light green eyes, and the skin that was so much darker than everyone else's in town. My ancestors had been both Indian and African, with a good portion of Scotch-Irish mixed in.

My toes tingled with cold, so I rose from the water and snatched my white terry-cloth robe from the ground. I slid my arms into it, and the silver glow of the moon went out as if snuffed by a huge heavenly hand. The wind whistled through the towering pines, sounding like an angry spirit set free of bondage.

I stood at the creek and watched the storm come. I

liked storms. They reflected all the turmoil I'd carried within me for so long.

However, this storm was different from those that usually tumbled over my mountains—stronger, quicker, stranger. I should have started running at the first trickle of wind.

Lightning flashed so brightly I closed my eyes, yet the imprint of the sky opening up and the electric sheen spilling out seemed scalded into my brain. The scent of ozone drifted by, and the thunder seemed to crash from below rather than from above.

I opened my eyes just as the lightning flared again far too soon. A horrible, screeching wail followed, and a trail of sparks tumbled from the sky in the distance.

"I got a bad feeling," I murmured, then watched the roiling sky for several minutes until the cell phone in my pocket began to buzz.

I don't know why I'd brought the thing. Half the time I couldn't get a signal out here. The trees were so high, the mountains so near. Often I got back to the house and realized I'd dropped the phone either at the creek or somewhere along the path. Nevertheless, I was too much my father's daughter to ever leave home without it. Dad had been the sheriff in Lake Bluff, Georgia, too.

"McDaniel," I answered, wincing as needles of rain began to fall, the wind picking up and driving them into my face.

"Grace?"

The connection crackled, the voice on the other end breaking up. Lightning flashed again, and I wondered if I should be out here with a cell phone pressed to my head.

Probably not.

I started for the house and—
Baboom!
Thunder shook the earth. The wind whipped my long, wet hair into my eyes. The world went electric silver as lightning took over the sky.

"Grace! You there? Grace!"

I recognized the voice of my deputy, Cal Striker. Cal had spent most of his life in the Marines; then he'd retired after twenty and tried to relax back in the old hometown.

Except Cal wasn't the relaxing type. I could understand why, after tours in the Gulf War, Afghanistan, and most recently Iraq, the pace in Lake Bluff had driven him bonkers. He'd begged me to hire him for the open deputy position. I'd been happy to.

"Right here, Cal." I wasn't sure if he could hear me. Above the wind and the rain and the thunder, *I* could barely hear me. "What's the matter?"

"We've got—" *Crackle. Buzz.* "Over on the—" *Snap.* "—problem."

Hell. *What* did we have on the *where* that was a problem? With Cal it could be anything. From a kitty cat up a tree to a domestic disturbance complete with shotguns, Cal handled every situation with the same calm surety.

Cal was a big fan of Chuck Norris, which had led to no small amount of teasing from the other officers, and someone had taken to leaving Chuck Norris jokes on Cal's desk. I thought most of them were hilarious. My deputy did not.

"You're breaking up, Cal. Say again."

Hurrying in the direction of home, I skidded a bit on the now-slick trail, hoping I wouldn't fall on my ass and wind up covered in mud. I didn't have the time.

I burst into my backyard and cursed. The house was dark. The storm had knocked out the electricity, probably all over Lake Bluff. The phones would be ringing off the hook at the station. I don't know why people thought the sheriff's department could do anything, but whenever when we lost power the switchboard lit up to tell us all about it.

"Grace." Cal's voice was much clearer now that I'd escaped the interference of the towering pines. "Look to the north."

I turned, squinted, frowned at the slightly orange glow blooming against the midnight sky, right about where that weird flash of sparks would have landed.

"I'm on my way," I said, and hurried into the house.

With no electricity and no moon spilling in through the windows, the place seemed foreign. Corners of furniture reached out and smacked my shins. I could stop and light a candle, try to find a flashlight, although it probably wouldn't have any working batteries, but I was possessed by a sense of urgency.

I kept seeing that orange glow in my head, and I didn't like it. Forest fires were extremely dangerous. They could sweep down the side of a mountain and right through a town. They've been known to jump highways and waterways, leaving behind acres of blackened stumps and devastated dreams.

I stumbled up the stairs to my room, found a towel, tossed the damp robe into the tub, then put on the same uniform I'd just taken off. As I shoved my .40-caliber Glock into the holster, I stepped onto the second-floor landing. The window rattled, and I turned in that direction, figuring the wind had shifted.

A great black shadow loomed, and my fingers tightened on the grip of the gun. Wings beat against the glass; a beak tapped. I couldn't catch my breath, and when I did I emitted a choking gasp that frightened me almost as badly as the bird had.

Then the thing was gone, and I was left staring at the rain running down the windowpane. How odd. Birds didn't usually fly during bad weather.

Heading downstairs, I dismissed the strange behavior of the wildlife in my concern for Lake Bluff and its citizens. I hoped the deluge had put out any fire caused by the lightning, but I had to be sure.

I ran through the rain and jumped into my squad car, then headed down the long lane that led to the highway. Once there, I hit the lights and the siren. I wanted everyone who might be stupid enough to be out right now to see and hear me coming.

My headlights reflected off the pavement, revealing sheets of water cascading over the road ahead of me. The trees bent at insane angles. My wipers brushed twigs, leaves, and pine needles off my windshield along with the rain. I glanced in my rearview mirror just as a huge tree limb slammed onto the road behind me.

"Great." I fumbled with the radio. "I have a ten-fifty-three on the highway just north of my place. Tree limb big enough to jackknife a semi."

"Ten-four, Sheriff."

My dispatcher, Jordan Striker, was mature beyond her twenty years and as sharp as the stilettos she insisted on wearing to work. She was Cal's daughter, and while the two of them didn't see eye-to-eye on much, they shared a sense of responsibility to the community that I admired.

Jordan's mom had hung around Lake Bluff after the divorce, but the instant Jordan turned eighteen, she was gone. I never did hear where.

Jordan dreamed of attending Duke University. She had the grades but not the money, which is how she'd ended up working for me.

"I'll send a car as soon as I can," she continued. "Everyone's out on calls. Storm's something else."

"Try the highway crew. We need to get that tree off the road. Some dumb ass who doesn't have the sense to stay in during a mess like this will run aground on the thing, and then we'll have a pileup."

"The world *is* full of dumb asses," Jordan agreed.

As I said, wise beyond her years.

I continued toward the place where I'd seen the orange glow. The sparks had appeared to fall near Brasstown Bald, the highest peak in the spine of mountains known as Wolfpen Ridge. Despite the name, there were no wolves in the Blue Ridge, hadn't been for centuries.

Static spilled from my radio, along with Cal's voice. "Grace, take the turn just past Galilean Drive. Careful, it's a swamp back here."

I followed his directions to the end of what would have been a dirt road but was now a mud puddle. Illuminated by the flare of headlights from his squad car, Cal wore a yellow rain slicker and the extremely ugly hat that came with our uniform. A hat I never wore unless I had to.

With a sigh I slipped into my own slicker and slapped the wide-brimmed, tree-bark brown Stetson wannabe on top of my still-damp hair.

"Where's the fire?" I asked as I joined Cal at the edge of the tree line.

"Not sure. I saw it. So did you. Hell, so did everyone in a mile radius. But by the time I got here, nothing."

Considering the wind and the rain, the fire had probably gone out. However, the proximity of the town required us to be certain. All we needed was for the thickness of the trees to protect one small ember, which would smolder and burst into flames the instant we turned our backs.

"You sure this is the place?"

Cal nodded. He wasn't a particularly tall man, maybe an inch more than my own five-ten, but he was imposing, still ripped, despite two years out of the Corps. I doubted I could even get my hands around his neck, if I was so inclined. Cal wore his light brown hair in the style of the USMC, and his face was lined from tours spent in countries that had a lot more sun and wind and sand than we ever could.

"Ward Beecher called it in," Cal continued. "Said all the trees were ablaze. He smelled the smoke."

I frowned. Ward Beecher wasn't a nut. He was the pastor of the Lake Bluff Baptist Church. I doubted he was much of a liar, either, and he lived not more than half a mile from this spot.

"There's nothing now." I walked around the clearing. The trees, the grass, the ground were all dripping wet; I couldn't find a single charred pine needle.

"'Cept this." Cal indicated an area in front of his car.

I joined him at the edge of a fairly large hole, which reminded me of photos I'd seen of meteor sites. Except there wasn't a rock of any noticeable size to be had.

"Could have been here forever," I said.

"Mebe."

He didn't sound convinced, but what other explanation was there? The hole was empty. Unless—

I went down on one knee, ignoring the mud that soaked through my uniform—I was already drenched— and studied the ground.

"You think someone was here before us?" Cal asked. "Took whatever it was that fell?"

I didn't answer, just continued to look. I was the best tracker in the county. My father had made certain of that. But sometimes, like now, being the best wasn't any damn good at all.

"The rain's washed away the top layer of dirt," I said. "An elephant could have come through here and I wouldn't find a trace of it."

I straightened, my gaze drawn to the tree line just as a low, bulky shadow took the shape of a wolf.

I didn't like that one bit. We'd had a little problem with wolves last summer.

Werewolves, to be exact.

I hadn't believed it, either—until some really strange things had started happening. Turned out there were werewolves all over the place. There was even a secret government society charged with killing them.

I'd thought they'd all been eliminated or cured—no one had died a horrific, bloody death in months.

But maybe I was wrong.

2

BY THE TIME I drew my Glock, the animal had melted into the trees on the north side of the clearing and disappeared. I ran after it anyway, even though I didn't have any silver bullets.

In this gun.

"What's the matter?" Cal followed; he had his weapon out, too.

"You didn't see the—?" I stopped. Had I really seen a wolf?

Yes.

Did I want to tell Cal?

No.

"Never mind." I put away the Glock. "A shadow. Maybe a bear."

Not a wolf in these mountains, but bears we had.

Cal narrowed his blue-gray eyes on the trees. "They don't usually come this close to people."

"Which might be why it took off so fast."

"Mmm." Cal holstered his weapon, but he kept his hand on his belt just in case.

I was kind of surprised he hadn't seen the wolf. The animal had been right in front of him; he should have at least detected a movement, even if he had been focused on the mysterious gaping hole in the earth.

I checked the ground but found no tracks. Though the rain still fell in a steady stream, a bear would have left some kind of indentation. A wolf should have, too.

"We may as well head back," I said. "I'm sure Jordan has a list of problems the length of my arm for us to deal with."

"Probably," Cal agreed. "What do you think that orange glow was?"

"A reflection?"

"Off a UFO?"

"Okay." Hell, stranger things had happened—right here in Lake Bluff.

Cal laughed at my easy agreement. "Anyone else live out here we could talk to? Maybe they saw something."

"My great-grandmother had a friend who lived—" I waved in a vague northerly direction. "Although I'm not sure how much she can see or hear anymore."

I hadn't been to visit Quatie in a long time. My great-grandmother had asked me to check on her whenever I was in the area, but I'd had a helluva year, considering the werewolves, and I'd forgotten. I needed to remedy that ASAP.

"Probably not worth going over there," Cal said.

"No," I agreed, but made a mental note to stop by another day.

We got into our cars and reached the highway without getting stuck. Then Cal went one way and I went the other.

I decided to drive straight to the mayor's house. Claire Kennedy was not only in charge of this town, but werewolves had nearly killed her, and her husband, Malachi Cartwright, knew more about them than anyone.

Myself, I'd been skeptical about the supernatural. Even though my great-grandmother had been a medicine woman of incredible power and she'd believed in magic, I'd been tugged in two directions. I'd wanted to be like her; I'd wanted to believe. But I'd also wanted to please my father—hadn't learned until much later that such a thing was impossible— and he'd been a cop, filled with skepticism, requiring facts. I'd been confused, torn—until last summer when I'd had no choice but to accept the unacceptable.

I turned the squad car toward Claire's place, uncaring that it was nearly midnight and she had a new baby. Claire would want to hear about this.

Before my tires completed twenty revolutions, headlights wavered on the other side of a rise. I was just reaching for the siren when a car came over the hill, took the curve too fast, and skidded across the yellow line. Out of control, it headed straight for me.

I yanked the wheel to the right, hoping to avoid both a head-on collision and being hit in the driver's side door. The oncoming car glanced off my bumper, but the combination of speed and slick pavement sent me spinning. I was unable to gain control of the squad before I slammed into the nearest tree.

My air bag imploded, smacking me in the face so hard my head snapped back; then everything went black.

∞

I awoke to the sound of the rain and the distant beat of something that could have been a drum. Maybe thunder.

No, that wasn't right.

I frowned and then groaned as pain exploded across my face and chest. Slowly I opened my eyes.

The squad was crumpled against the trunk of a towering oak, my face squished into the air bag. I tasted blood.

The car wasn't running. The radio was smashed. I felt for my cell phone, peered blearily at the display, which read: No service.

I was dizzy, nauseous. A quick glance into the rearview mirror didn't reveal much, although from the dark splotches on my shadowy face, I just might have broken my nose.

I released the seat belt and fought my way from the car. Then I stood alone on a deserted, rain-drenched road. The prick who'd hit me had taken off. He was going to be toast when I got hold of him.

The rain had already drenched me to the skin. I'd removed my slicker when I'd gotten in the car. My head had been too fuzzy to remember to put it back on before I'd climbed out.

The trees spun. I wanted to sit. Instead, I leaned against the rear bumper and grasped for a coherent thought.

I was stuck in the mountains with no way to contact

anyone. I could walk back to Lake Bluff; I'd probably have to. Just not right now.

Branches rustled. I blinked the rain from my lashes. Everything was still blurry. I could see my nose swelling up. I was going to have two black eyes. Wouldn't be the first time. I did have four older brothers.

Not that they'd beat on me—much—but I'd always tried to keep up with them, and with the lack of supervision that came from a father obsessed with his job and a mother who'd taken off when I was three, I'd often ended up bruised and bloody.

I'd also ended up tough, able to take care of myself and compartmentalize pain, which were exactly the skills I needed right now.

"Thanks George, Gerry, Greg, and Gene," I muttered.

I'd often wondered if my mother had chosen names that began with *G* for sentimental reasons or because she hadn't cared enough to be original. Unless she showed up one day, and I wasn't holding my breath, I'd never know. My brothers had refused to speak of her, as had my father.

Had her desertion screwed me up? Sure. Whenever I cared about someone, I knew it was only a matter of time until they left. So far, no one had disappointed me.

I moved closer to the edge of the trees. Even though I was dizzy, my head ached, and I wasn't sure just how "with it" I was, those trees were bugging me. They weren't swaying with the wind, as I'd first thought, but shaking as if something was coming.

I drew my gun. Would I even be able to hit anything in my condition? Would a lead bullet do me any good tonight?

Why hadn't I given in to my own unease and started loading all my weapons with the specially made silver bullets I'd ordered last summer? I was the boss here. No one would say anything.

To my face.

I spread my feet, clasped the weapon with two hands, trying to steady it. Whatever was coming was big.

I heard again that weird rumble—not thunder, not drums, maybe the wind, I wasn't sure. Then a shadowy figure appeared between the pines.

Too tall to be a wolf, too thin to be a bear—my mind wasn't firing on all cylinders or I'd have recognized a man even before he popped out of the forest and stopped dead, staring at my gun.

"Usually takes people a day or two before they want to shoot me," he said.

His accent was odd—not Southern, not Northern, but something in between. I couldn't see his face in the darkness, but he was several inches taller than me, with wide shoulders tapering to a lanky build. His hair was long, dark, and as soaked as mine.

I tightened my fingers on the grip as the world wavered. "What . . . what are you—?"

I'd meant to ask what he was doing out in the rain, but suddenly everything shimmered, whirled, and my entire body jarred as my knees hit the pavement.

"Hey," the guy said, hurrying forward. "You're hurt."

"What was your first clue?" I muttered, and then I passed out again.

I wasn't unconscious long, or at least I didn't think so. The storm still raged; the stranger rested on his heels next to me. His fingers flitted over my face, my neck, then pressed just below my ear.

I slapped him. "Watch it."

"I'm a doctor."

"That's what they all say."

He hesitated, as if he wasn't quite sure I was kidding, or maybe he just didn't find me funny. So few people did.

I still couldn't see his face. The moon remained hidden by the clouds, and we were hell and gone from any streetlights.

I lay on grass instead of pavement. The guy had had the good sense to drag me out of the road. If he'd wanted me dead, he could have left me there.

And why would he want me dead? As he'd said, it usually took people a few days to wish for that.

His hand fell away from my neck, and chilled from the deluge, I missed its warmth. Rain dripped from his head onto my own.

"You'll live," he said.

"Goody."

He sat back on his heels. "What happened?"

"Idiot driving too fast. Came over the hill, skidded into me; then I hit that tree and *kabam*—air-bag face."

He laughed, or maybe he coughed, I wasn't sure which. "I don't think you broke your nose, though you should probably have X-rays just to be sure."

"Why? Can anything be done about a broken nose?"

"Depends how broken it is. You probably don't want a permanent bump or a crook in the middle."

I could care less how I looked. I'd been told a hundred and one times I was beautiful and exotic. What I wanted to be was average, normal, loved, but it wasn't going to happen.

"Since you lost consciousness for a minute," he continued, "you're probably concussed."

"Wouldn't be the first time."

"Because?"

"I've got brothers."

"Ah, then you know the drill."

I did, if I could only remember, which, come to think of it, was a symptom of a concussion.

He must have seen my confusion, because he kept talking. "If you start to throw up, get to a doctor. Have someone wake you once in the night."

I snorted, which made my head and nose scream. The only someone at my place was me. Not that I'd be getting any sleep tonight anyway.

"Ice for your face," he finished.

The wind picked up and slapped a hank of his hair across his eyes. He lifted a hand and shoved it back. A stray shaft of moonlight sparked off his ring. I couldn't tell if the circlet was silver or gold.

He turned his head as if he'd heard something and a single, thin braid swung free, tangled with a feather of some kind. In the slight gray light his profile revealed a sharp blade of a nose and a slash of cheekbones any model would kill for.

This guy was as Indian as I was.

Had he walked out of the past? Was he a ghost? An immortal? How hard had I hit my head?

"Let me help you stand," he said.

I wanted to lie there a while longer, but a flash of red and blue lit the sky, and beneath me the ground vibrated with the roll of tires approaching from the direction he'd been staring. How had he sensed the car before I had?

I managed to gain my feet. My rescuer let me go, and I was pleased when I didn't fall down.

The squad came over the hill. I lifted an arm, but Cal was already pulling over in front of my mangled vehicle.

He jumped out, ran over. "You okay, Grace?"

"So he says." I waved my hand toward the stranger.

Cal's face creased in confusion. "So *who* says?"

I turned to ask the man's name, but no one was there.

3

Y OU'RE STARTING TO worry me," Cal said.

"I'm starting to worry myself."

I strode to the edge of the trees. Too much grass to distinguish any footprints. I found small areas of indentation, but with the rain they could have been from anything.

First the disappearing wolf and then the disappearing man. Were they connected?

"Yeah," I muttered.

"Grace?"

Talking to myself again. People who lived alone often did. I should probably stop, but I doubted I could.

"Never mind," I said. "How'd you find me?"

"Nine-one-one call from a cell. Probably the guy who hit you."

"Jerk," I muttered, although I was grateful someone had called. "I guess you'll have to take me home."

"I'm taking you to the hospital."

"No, you aren't."

"There's blood all over you!"

"Which is why I want to change my uniform before I go back out."

"You're not going back out. Not tonight."

"You seem to be under the impression that you're the boss of me," I said.

Cal's lips tightened, but when he spoke his voice was nothing but calm. Talk about the patience of a saint. "You can't drive around, especially in this mess, when you're dizzy. At least take the rest of the night off." He jerked a thumb toward my ruined vehicle. "You're going to have a hard time getting that thing to run anyway."

"I have a car of my own, Cal."

He mumbled something that I instinctively knew I didn't want to hear. Cal was just trying to look after me, but I wasn't very good at being looked after.

"Take me home," I ordered.

The short drive to my house was accomplished in total silence. When I tried to get out of the car, my head ached so badly my stomach rolled.

I glanced at Cal and sighed. "Okay, you win. I'll go to bed, but call me if anything serious happens."

From his somewhat sarcastic salute, there was nothing Cal would consider serious enough to wake me for tonight.

I hesitated. My father had rarely delegated authority. If he were here now he'd sneer and call me a girl. In my family, the ultimate insult.

"You need help getting inside?" Cal asked.

"Not since the mayor and I split a box of cheap wine when we were sixteen and I puked for three days."

"You two must have been a real treat."

"Oh yeah, we were swell."

I made it to the porch, then lifted my hand as Cal turned his car and went back to work.

I was mud splattered, blood spattered; my uniform had been soaked and partially dried so many times it was stiff and uncomfortable. My hair had come loose from its braid and slapped against my neck like wiry hanks of hay.

A long, hot shower eased the stiffness, the mud, and the blood from my body and face. I took a bag of ice to bed. It wasn't the first time.

I set my alarm for 3:00 A.M., happy that I woke easily when it rang. The ice bag was water. I tossed it to the floor and went back to sleep.

I dreamed of lightning and of birds trapped in a glass box so that the beat of their terrified wings sounded like distant thunder. My eyes snapped open as I realized what that odd sound had been in the woods last night.

"The wings of a really big bird." I shook my head and was rewarded with a dull ache behind my puffy eyes.

I was more concussed than I thought. I'd heard the wind, maybe thunder. There was no bird big enough to create the sound that had seemed to make the earth, the trees, the very air shudder.

Of course there weren't any wolves in Georgia, either, but last summer we'd had some. We might have some again, considering what I'd seen in the storm.

I climbed out of bed, got dressed, and went to see Claire.

Most nights it took me a while to fall asleep. As a result, I often overslept and had to race to work, hair still wet after I'd drunk a single cup of coffee in the shower.

This morning, dawn had just spilled over the horizon

as I drove my dad's faded red pickup down Center Street. A bread truck was parked outside the Good Eatin' Café. The *open* sign sprang to life in the Center Perk as I went by. The coffee shop specialized in the fancy lattes and teas popular in big cities—over the summer we earned a good portion of our income off the tourists—but the Perk also sold good old-fashioned java in a go-cup to appease the locals, like me.

A moving van idled in front of what used to be a doll shop, until eighteen months ago when the owner died. The store had been empty ever since. I made a mental note to see who'd bought the place and then welcome him or her to the neighborhood.

Claire owned the largest house in Lake Bluff. Not that she'd planned to, but when her dad—the former mayor—had died, he'd left her not only the family homestead but also his job.

Claire had never wanted to be the mayor. She'd wanted to be a news anchor, and she'd run off to Atlanta to do it. There she'd discovered that the talent and brains that had made her hot shit in Lake Bluff only made her average, or less, in the big city. She'd wound up a producer instead, and she hadn't liked it.

She did like being the mayor, and she was a good one. Much to her own, and pretty much everyone else's, surprise.

I was just glad to have her back. Claire and I had been pals since our mothers had left. Hers to Heaven, mine to Lord only knew where.

Our fathers had been friends, too—the mayor and the sheriff—and they'd thrown us together often, leaving one or another of my brothers in charge. Claire and I had survived. Then, as now, we'd depended on each other.

I parked in front of the white rambling two-story near the end of Center Street. Claire walked to work every day, as her father had before her. In a town of just under five thousand, nothing was very far away.

The door opened before I knocked.

"Who hit you?" Claire demanded. "And what did you say to make them?"

Her hands were clenched into fists, and she appeared ready to take on anyone who'd dared touch me. Not that she wouldn't get her ass kicked. Claire was a girl in the true sense of the word—soft, round, with the fire red hair, moon-pale skin, and clear blue eyes of her Scotch-Irish ancestors.

"Why do you think I said something?" I demanded.

"Because you always do?"

"Not this time. My face had an intimate encounter with an air bag."

Her fingers unfurled. "Are you okay?"

"Fine. But the squad car doesn't look half as good as I do."

She lifted a brow. "Lucky we can afford another."

Since Claire had taken over, the town treasury had done a complete about-face. Not only had our last Full Moon Festival been a huge success, despite the werewolves, but she'd also figured out a lot of other ways to bring tourists to town the whole year through, instead of only during that single week in August.

"There's something I have to talk to you about," I said.

Claire waved me inside and headed for the kitchen. "Coffee?"

"God, yes."

I glanced around for Oprah, the cat—named during Claire's talk-show-host phase— before I remembered that she'd developed an instant adoration for the baby and rarely left his side.

Whenever Noah slept in his crib, Oprah lay beneath it. If he fell asleep anywhere in the house, she stayed right next to him, and if anyone came in the room, she set up a squalling that would wake the dead yet never seemed to wake the baby. Oprah was the next best thing to a watchdog Claire could find.

"Where are the guys?" I asked.

"Still sleeping, thank God."

Claire had married Malachi Cartwright early last fall. Their son, Noah, had been born in May, which meant Claire was getting far too little sleep. Luckily, Mal took care of the baby during the day so she could take care of Lake Bluff.

Mal was an oddity here, and not just because he was a househusband. He had come to town with his band of traveling Gypsies to entertain at the festival. After a whole lot of spooky stuff had gone on, he'd stayed behind when the rest of his people left.

From the beginning a more unlikely pair could not be imagined—the mayor and the Gypsy horse trainer, the First Lady of Lake Bluff and the hired help. I could go on and on, making comparisons directly out of historical fiction. But the truth was, they'd been destined to meet, fated to fall in love, and they were the happiest couple I'd ever seen. I guess Claire had forgiven, if not forgotten, that Malachi had come here to kill her.

Claire set two mugs on the table, and we each took a chair. "What's going on?" she asked.

Quickly I told her about the previous night. The strange, flickering light. The fire that wasn't. The crater and the wolf.

"Not again," Claire muttered.

"I'm not certain I really saw it. When I checked for tracks, there weren't any."

"You expected to find tracks in a storm like the one we had last night?"

I shrugged. "You never know."

"Did you hear a howl?"

"Nothing but thunder and wind." And the rhythmic beat of the giant wings of an invisible bird. I decided to keep that to myself.

"There was also a man. He came from nowhere."

"As in now you see him, now you don't?"

"Not sure. He was in the woods. I couldn't make out his face clearly, but he was Indian. For a second I thought—" I broke off, remembering. "Grandmother used to tell a story about a band of Cherokee who'd hidden in the mountains to escape the Trail of Tears. They hid so well that eventually they become both immortal and invisible."

"I guess you *had* hit your head."

Though I'd thought the same thing, I couldn't resist needling her. I could rarely resist needling anyone.

"This from a woman who saw people turn into animals."

She toasted me with her mug. "Got me there."

I tapped my own mug against hers, then drank. "After my head cleared, it occurred to me that a wolf had gone into those trees and, not too long after, a man had popped out."

"Did the wolf have the eyes of the man?" Claire asked.

We'd discovered last summer that a werewolf resembled a real wolf in every way—except for the human eyes.

I tried to remember the eyes of the wolf, the eyes of

the man, but I couldn't. I would think I'd recall something as bizarre as human eyes in the face of a wolf, but with the residual effects of the concussion . . .

"I don't know," I admitted. "I have certain gaps in the gray matter since the air-bag incident."

Concern washed over her face. "You want an aspirin?"

"No, Mom, but thanks."

"Watch it, or I won't let you hold Noah when he gets up."

I had a serious weakness for Noah Cartwright. Who'd have thought that rough, tough, gun-toting, order-giving Grace McDaniel would go gooey over a baby? Certainly not me.

"Sadly, I'm not going to be able to wait for His Highness to get out of the crib." I stood, draining the rest of my coffee in one gulp.

"I'll mention what you told me to Mal." Claire and I went to the front door. "He's pretty good at spotting the unusual."

Considering Mal had been cursed to wander the earth for centuries, he'd had his share of experience with shape-shifters.

"That'd be great," I said.

I'd do it myself, but I had the distinct feeling I'd be a little busy with the human inhabitants of Lake Bluff for the next several days. Having never actually seen a werewolf, I was at a disadvantage. Not that I didn't believe they were real. Long before they'd shown up, I'd seen other equally amazing things, which had eventually made me a convert.

"I'll be in and out this week." I stepped onto the porch, marveling at the bright sunshine after such a terrible storm. "I'm going to have to check on all the people in outlying areas."

There were still quite a few old-timers who insisted on living in the mountains without a phone or even electricity. Hell, there were a few new-timers who thought it was all the rage. I thought they were nuts. Probably because every time a natural disaster occurred I had to check on them.

"Feel free to rack up the overtime," Claire said.

"Oh, I'd planned on it."

I headed down the hill where the sheriff's department shared a square of land with town hall. Instead of turning into the parking lot, I continued on to where the moving van had been parked earlier but was no longer. The front door of the store stood open, so I walked in.

I probably should have called out, but the place was empty. Had the moving van been taking things away rather than delivering them?

Smart thieves usually pretended they belonged somewhere, that what they were taking was theirs by right, and few people questioned them. What better way to clean out a place than to hire a moving van and dress like a mover?

I'd just turned, determined to find out if anyone had bought this place, when a floorboard creaked upstairs.

Slowly I lifted my head. I'd forgotten an apartment occupied the second floor.

Through the back door of the shop, in a small space that used to be a called a mudroom, lay a staircase. The stairs led up to a long, shadowed hallway full of closed doors, except for the last one at the opposite end, which gaped open. As I headed in that direction, I had the sudden sensation of being watched. A quick glance over my shoulder revealed nothing.

One door, two, three doors, four—I opened my mouth to announce myself and a whisper of air brushed the back of my neck.

Impatiently I turned, trying to stop my overactive imagination from harassing me by giving it a full view of an empty hallway.

The man was so close my breasts brushed his chest.

4

INSTINCT TOOK OVER, and I reached for my gun. He grabbed my wrist before I was halfway there. My left hand swung for his head, and he caught that one, too. Then we stared at each other, him grasping my wrists tight enough to bruise, our bodies so close every breath skimmed the front of me against the front of him.

He wore a black suit and tie with a shirt so white it glowed even in the dim light. But the suit wasn't what threw me—it was the long hair adorned with a single braid and an eagle feather.

At least I hadn't imagined him.

He didn't look Indian in this light, except for the feather. His skin was much fairer than mine, and his eyes were an oddly light shade—not brown, not green, not gray, but a swirling combination of all three.

"Hey!" I tugged on my hands.

He didn't budge; he didn't speak as his gaze wandered over my face. I struggled; I couldn't help it. Ever since my oldest brother, George, had held me down while Greg painted my face with maple syrup, I got a little wiggy when trapped.

I continued to thrash. He continued to ignore me. The friction created by all that rubbing started to feel better than it should. My nipples, despite the protection of a padded bra, responded, which only made my breathing and the subsequent friction increase.

I considered kicking him in the shin, but from the strength of his grip and the expression on his face, he'd continue to hold me anyway.

"You often sneak into private property and pull a gun on people?" he asked.

"Only when I see a previously abandoned storefront with an open door and then someone creeps up on me. You're asking for trouble."

"I hear that a lot."

"You're gonna hear more than that if you don't let me go. Catchy phrases like 'assaulting an officer' and 'held without bond.'"

His only response was a smile that flashed his slightly crooked but very white teeth. However, he did loosen his hold. I backed up, absently rubbing first one wrist and then the other.

My gaze caught on the eagle feather. In Cherokee tradition, only great warriors dared to wear the trappings of the sacred bird. Did he know that? Did he care?

"How's your head?" he asked.

"About to explode."

"It shouldn't hurt that badly still."

He moved so quickly I couldn't think, let alone escape, yanking me so close my nose scraped against his shirt as he began to probe my skull.

"Ow!" I shoved him away, even though he'd smelled

really good, as if he'd rubbed fresh mint leaves all over his skin.

He stared at me with a combination of bemusement and concern.

"My head's fine," I said. "Why'd you sneak up on me?"

"I didn't sneak."

"I didn't hear anything."

"I've always been quiet."

He was a lot more than quiet. *I* was quiet. My father had trained me to track both man and beast in complete silence, but this guy had tracked me. Something about him set my instincts humming—or maybe that was just my libido.

"Who are you?" I asked.

"I told you last night, or don't you remember?"

"You said you were a doctor, yet I find you creeping around abandoned storefronts manhandling women."

His lips curved. "You didn't mind."

If I could blush I'd have been beet red. As it was, my blood pressure went up so fast my pulse seemed to pound out a painful song behind my blackened eyes.

"I should take you in for squatting in an abandoned building."

"Do I look like a squatter?"

I took the opportunity to give him the once-over. In contrast to his expensive tailored suit, he wore sandals. His right ring finger sported the band I'd noticed last night, glaringly gold in the sunlight. I'd think it was a wedding ring, except he wore it on the wrong hand.

"Officer?" he pressed when I continued to stare.

He wasn't exactly handsome. The bones of his face were too sharp for that. But his hair was dark, his eyes light, and his skin just tan enough to make him memorable.

"Sheriff," I corrected.

His gaze lowered to my chest, and my pulse quickened again. " 'Sheriff McDaniel,' " he read from my name tag. "I'm Ian Walker, from Oklahoma."

Which explained the accent—not South, not North, but West, where most of the Cherokee had gone long ago.

"What brings you here?"

"To Lake Bluff or this building?"

"Both."

"I'll be opening an office as soon as I can get the place ready, and I chose Lake Bluff because . . ." His voice drifted off, as if he was trying to come up with a reason.

"Because?" I prompted.

"I traced my ancestors to this town. From the time before our people suffered on the Trail Where We Wept."

He used the Cherokee version of the historical term "Trail of Tears." They meant the same thing. Another example of the U.S. government's treatment of those whose only crimes had been to be here first and then arrogantly refuse to give up what was theirs just because they were told to.

"How do you know we're the same people?" I asked.

I could easily be descended from any tribe in the country. For all he knew I might not be Native American at all but African, Asian, Italian, Mexican, or any combination of the above.

"I ran across the McDaniels when I was researching my own family. You've been here since the beginning of time."

"Not quite that long." But close enough.

Legends say the Aniyvwiya, or the principal people, came from a land of sea snakes and water monsters near the place where the sun was born. In other words . . . east. But we'd been in these mountains so long that no one really knew when the first Cherokee had arrived.

"What clan are you?" Walker asked.

In ancient times, the question would have been unforgivably rude. Clan membership was a secret passed down from the mother to the children in a matrilineal society. To be without a clan was to be without rights, without protection, without family. Clan membership was everything.

Very few Cherokee knew their clan affiliation these days—partly because of the extreme secrecy that had been involved and partly because people no longer cared. However, I was one of the few who knew and who cared.

"Panther clan," I answered.

"A ni sa ho ni," he murmured. "Clan of blue."

Each of the seven clans had worn feathers of a different color to delineate them from the others. Panther, or the wildcat clan, was the clan of blue, referring to a certain medicine they'd made for their children.

When I was little and sick, my great-grandmother had often forced a disgusting blue concoction down my throat, and it always worked. I wished again that I could read her notes and discover what she'd put in that stuff.

"I'm A ni wo di," he said.

At my blank expression he frowned. "You don't speak the language of our mothers?"

I bristled at his tone. "I'm more Scotch than Cherokee."

I didn't bother to mention the African since no one really knew that for certain. Just because the Cherokee had once kept slaves didn't mean they broadcast the identities of the children they'd had with them. If secrecy was good enough for Thomas Jefferson, it was good enough for us.

"That's no excuse," he said.

"Who died and made you head of the Cherokee Nation?"

He contemplated me for several seconds, then dipped his head, the feather swinging past his ear along with the braid. "You're right. I just thought that someone descended from Rose Scott, one of the most powerful medicine women—"

"How do you know that?"

His lips quirked. "It's classified?"

"No." Although it wasn't exactly written about in the *Lake Bluff Gazette*, either. This guy knew an awful lot about me for someone who claimed to have been looking for *his* family tree.

"Your great-grandmother taught you nothing of the old ways?"

She'd tried, but my father had been adamant that there be no hocus-pocus or I'd lose my time with her. Since I'd known he was serious and that time meant the world to me, I'd balked at many of her teachings. Instead, she'd told me stories—legends of the origin of the clans, tales of the principal people being descended from animals.

As panther clan, we carried the spirit of the big cat within us. Some of us more than others.

Fascinated, I'd not only collected every stuffed and glass image of panthers that I could find, but I'd often pretended I was a panther, too. Slinking through the woods and the mountains, I'd often dreamed of actually becoming one.

However, I didn't want to talk about that, especially with him, so I flicked a finger at the feather in his hair. "You're bird clan?"

"That would be A ni tsi s kwa," he said. "Not A ni wo di."

"I don't speak the language," I said between my teeth.

He'd better not be wolf clan, or I just might rethink shooting him. At least I'd had the sense to load my gun with silver before I left home.

"I'm paint clan," he said.

"Medicine men. How convenient."

"I thought so."

My bad attitude didn't seem to faze him. He was a very calm guy.

"Too bad you had to give up the old ways when you became a doctor."

"Why would I do that?"

"I wouldn't think the AMA would be too happy about an M.D. who prescribes roots, berries, and bathing in a cool mountain stream."

"You'd be surprised."

"You do that?"

"If the illness warrants it."

My eyes narrowed. "Do you have a medical license?"

"Of course."

"From a real medical school?"

"Does Baylor College of Medicine suffice?"

Even I knew that was a good one.

"I also studied at the British Institute of Homeopathy in Canada."

I frowned. "Sounds like hoodoo to me."

"It's not."

I grunted, unconvinced. I enjoyed studying my heritage as much as the next guy. I was interested in the cures my great-grandmother had used. I might use them on myself, if I could figure them out, but I'd never presume to prescribe them to others. I considered a doctor who'd do so nothing less than a quack. People like Walker gave Native Americans a bad name.

I didn't trust him. I didn't much like him, although I did kind of like the way he smelled. I rubbed my forehead, wincing when I touched a bruise.

"Let me give you something for that." He inched past me and through the open door.

I caught a whiff of him again and had to bite back a sigh. I needed to get laid, then maybe this obsession would go away, but that wasn't as easy as it sounded.

In Lake Bluff everyone knew everyone and their mother, father, sister, and brother, too. I'd dated a few guys, slept with a few more. Every one had been a disaster of epic proportion.

If they hadn't expected special privileges from the sheriff's daughter, they'd definitely expected them from the sheriff. When they hadn't gotten them, each and every guy had turned into a whining child.

I'd sworn off locals, which meant the only sex I'd had in years had been during the festival when we were overrun with tourists. Sadly, I'd missed any kind of action last year due to our werewolf problem. No wonder I was so on edge.

Walker reappeared with a jar in his hand, unscrewing the top as he approached. The balm was pale yellow and carried a scent I didn't recognize.

He dipped a finger into the muck and spread some down my nose before I could protest.

"Hey!" I began, but he ignored me, smoothing the medicine over my bulbous nose and the bruised area beneath my eyes. The pain faded on contact.

"Close," he murmured, spreading one thumb over my brow bone.

What the hell? I thought. The stuff was already all over my skin. I let my eyes drift shut.

His fingers were gentle but firm. Everywhere he touched, the pain went away. He murmured words I couldn't understand, in the language of our ancestors.

Outside I heard again the low, rhythmic beat of wings. My eyes snapped open. His face was so close his breath puffed against the moisture on my face, and I shivered.

His eyes, eerily light, seemed to darken as his pupils expanded. I could see myself in them as he leaned closer.

My chest hurt; I wasn't breathing. He was going to kiss me, and I was going to let him.

My eyes fluttered closed again. I waited for him to take me in his arms, but the only place he touched me was in the light, feathery skate of his lips across mine.

I drew in a breath, captivated by the sensations. I was used to being handled differently. I was a tall woman who wore a gun. Guys never treated me as if I were spun glass. I didn't want them to.

My lips barely parted, his tongue flicked between, caressing both in one stroke. He lifted his mouth, I moaned in protest, but he pressed gentle kisses across my brow, beneath my eyes, down my nose. Wherever he touched, my skin warmed. I didn't want to open my eyes, to see his face, to remember who he was, who I was, how crazy kissing a stranger in an abandoned storefront on Center Street must be.

When he kissed me harder, deeper, his tongue delving in and stroking my own, my nipples went hard again; my whole body came alive.

He raised his head. I could feel him hovering, waiting and watching, his breath mingling with my own. Would we or wouldn't we?

Slowly I opened my eyes and stared at an empty hallway.

5

FOR AN INSTANT I doubted my sanity, until I caught and at last recognized the scent of the balm—fresh-cut grass beneath bright sunshine—then lifted a finger to my face. The tip came away shiny. Ian Walker was as real as the cream on my skin.

I strode to the open doorway. The room was cluttered with furniture, boxes, suitcases. I guess the moving van had delivered something. He stood near the window, shoulders slumped, head bent. What was wrong with him?

Then I saw the picture—a woman in a white dress, standing on a prairie as the wind ruffled her skirt. She was tiny, petite, young, with long hair like an inky waterfall against her smiling cheek.

The photo had been taken in black-and-white, then brushed with pastel colors, giving it the impression of age, although I'd seen the same technique used more recently, too.

Ian lifted his hand and shoved his own hair back

from his face. The wedding band flashed in the sunlight. No wonder he'd scooted off at the first opportunity. *Jerk*.

His shoulders slumped even more as he exhaled. He didn't turn around but continued to stare out the window as the streets below became busier and noisier.

If he could be this broken up about kissing another woman, maybe he wasn't such a prick after all. Then I remembered that kiss, what he'd made me feel, how my body still hummed with it, and my anger flared at the loss of something that could have been so good.

"Where's your wife?" My voice was as cold as my heart.

His shoulders twitched as if I'd slashed him with a whip. "Gone," he whispered.

The chill that had spread over me evaporated in the heat of embarrassment. Wedding ring on the right hand must mean widower, and I'd taunted him with the memory of his wife.

"I'm sorry—," I began.

"Not your fault. I forgot—" He stopped, shook his head, didn't finish.

I wondered how long she'd been gone. How she had died. If he'd ever get over her.

I was such an idiot. I didn't even like this guy. He'd kissed me once better than I'd ever been kissed before, and I was mooning over him like a lovesick teenager.

I'd been a lovesick teenager. Weren't we all once? I never wanted to be one again.

"Here." He snapped the cap back on the jar and held it out to me, though his gaze remained on the window. "Use it whenever the pain returns."

Right now my face felt great—as if I'd never been popped in the nose at all. I shrugged and took the jar.

"What's in this?" I asked.

"Rattlesnake oil."

I waited for him to laugh, but he didn't.

"You're serious?"

He turned. His skin pale, his pupils so large his eyes appeared black, fine lines bracketed his mouth. I re-arranged his age in my mind from late twenties to mid-thirties, which made more sense considering the medical degrees. If they were real.

"Rattlesnake oil is a common balm for rheumatism and arthritis," he said. "It works for bruises, too, if you say the right words."

I lifted my brows.

"Do you know anything about Cherokee medicine?" he asked.

"I thought we'd established I'm a cop, not a medicine woman."

"You're wrong."

I started to get annoyed again. Why did he have that effect on me? Maybe because he kept telling me what I was and who I should be.

"You think I wear this charming outfit because it flatters my ass?" I indicated the ugly brown uniform that bagged at the breasts and sagged in the butt. I didn't have a bad body, but you'd never know it by looking at me in this rag, which was probably the idea.

"You might be a cop," he said, "but you're a medicine woman, too. Even if you don't know the way. You were born to be who you are, and who you are is the great-granddaughter of Rose Scott."

I resisted the urge to roll my eyes again. "I'm sheriff of Lake Bluff. That's who I was born to be."

In truth, my dad had expected one of the boys to take over, but they'd hightailed it out of town the instant they'd turned eighteen. Good old Grace, who'd been begging for an ounce of Daddy's attention her entire life, had stayed and assumed the position when he died.

I didn't mind. I liked my job; I was good at it. Besides, there wasn't much call for medicine women these days.

"You'll discover your power one day." He tilted his head and the white of the eagle feather caught the sunlight and sparkled. "One day soon, I think."

I remembered how the small shaft of moonlight had glanced off the feather just last night. "What were you doing in the forest during a storm?"

"Is that a crime?"

"Not unless I can arrest people for stupidity, and as much as I'd like to, lawyers tend to frown on that."

"Lawyers frown on everything. Considering your accident, it was lucky for you that I was stupid."

"I'd have been all right. Why did you disappear?"

"I had things that needed to be done."

"Like what?"

"Things."

Before I could point out how uninformative that was, my cell phone buzzed. One glance at the display and I sighed. "Excuse me." I flipped the phone open. "What is it, Cal?"

"You okay?"

"Peachy. Cut to the chase."

"Sounds like you're back to normal. Nose broke?"

"I have no idea."

"Grace—," he began.

"My nose works, Cal. It's in the center of my face, and I can smell just fine with it." Against my will my eyes were drawn to Ian Walker, whom I'd been smelling far too much of. Walker lifted his eyebrows but said nothing.

"We've had a lot of calls since last night," Cal continued.

"I'm shocked."

Cal ignored me. He'd learned fast. "A lot of them dealt with birds."

"Whaddya mean?"

"Flocks of really big crows swooping low over cars. Birds flying into windows. Down chimneys."

"Is there a Hitchcock revival somewhere in the vicinity?"

"Very funny, Grace."

I hadn't been kidding. Every time a scary movie played in the area we had a rash of complaints that mirrored the plot. With every new *Friday the 13th* release— would they ever end?—people saw Jason all over the place.

"Could be the storm just threw them out of whack," I said. "Don't birds have radar?"

"I think that's bats."

"Whatever. We can't do anything about birds run amok. Anything serious I should know about?"

"Downed trees. Electricity out. Someone lost a carport to a falling branch."

"Injuries?"

"Nothing worse than that schnoz on you."

"Gee, thanks." I paused for an instant, thinking. A bird had smashed into my window last night. I'd thought it a fluke, but I guess not. I'd have to call the Department of Natural Resources and find out their take on it as well as— "Did anyone happen to see a wolf?"

"Why?" Cal asked. "Did you?"

"Maybe."

"But there aren't any."

"Could be someone has been keeping one as a pet and it got out during the storm."

"Could be," he agreed. "I'll ask around. You coming in soon?"

"Very," I said, and hung up.

"Pet wolves are more dangerous than real ones," Walker murmured. "They're often a wolf-dog mix, which makes them unpredictable. They aren't afraid of humans, but they're still wild in a lot of ways."

"How do you know so much about them?"

"I've known people who kept wolves. It never ended well."

I just bet it hadn't.

"If you've got a hybrid loose in these mountains you'd better catch it quick. Tame wolves tend to get themselves attacked by other animals, and then there's a danger of—"

"Rabies," I finished.

He nodded. "So you've got a wolf that isn't afraid of people, which is suddenly rabid."

I'd already been here and done this last summer. When a wolf that shouldn't exist in the Blue Ridge Mountains had attacked a tourist, we'd thought the wolf was rabid—never mind how it had gotten here. But when the tourist became extremely hairy and jumped out a second-story window before loping away, we figured that "rabid" was often a euphemism for "lycanthropic."

"I've got to go," I said, and did, ignoring the intent expression on Walker's face and the curiosity in his eyes.

A short while later I entered the Lake Bluff Sheriff's Department. The place was hopping.

We had nine full-time deputies and one part-time, along with three full-time dispatchers and one part-time on the payroll. Last night everyone had been called in, and from the crowd near the desks, most of them were still here. There had to be doughnuts.

I made my way through the outer area, nodding at the greetings. Sure enough, a box of bakery sat on a desk—more muffins and bagels than doughnuts, although I saw a few crullers with my name on them.

No one mentioned my swollen nose and dual black eyes. Cal must have warned them off. More and more I didn't know how I'd gotten along without him.

My office was a welcome respite from the chatter and the energy that come from having that many people in an enclosed space. I didn't like crowds. I did better one-on-one.

As soon as I'd taken the chair behind my desk, Cal appeared. "I've got every officer on the lookout for a vehicle with a dented front end. Also notified the repair shops in the county. We'll find whoever hit you and then took off."

"Thanks." I'd meant to do that myself, but I'd been a little distracted.

"I also checked the reports from last night," he continued. "No wolves. Just more of the really big crows and strange bird behavior."

"Wait a second," I said. "Really big crows—you mean ravens?"

"What's the difference?"

The knowledge wasn't common. The only reason I knew was because I'd done a report in eighth-grade science. Never thought that bit of trivia would come in handy.

"Ravens and crows aren't the same," I said. "You

could call a raven a crow, since they're in the crow
family, but all crows aren't ravens."

"How can you tell them apart?"

"Ravens are about the size of a hawk and crows are
more like pigeons."

"So people's complaints about really big crows are
probably not about crows at all."

"Probably not, although I hardly think it matters in
this case."

"True." He moved on. "I sent some of the guys out
to check on the folks who don't have phones."

"Good." I began thumbing through my messages.
Cal's silence made me glance up. The expression on his
face made me set the messages down. "What?"

"One of them was dead."

"Who?"

"Orel Vandross."

"He was still alive?" The guy had to be a hundred.

"Until yesterday. According to the report, the officer
found him in his bed."

"That's the way to go—in your own bed near the
century mark."

"Definitely. The funeral home picked him up. There
won't be a service. His family's gone and his friends,
too."

"That's too bad."

"I don't think he'll care."

I cast Cal a sharp glance. Sometimes his gallows humor, no doubt learned on the front lines of several
nasty wars, startled even me.

"I had another joke on my desk this morning," Cal
said.

"Already?"

The Chuck Norris joke bandit had struck just yesterday with the ditty *When the boogeyman goes to sleep he checks his closet for Chuck Norris.*

Cal handed me a sheet of paper and I steeled myself before reading: *Chuck Norris ordered a Big Mac at Burger King, and got one.*

I bit my lip to keep from laughing. Cal didn't seem at all amused.

"I don't get it," he said. "Why would Burger King make a Big Mac?"

The man was so literal sometimes, he scared me.

"Anyone see who put that on your desk?" I asked.

"No, and I haven't had a chance to check the security camera. Not that it'll make a difference."

No matter how many times we ran over the security tapes, we never saw anyone put the jokes on Cal's desk. Which was impossible. Nevertheless, new jokes continued to appear.

"I'm going to call the DNR about the ravens," I said. "Can you do something for me?"

"Sure."

I wrote "*Ian Walker, Baylor School of Medicine* and *British Institute of Homeopathy—Canada*" on a piece of paper and handed it to him.

Cal frowned at the words. "What about them?"

"There's a new doctor in town. Or at least he says he's a doctor. Those are his credentials. Can you verify?"

"Shouldn't be a problem." Cal turned to go, then paused, peering at me closely. "I thought your face would be a lot worse today."

"You think this is good?"

"Considering how it looked last night, hell, yeah." He headed out.

I frowned, and for the first time since I'd been air-bagged, the motion of my face didn't cause pain.

Reaching into my desk, I withdrew the mirror I kept there just in case I had to check my teeth for spinach or my nose for—well, what we check our noses for—and held it up.

My bruises were fading toward yellow, and my nose was half the size it had been an hour ago.

I lowered the mirror and stared at the jar of balm on my desk as if it were an actual rattlesnake instead of just the oil.

How could it have worked so fast?

6

M Y HEART WHISPERED, *Magic*. My mind scoffed.
Too much in my life and my job contradicted
any sort of fairy tale. But I'd also seen amazing, unex-
plainable things whenever I'd been around my great-
grandmother, not to mention everything that had
happened in Lake Bluff last summer.

So, on the one hand I figured the balm was just really good balm; on the other I wondered if the words
Walker had murmured had been an equally powerful
spell and, if so, where he had learned it.

Regardless, I rubbed more rattlesnake oil into my
face before I picked up the phone and called the Department of Natural Resources.

After a few transfers I reached the office of Alan
Sellers, bird geek. Quickly I told him what had happened in Lake Bluff.

"Odd bird behavior after a strong storm isn't un-
heard of," he said in a nasal whine that had me imagining his colorless hair, pasty skin, and watery eyes.

"So it's nothing to worry about?"

"Worry in what way?"

"Coordinated attacks. Bird rabies?"

His laugh disintegrated into a cough. I revised pale skin to the gray cast of a lifetime smoker. "You've heard the term 'birdbrain'?"

"Far more than I'd like," I muttered. It had been one of my brothers' favorite insults.

"Although recent studies have revealed that birds aren't as dumb as originally thought, coordinated attacks are beyond the capacity of most species. A flock may follow the leader, they can even communicate information about where to find food, but they don't have the brainpower to mount an attack."

"So Hitchcock was full of shit?"

"Most movies are."

Smart man.

"Also," he continued, "rabies is a disease passed from mammal to mammal, so birds can't get it. You say you have both crows and ravens?"

"Hard to know for sure. We've had reports of really big crows, which I took to be ravens. Crows have never been all that common in Lake Bluff."

"They usually congregate near larger towns; ravens like the mountains and forests. A sudden increase in crows in a rural area often follows a radical increase in the timber wolf population. I highly doubt that's the case in the Blue Ridge Mountains."

I opened my mouth, but nothing came out.

"Sheriff?" Sellers asked. "You there?"

"Yes. Sorry. Why would timber wolves increase the crow population?"

"No one knows for sure, but the two species have always worked in tandem. The crow leading the wolf to prey, and the wolf leaving carrion for his feathered friend to eat later—like payment, although we know they aren't so advanced in their thought patterns."

"Birdbrains," I muttered.

"Exactly. Wolves are quite a bit smarter, of course, but I don't think they have sufficient brainpower to account for a system of checks and balances. Of course there are quite a few Native American folktales that ascribe humanlike behavior to the beasts and the birds. I'm sure there has to be one somewhere that explains why the crow and the wolf are friends, although I haven't found it yet."

The slowing pace of his voice revealed he planned on remedying that lack of knowledge ASAP.

Too bad I couldn't ask him if werewolves followed the buddy system with crows, unless I wanted to be branded a nut job. Luckily, I did have a resident expert.

After thanking Sellers, I disconnected, considered calling Malachi Cartwright, and decided to walk over. That way I'd get to see Noah.

"I'm taking a stroll around town and then stopping at the Cartwrights'." Sharon Brendel, the dispatcher on duty, nodded. "You can raise me on the radio or my cell if you need to."

"How well do you know him?" Sharon asked dreamily.

Although she was probably only five years my junior, Sharon seemed very young to me. Probably because I'd never dreamed about anything the way Sharon did. Not my future, not boys, and certainly not men. I'd learned early and often that men were not very dream worthy.

"You mean Mal?" I asked.

"Mmmm." The girl actually licked her lips.

I had to resist the urge to laugh in her face. Malachi
was way too old for her—by about two hundred years.
Not to mention he was totally, hopelessly, in love with
his wife. From the moment Mal had seen Claire, and
vice versa, there'd never been anyone else for either
one of them.

A prickle of jealousy burned just below my breast-
bone. I was happy for Claire. She deserved some joy in
her life, as did Malachi. But I'd never realized how
lonely I was until Claire had come back and then gotten married. I wanted what she had so badly I ached
with it.

Out on the street the sun shone with the wattage of a
nuclear blast. I slid my wraparound sunglasses from
the pocket of my uniform and onto my nose. No pain.
God, that balm was good.

I hadn't gone half a block when an ambulance
wailed down Center Street, pausing at a small white
house only a few paces ahead of me. The paramedics
jumped out and ran inside. There was no way I could
walk past and not stop to see what was wrong.

Marion Garsdale appeared to have fallen asleep on
her couch. It wasn't until I got closer that I saw she was
dead. I should have figured it out from the sudden lack
of hustle on the part of the paramedics.

"What happened?" I asked.

They glanced up—two young men who appeared
just out of high school, although they had to have had
some training for this job and could not therefore be
"just" out.

"Sheriff." The dark-haired one, who must be at least
a quarter Cherokee, straightened.

He was someone's kid; I just couldn't recall whose.
My dad had always known everyone's name, their

children's names, and their children's children's names, as well as their dogs'.

"She was gone when we got here."

He seemed a little nervous, as if afraid I'd blame him for something. But what?

I came closer, staring down at the face of Ms. Garsdale. Her eyes wide open, her mouth had frozen in an equally wide *o* of shock. I guess no one is really ready to go, despite any hopes to the contrary.

Ms. Garsdale had once taught English at the high school. Though she seemed like a caricature of an English teacher with her white hair, flowered print dress, and thick glasses on her thin nose, she had in fact been quite the hippie.

Her hair, when unbound, reached to her waist. The flower print dress had once been the height of fashion— a seventies maxi—and her glasses, while thick, were still the same granny frames that had once been popular in her days at Berkeley. I'd always liked her.

"I thought dead people were supposed to be peaceful," the dark-haired kid said.

I cut him a quick glance. He was paler than he'd been before. His blond sidekick appeared more green than white.

"First one?" I asked.

"We've been on calls before, Sheriff," the Indian boy said.

"I'm sure you have, but no one's been dead, have they?"

Both shook their heads so frantically their moppy haircuts flew over their eyes. Why did every kid want to look like a greasy, grimy rock star? I didn't see the appeal. But I wasn't a seventeen-year-old girl any longer. Thank God.

"What's the procedure for a death?" I asked.

"We need to have a doctor pronounce her."

"Here?"

"No. We take her to the hospital. Then she'll be DOA."

"Wouldn't it be easier to have someone pronounce her at the scene?"

"We'd have to call a doctor and wait for one to show. That's not a good idea, especially when a lot of times the families are watching and wailing."

"Speaking of—" I glanced around the empty house. "Who called you?"

The blond kid found his voice. "Neighbor. Said she heard shrieking last night but thought it was the wind from the storm. This morning Ms. Garsdale didn't show for coffee like she usually does, and when the neighbor knocked, no one answered, so she used her key and—" He spread his hands.

"The neighbor said she heard shrieking?" I asked.

Blondie nodded.

I stared at Ms. G. She'd never been the shrieking type, and if she'd died while reclining on her couch, what was there to shriek about?

"Which neighbor?" I asked. "North or south?"

"North," the two said as one.

"Don't move her," I ordered. "In fact, don't touch anything. Go back to your ambulance and play games on your cell phones until I tell you to do otherwise."

Their eyes widened, but they did as I told them.

I recognized the woman next door immediately. "Ms. Champion," I greeted. "Can I ask you a few questions?"

Without a word, she opened the door wider and stepped back.

Ms. Champion and Ms. Garsdale had been friends forever. They'd met at Berkeley and taken jobs in Lake Bluff the same year. Ms. C. had taught music.

Since they'd never married and they'd bought houses right next to each other, a lot of gossips whispered the *l* word. I suspected if neither Claire nor I had married, the same would have been whispered about us in a few years. Such was the way of things in small towns. I wouldn't have cared, and I never noticed Ms. C. or Ms. G. giving a shit, either.

Ms. Champion motioned me to a seat on her couch. She took a chair on the other side of the coffee table. She still wore her robe and slippers. Her hair was as short as Ms. G.'s was long and as black as Ms. G.'s was white.

"Can you tell me what happened?" I asked. Ms. C. seemed shaken, and I couldn't blame her. The average Josephine didn't often see dead people.

"She didn't come this morning. I figured she'd overslept, so I went over."

"Did she often oversleep?"

Ms. C. nodded. "She'd stay up late and watch shows, then fall asleep on her couch."

Which appeared to be what had happened, except—

"Did you turn off the TV?"

Ms. C.'s bright blue eyes jerked to mine and she frowned. "No. It wasn't on."

"You heard something last night?"

Her frown deepened. "Terrible shrieking. Like something was dying right outside my house. I had to put my hands over my ears, it was so awful."

Bing!

If I were a cartoon, there'd be a lightbulb blinking

over my head. The shower of sparks, the horrible sound, the fire that wasn't.

"What time was this?" I asked.

"I'm not sure. My electricity was out."

Which could explain Ms. G.'s turned-off TV.

"Probably three A.M. or thereabouts," Ms. C. continued.

Which was a lot later than I'd heard the sound, but who was to say Ms. C. could remember the day of the week, let alone what time it had been when she'd heard something in the middle of a storm without benefit of a clock?

"You didn't think the shrieking might be coming from Ms. G.'s place?"

She shook her head. "Marion never raised her voice."

I didn't want to point out that she might have if she was being attacked. Why upset the woman any more than she was already?

"The door was locked when you got there?"

"Of course." She straightened, appearing concerned. "Not that Lake Bluff isn't safe, Grace. I mean Sheriff."

I waved my hand. Ms. C. had been around since long before I wore diapers, let alone a sheriff's uniform.

"Okay, thanks." I stood, held out my hand, and she took it. But instead of shaking, she sandwiched mine between both of hers. Her skin was paper-thin, soft, and mapped with roads of blue.

"I'll be fine," she said. "I'd resigned myself to losing her soon."

"What?"

"When she had the diagnosis, I was upset, but I had time to make my peace."

"I don't understand."

"Marion had congestive heart failure. The doctors

didn't give her long, although she'd been doing so well . . ." She spread her hands. "I'm glad she went in her own home in relative peace."

There went whatever theory I'd had about the shrieking being connected to some unidentifiable monster that was killing little old ladies.

I returned to Ms. G.'s house. Just to cover all my bases, I walked around the yard, and didn't find a single track. Big shock with all the rain.

Then I checked every window—locked, with no sign of forced entry—and I did the same for the doors. Beyond Ms. G. being dead, nothing was out of place— neither outside nor in.

I should have been happy that she'd gone to her reward without any help, but I had a funny feeling, and I'd learned long ago that my funny feelings were often premonitions.

7

BACK AT MS. G.'s I discovered Ian Walker bending over the corpse as the two baby paramedics looked on.

"What are you doing here?" I demanded, even though his stethoscope made it fairly obvious.

"Pronouncing her," he said. "Now she can go directly to the funeral home instead of making a detour to the hospital."

I scowled at the boys. "What did I tell you?"

"But he's a doctor," Blondie said.

"I'm the sheriff. What I say wins." I cast Walker a quick glance, but he was still messing with Ms. G. "The jury's still out on if he's really a doctor."

That made him glance up, but instead of being angry or even annoyed, he appeared amused. "Oh, I'm a doctor all right."

"I'm just supposed to take your word for it?"

"Sheriff, I'm sure you've checked my credentials, or

had one of your underlings do it. If you don't have my info yet, you will soon. If I'm lying, you'll arrest me. Since I've got better things to do than sit in a cell, believe me when I say I have a medical license and I know how to use it."

"Just because you were certified as a doctor in Oklahoma doesn't make you one here."

"I'm a doctor everywhere, regardless of if I'm licensed in that particular state or not."

I narrowed my eyes. "You're not licensed?"

"I didn't say that."

I'd had enough. Not only was the scent of him reminding me of the kiss we'd shared, but it also was making me want to kiss him all over again.

"You two go play cell phone." I jerked my thumb toward the door, and the kids left.

I had a shoulder mike, which would raise Cal quickly, but what I had to ask him I didn't want everyone else to hear, so I yanked my own cell phone off my belt, and seconds later my deputy answered.

"I don't suppose you checked those credentials yet?" I asked.

"Of course."

"And?"

"Top of his class at both places."

"His license to practice in Georgia?"

"Funny you should ask." I scowled at Walker, but he didn't appear concerned. "He's got one."

"Why would that be funny?"

"His application was scooted through damn quick. He must have friends in high places."

"Terrific," I muttered.

"What's the rush?"

"He's running around town pronouncing people. Wanted to make sure he was legal before I let him sign any death certificates."

"Who's dead?"

"Ms. G."

"Ah, hell," Cal muttered. "I liked her."

"Me, too." I disconnected, then contemplated Walker. "You're good."

I heard the words an instant too late and wanted to snatch them back before he made some sexual innuendo. But Walker wasn't the type. He merely contemplated me with an expression that said, *Told you so.*

"How did Ms. G. die?" I asked.

"I can't say for certain without an autopsy, but if I had to make a guess, I'd say it was her heart. Did she have a history of problems with it?"

He *was* good.

"Congestive heart failure, or so her friend next door told me."

He sighed as if I'd said something he expected but didn't much like. "Well, that would explain it."

"What about her face? She looks . . . scared."

Which was what I couldn't get past. Ms. G. had died at home in a way she'd been warned she might, yet her expression said otherwise, and that made all my nerve endings hum.

"She was alone," he said. "Probably in pain; she could have gone into shock. No matter how prepared we might think we are, when the time comes, we aren't."

Walker moved back to the couch, brushing his hand over Ms. G.'s eyes and chanting a short, quick chant in Cherokee. When he turned, his face appeared drawn. But why would he be upset over the death of an elderly woman who'd lived a full life, one he hadn't even known when she was alive?

"You okay?" I asked.

"Yeah." He rubbed his forehead. "Why wouldn't I be?"

"You seem upset."

"Death pisses me off."

"You can't win them all, especially when you weren't even her doctor."

"I know. It's just—" He shrugged.

Walker was a mystery. He seemed to mourn Ms. G.'s passing with a sorrow that mirrored my own. Although I was no longer completely suspicious of him, I *was* totally curious.

"What did you say?" I waved at Ms. G. "The chant?"

"The Cherokee equivalent of last rites."

"She's not Cherokee." Or Catholic.

"Doesn't matter. I told her spirit to go to Usûñhǐ' yi."

"Translation?"

His lips curved, reminding me of how they'd tasted on mine. "The Darkening Land in the West."

"Where the spirits go after death."

"You do know something."

My eyes narrowed. "There's no need to get snotty."

"You can, but I can't?"

"Now you're catching on. Why would you send a little old white lady's spirit to the Darkening Land?"

"You don't want her hanging around here, do you?" I snorted, and his head tilted, making the eagle feather swing free. "You don't believe spirits can come back from Tsûsginâ'ǐ?"

"Hard to say when I don't know what Tsûsginâ'ǐ is."

"The ghost country."

Something in my expression must have revealed my skepticism.

"You don't believe in Heaven? No Hell below us, above us only sky?"

"A John Lennon fan," I murmured. "Imagine. You have a lot of strange beliefs for a man of science."

"And you have a strange lack of belief for a descendant of Rose Scott."

"I didn't say I didn't believe in Heaven, even though I've seen no evidence of it."

"Belief in something for which there's no evidence is called faith, Sheriff."

"So I hear."

I *did* believe in things I had no proof of.

Werewolves, for instance.

8

I FINALLY MADE it to the Cartwrights' around noon. The day, as usual, got away from me.

I tapped on the front door, unwilling to ring the bell for fear I'd wake Noah from his nap. Then I heard voices in the backyard, so I skirted the wide veranda and found Malachi pushing Noah in his red plastic baby swing. For a minute I just stood at the corner of the house and watched.

Mal had the dark hair, dark eyes, and bronzed skin of his Gypsy heritage. Combined with the brogue of Ireland, a place he'd once called home, he'd been a lethal combination of looks, charm, and danger. Claire hadn't stood a chance.

He'd come to town searching for a way to break a curse of immortality and found it in her. He'd also found love and a family.

Since last summer, Mal had cut his hair and removed the earring from his ear, but he still stood out as a stranger in Lake Bluff, though folks had accepted him for Claire's sake.

My gaze turned to Noah. The kid was only two months old; I don't know why I had such an incredible crush on him. Could be because he was too young to run out on me.

Today a tiny Braves baseball cap covered his bright red hair. His blue eyes were scrunched up as he did his best to keep his gaze focused on his father's face.

"Will ye be fallin' asleep soon, son? You've worn me out, and the day's not half yet gone."

The light shone so brightly it hurt my eyes, typical of the day after a horrific storm. It was almost as if the sun had to prove itself stronger than the wind and the rain and the moon.

"I can take over," I said.

Noah kicked his bare feet at the sound of my voice and gurgled. Mal didn't even turn around. He'd been aware I was there from the moment I'd set foot on their front walk. In truth, he'd probably known I was coming for a visit before I did.

In the Gypsy tradition only the women had the gift of sight; however, Mal had a few gifts of his own. According to him, those who possessed the pure blood of the Rom—the name the Gypsies called themselves— were magic.

I'd witnessed a few parlor tricks—appearing and disappearing coins—as well as a near-supernatural ability with animals and, according to Claire, a very convincing knowledge of things yet to come.

I moved forward, taking Mal's place behind the swing. Noah's eyes followed me, and he kicked harder as I got closer. His father sat in the grass and stretched out with his hands behind his head.

Mal and I hadn't gotten on at first; I'd known he was up to something. But in the end, he'd sacrificed everything for Claire, earning not only my thanks but also my friendship.

"I heard you saw a wolf last night," he said.

"I'm not sure what I saw. Any tingles on your end?"

"I haven't had a vision, if that's what you're askin'."

"I don't know what I'm asking. Claire tells me you know things. I've seen how you are with animals." I shrugged, then gave Noah another soft push. His head was beginning to sag against the headrest. Nap time would soon be at hand. I could use a nap myself.

"I've had dreams that come true, but I've had just as many dreams that didn't. Since I stopped living as a Gypsy, the ability's fading." He held out his hands as if he wasn't sure what to do with them. "I dinna mind. The magic for me now is in Noah and Claire."

I smiled, leaned over, and kissed Noah's sweet cheek. He murmured sleepily. "Well, if anything comes to you—"

"I'll call."

"Thanks."

"I don't suppose you've contacted the *Jäger-Suchers*?"

I paused. That hadn't occurred to me.

Last summer the *Jäger-Suchers*, translation "Hunter-Searchers," a Special Forces monster-hunting unit, had come to town. We wouldn't have even known they were there, as they'd planned to slip in, shoot the were-wolves, then slip out again unnoticed—their modus operandi—but things had gotten more complicated, and they'd been forced to reveal themselves.

I knew that the *Jäger-Suchers* had resources beyond anything a small-town sheriff might. I still didn't want to call them when I wasn't exactly sure if anything supernatural was going on.

"I think I'll wait," I said.

"Wait too long and they'll just show up and take over."

"Like they won't do that anyway," I muttered. The *Jäger-Suchers* had a lot in common with the FBI when it came to sharing cases. They didn't.

A shadow passed over the yard, and I glanced up just as a great bird seemed to sail through the rays of the sun. Something tumbled out of the sky, sifting slowly downward on the current. Mal snatched the feather from the air before it got anywhere near the ground. "I didn't think you had any eagles here."

I stared at the feather, white with a dark tip. I couldn't recall the last time I'd seen one, and now I'd seen two in as many days.

"We don't," I answered. "Not really. They live in the south, though sometimes, in the winter, they'll travel to the mountains."

"Mmm," Malachi said, twirling the feather around in his nimble fingers.

"What do you think it means?" I asked.

His eyes met mine. "There's an eagle where one isn't supposed to be. What do you think it means, Grace?"

In the lives of most women, that would mean a bird whose sense of direction was on the fritz. In mine it meant the very real possibility of a shape-shifter.

"Hell," I muttered. I was going to have to call the *Jäger-Suchers*.

                               ∞

I headed to my office, trying to figure out a way to avoid the inevitable. The only thing I knew about shape-shifters was that touching some of them in human form with silver caused a nasty burn, and if you shot them with a silver bullet, whether they were on two legs or four, great balls of fire were the result.

Some of them, but not all. An unpleasant fact we'd learned the hard way last summer. Those cursed to shape-shift, rather than having been turned by another shifter, followed different rules depending upon the nature of the curse. However, it wouldn't hurt to try the silver test; it was all that I had.

Since the only new person in town was conveniently the same person I'd seen step out of the woods after the wolf had gone in, *and* he was the same person who'd shown up in town wearing an eagle feather in his hair, *and* he was a self-admitted member of a clan of medicine men, I had a pretty good idea where to start.

"Is he an eagle or a wolf?" I murmured. Did it really matter?

What good was a were-eagle anyway? I could see the advantage of a werewolf—faster, smarter, stronger, they had the abilities of wolves, with the addition of human intelligence and a lack of human compassion. Werewolves were the perfect killing machines.

So if a man became an eagle, he'd theoretically have human intelligence with the abilities of a bird. Big deal. Sure the eagle was considered a great and terrible war beast by most Native American tribes, mine included. But that basically meant eagles could kick the crap out of every other bird on the planet. Humans? Not so much. What then was the advantage?

I guess I'd just have to pin one down and ask him.

Unfortunately, it appeared that everyone else in town had the same idea—not that Walker was a werewolf or even a were-eagle, but that they wanted to meet him, talk to him, welcome him to the neighborhood. His storefront was packed.

I approached the nearest loiterer, a member of the town council and former bank president, Hoyt Abernathy. "What's up?"

Hoyt shuffled his feet, clad as always in a pair of slippers. When Hoyt had retired from the bank, he'd made a dress-shoe bonfire and worn nothing but soft soles ever since. In my opinion, a fantastic idea.

"Folks heard about poor Ms. G.," he said, in a voice reminiscent of Eeyore on a very rainy day. To Hoyt everything was an indication of upcoming disaster. In a lot of cases, he was right.

"And?" I asked.

"They wanted to pay their respects, thank the new doctor."

"What did *he* do?"

"Helped out one of our own in her last hour of need."

"She was already dead when he got there," I pointed out.

Hoyt shrugged. I scowled at the sea of people in line ahead of me.

Though I wanted to march right in and toss a silver bullet at Walker's head, I was going to have to wait.

Probably a better idea to do this in a more private place anyway. What if he exploded on Center Street? How in hell would I explain that?

I'd do better to ask Walker over to my place tonight for a get-acquainted drink. After the kiss we'd shared, he'd probably think it an invitation, and if his reaction this morning was any indication, he'd turn me down—unless I went about asking him just right.

Sadly, since I'd been elected sheriff, I had no patience for bullshit, and I'd lost any social graces I'd once had. Although most people who knew me would argue that I'd never really had any. Maybe a note would be a better idea than letting my mouth run free.

I caught a glimpse of Walker beyond the crowd, his long dark hair a delicious contrast to his stuffy suit and tie, and the idea of my mouth running free took on a whole different meaning.

Why did I keep having these flashes of lust? The guy could be part wolf, part eagle, 100 percent monster.

Maybe that was the attraction. For years I hadn't felt a thing beyond a passing interest in any man from Lake Bluff, the same went for any of the tourists, but Walker, with all his secrets and contradictions and baggage, fascinated me.

I scribbled a note, then waded through the crowd making official noises. Unfortunately, by the time I got to the front of the line, everyone had gone silent, wondering why I was here. Walker was no help; he merely contemplated me with a slight curve to his lips and a lift of his brow.

"I . . . uh—" Hell. I couldn't exactly hand him the note like a ten-year-old with a crush on the new kid, and I couldn't ask him over to my place tonight without the same problem.

"Thank you for your help today." I held out my hand. He took it, and I pressed the note into his palm.

Not even a flicker passed over his face when the paper transferred between us. No doubt he'd had this happen to him before, which only embarrassed me more.

"You're welcome." Ian released my hand and casually put his into the pocket of his pants.

I turned away, nodding at the townsfolk, noticing people from every walk of life—old, young, rich, poor, white, black, and Indian—although the majority had to be twentysomething single women. A new man in town, they couldn't help themselves. They probably thought I couldn't, either.

I was not a desperate old maid hitting on the new young stud. I *wasn't*. I'd invited him to my house to figure out what he was.

Man or beast? Human or monster? What if he came to my place in animal form?

I gave a mental shrug. That would only make it easier to shoot him. Because, despite my tough exterior, my determination to keep Lake Bluff safe from anything that might threaten it, I still wasn't certain I could put a silver bullet in a man just to be sure.

The rest of the day was full of both the mundane tasks of a small-town sheriff and the atypical happenings that came with tourists and the aftermath of a hellish storm.

I mediated a dispute between two neighbors over dog poop—they both had dogs; how in hell did they know that each other's pet was pooping in the opposite yard, and what possible difference could it make?

I had a case of shoplifting (local kid), a case of bullying (a tourist), and four calls from former residents whose loved ones weren't answering their phones after the storm.

I arrived home with an hour to spare before the appointed time with Walker—if he showed up. No messages on my machine telling me anything one way or another.

I was hot and sticky, compliments of a scalding day in Georgia and a lack of air-conditioning in my dad's old pickup. I smelled bad courtesy of both, as well as the little girl from Michigan who'd gotten lost, eaten too much ice cream, cried bloody murder, then upchucked on the front of my uniform.

The shower was heaven. I washed twice with scented soap and worked conditioner into my hair all the way to the ends; then I stood under the lukewarm spray and let my blood settle.

I opted for a loose white cotton skirt that fell to my ankles and an equally lightweight fuchsia top. I didn't bother with shoes—not after a day in cop boots. I had just enough time to walk to the water and stick in my feet.

I saw no reason to drag along my gun; the sun was still up, although I did tuck a bit of silver into my pocket for later. I planned an impromptu shape-shifter test.

As soon as I left the yard and the trees closed in behind me, I took a deep breath full of the scent of grass, leaves, and sun. I loved Lake Bluff, but here in the shadow of the mountains was where I truly lived.

Tiny animals scuttled in the bushes. Birds rustled in the trees. A snake slithered through the fallen leaves, hurrying away from me as fast as it could.

I reached the creek, lifted my skirt, and stepped in. The chill of the water on my tired feet was bliss. I wished I could throw off all my clothes and sink in as I had last night.

At the creek I felt the closest to E-li-si. When I went to the water, I could almost hear her speak. Under the moon and the stars, I missed her the least.

The sun tipped toward the horizon. Soon shadows would spread from the mountains through the trees, dappling everything with the approaching coolness of night. Dusk was my favorite time of the day. If I didn't spend it here at the water, I usually spent it on my porch just watching the evening come.

I glanced at my watch. Best be on the porch tonight. Best to get out of the woods before the sun died and the really dangerous things began to roam.

I turned and froze.

Like that wolf.

9

SHIT," I MUTTERED.

The animal tilted its head, growling as if it understood the word and did not approve.

I took a step backward; my foot slipped on a flat slick rock, and I nearly fell. The wolf gave a sharp yip, but it didn't attack, just continued to stare at me, half in and half out of the underbrush.

I couldn't run, couldn't hide. The only weapon I had was the silver bullet. Fat lot of good it would do me without a gun. I could toss the bit of metal at a person, and if they caught it and smoke began to pour from their hand, they were a shifter. However, the wolf was a little short on fingers for that test.

I hadn't thought I needed a gun before sundown. Frowning, I glanced at the sky, then back at the wolf. What the hell?

The sun was still up, and while I knew there were monsters that walked in the daytime, werewolves weren't one of them.

I peered at the wolf more closely. Black with silver threads in its fur. Long, spindly legs. Dark, dark eyes, with not a hint of white.

Just a wolf.

I sighed with relief, although there was still the issue of a wild animal choosing to come near me—not something a healthy wild animal would do—and the strangeness of this thing being here in the first place.

"Nice doggy," I murmured.

The wolf snorted. I could swear the animal understood me.

"I don't suppose you want to turn tail and run away from the big bad sheriff."

The wolf blinked once but didn't move.

"That's what I figured."

I cast my gaze around for some kind of weapon. Plenty of big rocks, but I'd never been much of a softball player. To hit the thing, I'd have to get much closer than I wanted to.

I spied a long branch—thick enough to do some damage—and slowly lowered myself until I could pick it up. The beast's upper lip curled.

"I won't hurt you if you don't hurt me," I said.

The animal charged.

Despite my lack of talent with a ball and bat, I hauled back and swung away. Not only did the branch pass right through the wolf, but the wolf passed right through me also.

For an instant I stood there gaping, shivering at the sudden chill; then I spun around. The animal sat placidly behind me, tongue lolling.

I couldn't see the grass through its body, nor the creek on the other side. The wolf seemed solid.

I poked at it with the stick. The end swept right

through its body. The animal lifted a paw and swatted at the branch, leg swooshing from one side of the stick to the other with no resistance.

"What are you?" I whispered.

The wolf cocked its head, staring at something behind me.

"I know that trick," I said. "I turn, and you jump me." Or maybe I should say *jump through me*.

"Can we have a drink first?"

I spun around despite my resolve not to. Ian Walker stood at the edge of the trees.

"I was talking to—" I glanced at the wolf, which was, of course, gone.

I didn't bother to check for tracks. Been there, done that, saw the movie.

"I . . . uh—" That seemed to be the extent of my conversation around this man.

"Did the wolf come back?"

I glanced his way; he nodded at the club. I dropped it to the ground. "Did you see anything?"

"No. But you obviously did."

"Maybe." I looked around the empty clearing. "Then again, maybe not."

"You want to explain that?"

"Not really."

He moved forward, lifting one arm, which held a six-pack, and another, which held a bottle of wine. "I didn't know what you liked."

"Thanks. But I invited you—"

He shrugged. "My mother taught me never to arrive at anyone's home empty-handed."

"We can go back—"

"No. I mean, if it's all the same to you, I'd like to sit here. I don't get much chance to go to the water."

I started at the term, but why shouldn't he know it? Despite his light eyes and skin, he was Cherokee, too. Or so he said.

Walker leaned over and set the beer and the wine in the creek, then sat on the grass and took off his shoes. He'd changed from the suit he'd worn in town to a pair of jeans and a blue button-down shirt. The color only served to make his eyes glow eerily golden in the fading light.

The sharp crunch of a beer can being opened made me jump. Walker held one out to me. "I didn't bring a corkscrew," he said. "Or a glass."

"This is fine." I took the beer but hesitated at sitting next to him. I'd asked him here to see if he was a shape-shifter. I needed to do what I'd planned before I got too close.

"I—uh—found this," I said, and before I could change my mind, tossed the bullet at his head.

He snatched the lump of silver out of the air before it hit him between the eyes. After shooting me a puzzled glance, he opened his palm and stared at the metal. No smoke rose from his burning flesh. *Yippee.*

"Strange bullet," he mused. "You find this out here?"

"Yeah," I lied.

"Huh." He put it into his pocket and took a swig of beer. "Thanks."

I blinked. I hadn't meant for him to keep the bullet, but I guess it didn't really matter. I had a hundred more just the same.

"You going to have a seat?" He tilted his head. "Or make me get a crick in my neck talking to you."

"Sure. I mean no." What was it about this guy that turned me into a gibbering idiot? I began to sit next to him, and he jumped to his feet.

"Wait." He yanked off his shirt and spread it on the ground. "You can't sit here in a white skirt."

I tried not to stare at his chest, but it was a really great chest. Ridges and dips, smooth, flawless, the dark circles of his nipples like melted caramel against the paler skin. I fought back a groan—two years of celibacy—then took a quick sip of beer to stop the drool from running down my chin.

"Grace?" He patted his shirt, which was far too close to him for my comfort.

I smiled, set my beer down, then pulled the shirt farther away under the guise of smoothing it. However, when I sat, he merely scooted closer, tilting his can toward me. "Cheers," he said.

I grabbed mine, clinking it against his a little too hard, so that beer sloshed onto my wrist. I licked it off, caught him watching my mouth, and stopped. Silence that wasn't really silence descended. In it I heard all sorts of things.

Want me. Kiss me. Do me.

"I was surprised you came," I blurted, then bit my lip at the dual meaning to the sentence. Why did everything have to remind me of sex around him?

Luckily, he didn't have the same problem, because he answered with an easy curve to his lips. "If you didn't think I'd show, why did you ask?"

I'd asked Walker here to test him for shape-shifting, but I couldn't exactly say that. "I—I'm not sure."

"Are you uncomfortable?"

"What?" *Yes.* "Why?"

"The wolf. We'd discussed it being rabid."

Oh, the wolf. Right.

"I don't think it is," I said. I wasn't sure what the beast was, but "rabid" wasn't on the list anymore.

"They say the wolf is a messenger from the spirit world," he murmured.

I started again, sloshing beer, *again*. This time I left the spill where it was.

"Why would you bring that up?"

"A wolf that appears and disappears in a place no wolf should be. Don't tell me you hadn't thought of it yourself."

I hadn't. Until now.

The wolf wasn't a shifter—or at least not any kind of shifter I knew about—so maybe it *was* a messenger. Since I was the only one who'd seen the thing, I had to think the message was for me.

"What do you know about messenger wolves?" I asked.

"Only what the legends say."

"Which is?"

"Your great-grandmother never told you?" I shook my head and he frowned. "What *did* she tell you?"

"Family stuff mostly."

Since my mother had taken off and my grandmother died before I was born, Rose had been concerned that the family history would die with her. Unfortunately, all that time spent on who was related to whom had left precious little for lessons in language and mysticism, even if I'd been open to them.

"This is what the old men told me when I was a boy," Walker began. "When someone from the Darkening Land must commune with those still of this world, a messenger wolf is sent from the west."

I glanced at the trees where the animal had appeared. Yep, west all right.

"To the Cherokee the wolf is sacred," Walker continued. "He is not to be killed for fear we might extinguish."

"I never heard that."

"Have you ever killed a wolf?"

"Not yet." I paused, thinking. "How would you kill a spirit wolf anyway?"

"I always figured the messengers were actual wolves," he said, "hence the taboo on killing them. Unless you're a wolf killer."

"Is that like an eagle killer?" My gaze rested on his feather.

"Exactly."

In Cherokee tradition, only certain people could kill an eagle—those who'd been trained in the method and the prayers that would allow such a great warrior bird to be taken without having a curse fall on the hunter and all his descendants. I'd heard the same rules applied to wolves—kill one and be cursed forever, along with your children.

"Are you an eagle killer?" I asked.

Though the title was one of honor, the words sounded more like a taunt. I hadn't meant for them to.

"I'm not," he said.

"You know only great warriors are supposed to wear the feather of an eagle?"

He turned away, resting his gaze on the slowly falling sun. "I know," he whispered.

I meant to ask what he'd done to be considered a warrior, but when he faced away he presented me with his back, and I saw the tattoo.

High up on his left shoulder blade flew the image of an eagle, talons outstretched as it swooped down on unsuspecting prey. I'd never known a Cherokee to have a tattoo. Slowly I reached out and touched it.

He moved so fast I didn't have time to draw back, let alone get away. The beer I'd been holding fell to the ground, tipped over, and melted into the grass. My hand was left hanging in the air where his shoulder had been; his fingers closed around my wrist.

"What—?" was all I managed before he kissed me.

I didn't fight; I didn't want to. His mouth was already familiar, his taste one I already craved. The air hummed with awareness, or maybe just cicadas.

His tongue tasted of beer, not unpleasant considering the heat and my thirst. I licked the inside of his mouth. His lips were cool; I wanted them to touch me everywhere.

Wait. There was a reason I shouldn't be doing this.

I tugged on my wrist; he let me go, his mouth stilling on mine as our breath mingled. Instead of pulling myself away, pushing him away, I let my hand trail over his beautiful skin, down his belly around to his back, then up to his shoulder. My finger worried the area of the tattoo—it felt almost feverish—so much so that I remembered everything I should never forget.

Sometimes people weren't people all of the time.

A shadow passed over the dying sun. An eagle lazily circled the creek. And if the eagle was up there and Walker was right here—

Well, there could be two, but since there weren't even supposed to be any . . .

My mind filled with all sorts of interesting codas to that sentence, even as my libido screamed for the only one that mattered—*forget about shape-shifters and kiss him again*—still, I hesitated.

Earlier a simple embrace had sent him to a darkened room where he had mourned next to a picture of his lost wife. I didn't want to upset him further, but I also believed that he needed to move on. Probably because I wanted him to move on to me.

I stood, and Walker eyed me warily, as if he thought I would stomp my feet and order him to leave in my best Scarlett O'Hara voice. I might be Cherokee, but I was also Scottish and Southern. I could Scarlett with the best of them.

Instead, I pulled off my shirt, my skirt, my underwear; then I held out a hand for his. "You say you never get to go to the water?"

He shook his head mutely, his gaze wandering from my thick dark hair tumbling over my breasts to my waist, past where other thick dark hair swirled, all the way to my toes, which wiggled in the steadily cooling grass.

Mist tumbled from the mountains, skating across the tops of the trees, reflecting every shade of sunset. Soon it would settle over the water, going silver along with the moon. I wanted to bathe in that mist, sink into the creek, as Walker sank into me.

I flexed my fingers, and spellbound, he put his hand into mine.

10

HE WOULD HAVE walked into the water still wearing his pants if I hadn't stopped him with a hand on his chest. The heat of his skin distracted me, the smoothness of it beneath my own, and I lifted both arms, running my palms across his pecs, over his shoulders, down his biceps.

The scent of him mingled with the scent of the trees, the mist, the water. I had to taste him or die, so I put my mouth where my hands had been, running my tongue from his collarbone to his nipple, then tracing the line of his ribs.

His fingers clenched in my hair, not pulling me away but holding me close. Slowly I straightened, cupping him through the thick material of his jeans, sliding my thumbnail down the zipper until he moaned.

"The water," he said almost desperately.

"We'll get there." I flicked open his jeans and reached inside.

Hard and hot, thick and full, he pulsed against me. "Grace, I haven't—"

I squeezed him once and he came, spurting against my belly. "You have," I murmured, continuing to work him in my fist.

His face was beautiful in the fading light, his profile harsh yet familiar, eyes closed, mouth slightly open and relaxed. Leaning up, I brushed my lips against his, and his eyes opened, staring straight into mine. "I'm sorry," he whispered.

"I'm not." I'd followed my instincts, and they'd been right. He hadn't done this in so long, he had no control. Now he would.

I waded in until the water reached my waist, then turned and waited for him. He stood on the bank, staring at me as if I were a water nymph emerging from the depths.

As I did every time I came to the water, I lifted my hands to the moon and said the words of my great-grandmother. When I lowered my arms, he still watched me.

"There is another world beneath our own," he said. "It's like this one in every way, except the seasons are opposite. Which is why the moving waters are warmer in winter and colder in summer than the air."

I smiled, enjoying the way he told the tales he'd heard from the old ones whenever something reminded him of them.

"To reach the other place we walk the trails of the springs that come down the mountains. The doorway lies at their head where we can slide in and the beings there can slide out. You're so beautiful, Grace, you seem from that other world."

I shook my head, and my hair skated across the surface of the water, tossing droplets every which way.

As a child I'd been stared at and pointed at so much that by the time I'd grown into my legs, my mouth, my nose and teeth, I no longer believed I was anything but strange.

"I'm cold," I said, as my nipples tightened, and my body seemed to come alive in a rush of blood just beneath my skin. "Warm me."

Ian stepped into the creek and immediately went below the surface, bobbing up, then dunking himself again. Once, twice, he kept at it until he'd doused himself seven times. Most every Cherokee ritual involved the sacred number seven.

At last he burst from beneath and stayed there. "Before you come to the water you should fast." He cast his eyes to the rising moon. "The ritual is performed at daybreak."

I reached out and pulled him closer. "Forget about the old ways for a minute."

I slipped my arms around his waist and licked a cool drop from his hot skin. At first I thought steam rose from his body, until I realized the mist skimmed across the surface of the creek like a snake, swirling around and over us.

"Grace," he began. "I haven't been with anyone . . ."

His voice faded, and his face darkened. He stiffened as if he might pull away, and I kissed him. Open-mouthed, lots of tongue, as I gripped his biceps and poured all that I wanted, all that I needed, into this single embrace.

He hadn't been with anyone but his wife—maybe ever, but considering his reaction to just the sight of my body, the touch of my hand, definitely since he'd lost her.

Walker was a naked man in the water with a naked woman. Eventually he kissed me back. He didn't stand much of a chance.

I believed he needed to connect with someone; I certainly needed to, and not in a nudge-nudge, whisper, snicker, connect-with-me-baby kind of way. I needed a *connection,* the sharing of bodies, some kindness and awareness in a world where there's so very little.

If, in some tiny corner of my mind, I thought, *Maybe he's the one, the one who won't leave,* I didn't know it then. Then all I knew was the taste of his mouth, the sleek, wet expanse of his skin, the scent of the water and the wind and the night. We both belonged right here, right now, with each other. I'd worry about later . . . later.

His hands raced over my body, slipping, sliding both above and below the water; the sensation of his hot flesh and the cool creek, his slightly roughened fingers on skin that hadn't been roughened at all, made me moan. He traced a palm over my hip and swooped up, cupping one breast, then the other, before scraping his thumbnail over each peak.

My head fell back, my eyes half-open so I could watch his head descend and his lips close over me. His tongue pressed my nipple against the roof of his mouth, suckling me as one finger dipped below the surface of the water and stroked.

The moon was satin on my cheeks, his mouth like silk. The lap of the creek, the pressure of his hand, I came apart in his arms just as he'd come apart in mine. He held me as I gasped, and pressed soft kisses across my chin, even as his fingers drew out the magic.

I lifted my head and met his eyes. "Sorry," I said, and he smiled, hearing the echo of himself.

"That was . . ." He paused, uncertain.

"Amazing? Astounding? Fantastic?"

"Yes."

"How about one more?" I headed downstream, tugging him along after me.

"Life-altering? Mind-boggling? Mood-shifting?"

I glanced over my shoulder, smiling at the happiness on his face. Until now, he'd only looked sad.

"When I said, 'How about one more?' I didn't mean an adjective."

The water deepened until it was over our heads. I dropped his hand and began to swim.

"What did you mean?"

He swam, too, following me around the bend and into the secluded cove where the water remained warm nearly the whole year through. I don't know if an underground spring fed the pond or if the smaller, somewhat enclosed area held the heat of the sun longer than the moving length of the creek. Either way, this was my secret place. I'd never brought anyone here, not even Claire.

At the center, I let my feet drift to the soft bottom, then rose into the moon-shrouded air like a mermaid. The water lapped at my rib cage. Droplets shone like pearls on my skin.

"I meant, how about one more?"

"Oh!" He dragged his gaze from my chest to my face. "Yes."

I floated across the few feet separating us, stopping when I was so close my breasts brushed his chest. Then I bobbed up once and sank beneath the surface.

11

GRACE!" HE GRABBED at me, but I was too quick. As soon as my mouth closed around him, he understood I'd meant to submerge.

I could hold my breath for a very long time, even without the added incentive. The water was warm, welcoming. Beneath the surface everything was dark.

He was already hard; I wasn't surprised. Even though I'd taken the edge off earlier, he was still a desperate man. I'd never known I had a thing for desperation until I'd tasted it in him.

Lazily I ran my tongue along his length, then drew him deep within. The swirl of water past my face revealed movement even before his hand cupped my head, showing me the rhythm. In and out he pumped against my lips. Long before I was ready, he urged me upward. I shook my head, suckling him hard, grazing him with my teeth before I gave in and burst from the water.

His hands found my arms; he dragged me against

him, the poke of his erection insistent. He tasted of need. I wrapped myself around him and held on.

He fell back, taking me with him, and side by side we floated, kissing, touching, arousing. My shoulders bumped against the mossy bank, and I twirled with the current until he was braced against it, then slid up his body until we were face-to-face. His hands spanned my waist; my legs opened, then closed around him.

He seemed to know my body better than, or at least as well as, I did, slowing, shifting, taking the pressure away from one place and applying it to another.

His lips traveled everywhere, first soft, then hard, a nip of the teeth, a stroke of the tongue, just enough, not too much. There, yes there. Again.

I wanted the release; I begged for it, too. He made me wait, nearly gave it to me, then made me wait some more. The moon shone, round and impossibly white on my upturned face as I rode him, desperately seeking something.

His body convulsed, triggering an answering convulsion in mine. The sharp, hot puff of his breath against the damp skin of my breasts made my nipples tighten, the reaction echoing in the deepest part of me.

In the aftermath, I lay draped over him. He was strong; he kept us both above water. The warmth, the gentle lap of the waves that slid into the cove from the moving creek, lulled me. I almost fell asleep.

"Is this where you bring all the guys?" he murmured.

I stiffened, lifted my head, and met his curious eyes. I could see how he'd think that. We'd only just met and now we were naked. Maybe I *was* a slut, but most men had the sense not to say so.

"You're the first."

He frowned. "I don't think so."

"Ass." I shoved myself off him, scooting backward in the water. "I didn't mean first, first. I meant first person I've ever brought here. This place is special, but you, Doctor, are not." I began to swim home.

He caught me before I reached the colder, faster rushing water of the creek, grabbing me around the waist and hoisting me against him. I struggled, but he was bigger, stronger, more determined than me.

"Hey," he murmured, putting his forehead against mine. "I'm sorry. That was . . . stupid."

"You think?" I kicked him in the shin. Since I had no leverage and the water dulled the blow, it was a childish gesture, but I felt better.

"I'm sorry," he said again. "I'm no good at this."

"What? Speech? Social niceties? Tact?"

"All of them. Since my wife—" He sighed, his chest rising and falling against my own. "I haven't been with anyone and I've never been very good at keeping what's in my head from shooting out of my mouth. I like you and I didn't want—" He broke off. "I'm making a bigger mess of this now than before, aren't I?"

"I don't think that's possible." I pushed against his chest, and this time he let me go. "Listen, I don't sleep around. This is a really small town, and it's bad for business." I shoved my hand through my dripping hair. "Sleep with a guy, he expects privileges."

"What kind of privileges?"

His face had hardened, his biceps, too, as his hands curled into fists. I found myself charmed by his defense of me, as well as the flex and flow of his muscles. God, I was pathetic.

"Fixed parking tickets. Free rein to speed wherever and whenever. Leniency for all his kith and kin."

"Seriously?"

"Seriously."

"I can see why you'd be leery. So why me?"

I didn't want to explain about two years of celibacy, exacerbated by the way he smelled, the way he looked, how he'd made me feel when he'd touched me. I was pitiful, but I didn't want him to know that.

I let my gaze wander from the top of his sodden feather to where his spectacular chest disappeared into the water. "Why not you?"

"You don't think I'll ask for favors?"

I tilted my head. "Will you?"

"No."

"We're adults," I said. "We both needed the release. We can just leave it at that and go back to being . . ." I spread my hands. "Whatever."

"You think I can go back to being *whatever* with you, after this?"

I held my breath. I so didn't want to go back to being "whatever" with him, but I'd had too many years of being the one left behind, even figuratively, to put myself on the line like that ever again.

I thought about the guys who had come before. Not a one of them had ever had a problem with a few days of sex and then never seeing me again. Of course none of them, for several years anyway, had lived in Lake Bluff. Not that any of the townies had had a problem calling it quits with me, either.

For that matter, neither had my mother. . . .

When I didn't answer, he made an aggravated sound. "I'm not a robot, Grace. If I share myself with someone, I do it for a reason."

"Sex."

"I'm not made that way."

"You're a guy. Don't tell me you haven't had meaningless sex and walked out the next morning."

"I didn't say that. But this wasn't meaningless and you know it."

I did, although I wasn't exactly sure what it was. Not love. But something a step above a quickie in the night.

Something swirled through the water near my hip. I jumped, thinking snake, until his hand slid into my own. "Why don't we see where this goes? We kind of went at things out of order, but what would you say to a date?"

My face must have revealed my confusion, because he continued with a laugh in his voice, if not his eyes. "You know, dinner, a movie, maybe a walk beneath the moon?"

"Sounds vaguely familiar."

"I thought it might. Tomorrow night?"

I nodded. I couldn't believe we were standing in my pond, discussing dinner and a movie while naked. Talk about back assward.

Walker stared up at the towering hills, navy blue against the indigo night. "I'd like to see Blood Mountain sometime. Have you been there?"

"Sure. My great-grandmother used to take me."

His gaze lowered. "Why?"

"It's beautiful. We had a picnic."

Waterfalls and hiking trails surrounded the peak. We'd eaten on the banks of Lake Winfield Scott. It was one of my fondest memories.

But we hadn't gone there just to eat in the sun. According to Grandma, Blood Mountain was sacred. Our ancestors had once worshipped it. On Blood Mountain the greatest of magic was born. She'd done some awe-some things there, things I'd never told anyone about.

"The history books claim the mountain was named because of a battle between the Cherokee and the Creek."

"People still find arrowheads," I said. Though no one had been able to decide for certain what year the battle had occurred.

"The Cherokee won."

"Of course."

He smiled. "And the Creek gave them Blood Mountain. It's a holy place."

A spooky place, that's for sure. I'd often wondered if the blood that had been spilled there had turned the very earth and the air of that mountain into something otherworldly.

"Usually the Cherokee revere the highest point," Ian mused, "like Brasstown Bald, so it's odd they took such a shine to Blood Mountain."

"Not really," I muttered, thinking of the way the light hit the lichen and rhododendron, turning the mountain the shade of freshly spilled blood.

"What was that?"

"Nothing. It's a great place. Lots of hiking trails. Neat-o."

Ian lifted a brow. "I'll take your word for it."

A sudden and disturbing thought muscled into my head. "I left my phone at the house." The whole town could have gone up in flames while I'd been banging the new doctor. That would play great during the next election. "I have to go."

Ian tugged on my hand, and I paused, glancing at him. "You have every right to a life, Grace. That's one thing I learned—though a little too late for Susan."

"That was her name?"

He appeared startled he'd said it out loud. "Yes. I shouldn't talk about her so much."

"Yeah, you've been a real chatterbox on the subject."

"Feels like it."

"I don't mind, Ian. You obviously loved her; you lost her; you miss her."

"Obviously," he murmured, then dived into the creek and swam away.

⚭

I offered Ian the use of my shower, but he seemed in a sudden hurry to leave.

His taillights disappeared down the drive; then the sound of his tires rolling faster and faster across the pavement of the highway that led to town drifted on the wind. Despite our supposed "date" tomorrow night, I wondered if I'd ever set eyes on him again.

I shrugged it off. I was used to seeing men's taillights. So why did it seem so much worse this time?

Because I'd felt something, just as he'd said. A kinship. Perhaps just the shared heritage and the interest in our past, maybe more. Did it matter? I had a full life—a busy job, a friend or two, a community. I didn't need Ian Walker any more than he needed me.

Inside, I checked all my phones and messages.

Relieved to find nothing that couldn't be handled tomorrow, I headed for the shower, but before I got there a slight scratch at the back door drew my attention.

I glanced out the window, didn't see anyone, shrugged, and turned away.

Yip.

My eyes narrowed as the scratching began again.

Not wanting to meet whatever was out there while I

was stark naked, I grabbed some jeans and a tank top from the clean pile atop the dryer, found my gun where I'd left it in the junk drawer, loaded it, and slowly opened the door.

The wolf sat right on my porch.

I tightened my finger on the trigger. The animal tilted its head, unconcerned. Since a stick had passed right through it, I had no doubt a bullet would do the same. I eased my finger away.

"What do you want?" I asked.

The beast tilted its head in the other direction. There was something about the eyes that disturbed me. They weren't human; they didn't seem crazed or evil, but they did seem familiar.

"Do I know you?"

Yip!

Swell, was it one yip for yes and two for no or the other way around?

The wolf got to its feet and my finger went back to the trigger. Spirit wolf or not, I didn't plan to let the thing jump me without trying to stop it.

However, the animal whirled and trotted down the steps, pausing at the bottom to peer over its shoulder at me as if waiting.

All I could do was stare. The wolf had passed right through me earlier, yet it was capable of scratching at the door. How could that be?

The beast ran a few feet toward the woods, then waited. I contemplated the Lassie-like behavior. "You want me to follow you?"

Yip.

I was starting to think one was for yes.

According to Ian, a wolf was a messenger from the spirit world. If so, I really wanted that message.

The animal whined, scratched at the ground, trotted to the tree line, then halfway back again.

"What the hell?" I slipped my feet into the sandals on the porch, shut the back door, and followed my messenger into the mountains.

12

THE WOLF LED me through thick towering spruce, so close together the silver light of the moon barely penetrated their branches. I glanced back, but the trees had already swallowed the white gabled roof of my house. I did see a few of the bats that I couldn't seem to oust from the attic flitting in front of the moon.

The night had cooled, but the air was muggy, hard to breathe, especially when we continued on for the better part of an hour.

I'd been this way before. My great-grandmother had lived at the foot of the mountain, preferring a remote cabin to putting up with my father, whom she'd never had much use for.

According to Rose, men were good for two things: providing children and hunting. Other than that, they could go to the Devil. I guess it was lucky for them both that my great-grandfather had died young. I didn't think Rose had ever been easy to live with.

At first I wondered if we were going to her cabin—maybe someone was squatting. Why such a minor offense would warrant a messenger from the Darkening Land I had no idea, but when I took a step in that direction the wolf growled and kept on what appeared to be a straight arrow to someplace else.

My mind began to wander. Where were we and why? What possible message could there be for me up here where the mist began?

The sudden silence made me pause. I looked ahead, to the side, even behind me, but the wolf was gone.

"Nice one, Grace." I rubbed my sweating palm against my thigh and took a better grip on the gun. This suddenly smelled very much like a trap.

The wind lifted my hair, which had dried once again into stiff-straight hanks, and slapped them against my face. The trees rattled like dry bones, and dead needles tumbled from the sky like spruce-scented rain.

The underbrush moved, first here, then there. Ah hell, everywhere. I turned a slow circle, searching the darkness, twitching at every slinking shadow.

Something flew across the moon—a bat, a bird, a beast? I glanced up, but it was already gone, and when I lowered my head a human-shaped silhouette emerged from the night.

An old woman, bent but still strong, her hair long and black, with strands of silver lit by the moon. Clothed in what appeared to be traditional Cherokee dress, a sleeveless shift made of deer hide, belted at the waist and ending at midthigh, complemented by a knitted underskirt with beaded fringe that fell to the ankles. Her feet were covered in soft moccasins to the knees.

I was again reminded of those who had disappeared into these mountains during the removal, hiding so well from the white soldiers that to this day no one had ever found them.

The woman lifted her head, and the outline of her face was familiar. "E-li-si?" I whispered. "Grandmother?"

"Gracie?"

The voice wasn't hers. How could it be?

"Quatie." I stowed the gun and hurried forward to help the woman who'd been my great-grandmother's best friend. "What are you doing out here in the dark?"

Quatie was a full-blooded Cherokee, very rare in this day and age. She'd lived in Lake Bluff her entire life, as had her mother and grandmother and great-grandmother before her. She knew every tree, every trail, every stream and hill. But she was old, arthritic, and half-blind.

I took her arm. She was thinner than I remembered and less steady on her feet than I liked.

"I could ask the same of you," she said.

My gaze flicked to the trees. "Did you see a wolf?"

Her laughter was more of a cackle before it turned into a long hacking cough. I supported her until she was able to straighten, then speak. "Messenger?"

I wasn't surprised that Quatie knew what a wolf meant. The surprise would be if she hadn't.

"What did she come to tell you?" Quatie asked.

"She?"

"Who would bother to come all the way back from the Darkening Land with a message for you?"

"E-li-si," I whispered.

Quatie patted me on the arm. "What did she say?"

"The wolf's supposed to talk?"

She shrugged. "I've never seen one."

"What do you know about them?"

"Only what my own grandmother told me. A messenger from the Darkening Land is not of this world. Once their message is delivered, they will return to the west. Until you understand the message, expect visits from your *e-li-si*."

Now that I had a hint of who the messenger was, I had a pretty good idea of the message.

The wolf had first appeared on the night of the Thunder Moon, when magic happened, and she had shown up not far from here. Grandma and Quatie had been friends. Quatie was obviously ill, fading. She needed help, and Grandma had come to make sure I gave it to her. She'd led me to Quatie and then disappeared. I doubted I'd see the wolf again.

Which was fine with me. Messenger wolves were spooky, even if they were Grandma in disguise. Too Little Red Riding Hood for my comfort.

"I'll walk you home," I said.

"No need, child. I come out here every night for a little exercise before bed."

I frowned. What if she fell and broke a hip? She could be on the ground for days, weeks, before anyone found her. We might not have wolves, but we had bears. They'd love to come across a crippled little old lady buffet in the forest.

"Don't you have any relatives who could stay with you?" Despite her protest, I walked with her in the direction of her cabin.

"Why would anyone want to stay with me out here?" She patted my arm again. "And I'm not leaving. The place belonged to my own great-grandmother. My children are in their seventies, their children in their fifties." She waved an arthritic hand as if to say, *And so on.* "No one wants to spend time with an old woman who has no indoor plumbing."

"I do," I said.

"No, you don't."

She appeared almost scared, or maybe just embarrassed. I was the one who should be embarrassed. My great-grandmother had asked me to check on Quatie, and I'd done a shit-poor job. No wonder my *e-li-si* had come from the Darkening Land in the guise of a wolf. I was lucky she hadn't ripped me limb from limb. If a spirit wolf even could.

We reached Quatie's cabin. Though the building lacked certain amenities, like plumbing and a furnace, it possessed a good foundation, a solid roof, and weathered log walls, which had been chinked recently. The place appeared cozy, friendly, warm.

I caught a whiff of tobacco. Had Quatie walked into the woods to smoke? Why, when she lived alone?

Perhaps she'd been performing a ritual. Many of the Cherokee spells involved blowing smoke to the four directions.

I didn't ask what she'd been doing. Some spells were secret, known only to the one who'd invented or inherited them. These were sacred and could be ruined just by talking about them.

The place was the same as I remembered—one room that served as a bedroom, sitting room, and kitchen. What more did Quatie really need? Scattered across every surface were papers scrawled dark with the Cherokee alphabet.

Quatie and my great-grandmother had always conversed in Cherokee and written everything that needed to be written the same. They'd both been terrified that the language would be lost.

"Quatie, could you teach me Cherokee?" I blurted.

That would kill two birds with one stone; I'd learn the language and I'd be able to keep an eye on her.

"No, Gracie."

I blinked, stunned. I hadn't expected her to refuse.

"My eyes are going. I can barely read the books. My hand shakes too much to write anymore, and I'm just too tired and impatient to teach."

"Oh," I said, my voice faint with disappointment.

"You know more than you think. From the day you were born, Rose spoke to you in our language. If you let yourself, you will remember."

I had my doubts, but I nodded anyway.

"I'd better get back," I said. "Let you sleep."

"I don't sleep much anymore, but I think I will lie down. That walk nearly did me in."

"Maybe you should take it a little easier. What if you fell out there?"

"Then I fall."

"And if you fall and die?"

"Better to die against the earth, beneath my brother the moon and a hundred thousand *năkwĭsĭs,* than to fade away hidden from the sun."

"Năkwĭsĭs," I said softly. "Stars."

"See? You do remember."

I wasn't sure if I remembered or if I'd just figured it out from the context. Regardless, I liked how knowing the word made me feel. As if I'd connected to my past and in doing so made possible a brighter future.

"You're taking good care of her papers, aren't you?" Quatie asked.

"Of course." They were irreplaceable—in both emotional value and ancient lore.

"They're in a safe place?"

"Very."

I thought of the false bottom in the right-hand drawer of my father's desk—the one I'd only learned about from his lawyer after he'd died. In it I'd found all the pictures of my mother that had disappeared soon after she'd died. Now the photos were in my bedroom and my great-grandmother's papers were in the drawer.

"I'll come back in a few days," I said. "Is there anything you'd like me to bring for you?"

"I hear there's a new doctor in town."

My eyebrows lifted. The gossip grapevine never ceased to amaze me. The proof of its far-reaching voice also soothed my guilt just a little. If Quatie was getting the news that quickly, then she was in contact with townsfolk other than me, and if there'd been anything seriously wrong up here, I'd have heard about it just as fast.

"There is a new doctor," I agreed.

"He knows the old ways?"

"So he says."

"I'd like to meet him."

"Are you ill?"

Quatie glanced up and her lips quirked. "Child, I'm *old*."

"You've never gone to a doctor before." Or at least I didn't think she had.

"Rose took care of me. Her cures were all I needed. But since she's been gone, I've just made do. I'd like to hear what this young man has to say."

"I'm sure that could be arranged. I'll bring him with me the next time I come."

Quatie's eyes brightened. "He'll come here?"

"Of course." There was no way Ian would make an

arthritic old woman come to see him. I didn't know him well, but I knew that much.

"That would be lovely. Thank you."

"No problem." Quatie shifted in her chair and her mouth tightened with pain. "You're sure you're going to be all right?"

"I'll be fine, Gracie, and my great-great-granddaughter is coming soon."

"Really? When?"

She glanced out the window. "Hard to say."

I had the feeling there was no great-great-granddaughter, or at least not one who was coming to visit. Quatie just didn't want to burden me.

I'd come back in a few days with Ian. Who knows? Maybe that would be all it would take to keep Grandmother in the Darkening Land and off of my back porch.

13

I RETURNED TO my house without incident. No wolf in the woods. No bats in the belfry. No messages on my voice mail. A good night.

Nevertheless, I slept badly—my dreams full of Ian Walker's body entwined with mine, wolves howling somewhere in the darkness, and the whisper of words in Cherokee that I could almost, but not quite, understand.

The shriek of a diving bird woke me to a misty dawn. I sat straight up in bed clutching my chest, my breathing too hard and fast, so that at first I didn't realize the shriek was nothing more sinister than my phone.

I snatched it up. "McDaniel."

"Having trouble with the wildlife again, Sheriff?"

I recognized the voice at once because it made the hairs on the back of my neck lift like the ruff of a dog. "Dr. Hanover, what an unpleasant surprise."

Malachi had been right. If I waited too long to contact the *Jäger-Suchers,* they'd just contact me. Or worse, show up.

"Are you in town?" I asked.

"If I were in town, I'd knock on your door, or perhaps break it in."

She could, too. Dr. Elise Hanover was both a virologist and a werewolf.

According to everyone who knew her, she was "different," a werewolf that wasn't evil, as long as she took her medicine—a serum she'd devised to keep the bloodlust at bay. Though she was able to cure some of those afflicted with lycanthropy, she'd never been able to cure herself. I would have felt sorry for her if she didn't irritate the hell out of me at every opportunity.

"What do you want?" I asked.

"I'm following up on a report we had from the local DNR. Birds run amok? Imagine my surprise to see your name on the complaint."

"How do you always know every damn thing?"

"Just a service of your federal government, ma'am."

Sometimes the services of my federal government were downright creepy.

"If I'd wanted *J-S* help," I said, "I'd have asked for it."

"You don't have to ask; we freely give."

I snorted. "Force yourself in and do whatever you like, you mean."

"Goes without saying."

My lips twitched. She was kind of amusing when I didn't have to look at her. Elise was a perfect example of Aryan beauty. Hitler would have loved her.

"Listen," I said. "This wolf's a messenger wolf—a spirit, maybe a ghost. No worries."

Silence came over the line. *Shit.* I hadn't complained about a wolf but birds. I should never be allowed to speak without first drinking at least two cups of coffee.

"There's a wolf in Lake Bluff and you're asking questions about ravens and crows?"

"The wolf's nothing. My great-grandma came back from the Darkening Land. Wants me to keep an eye on her friend. Forget it."

"I've often wondered what people would say if they listened in on some of my conversations. This one's a beaut."

"Lucky no one can listen in, then."

The *Jäger-Suchers* had all the best toys in security and electronics.

"I've dealt with ghost wolves before," Elise said. "They aren't anything to screw with."

"Ghost wolves?"

"Ojibwe legend. Witchie wolves guard the resting places of warriors, and they aren't nice about it."

"How much damage can be done by a non-corporeal animal?"

"You'd be surprised," Elise murmured. "You do realize that crows are an indication of werewolves?"

"And ravens?"

"Them, too."

"I'd heard that crows increase in rural areas when the timber wolf population increases. I wasn't sure about werewolves."

"Works the same way."

"I've only seen one wolf and, as I said, not really a wolf. You don't need to get your knickers in a twist, Doctor. I know what I'm doing."

"That remains to be seen. So what, exactly, have your crows and your ravens been up to?"

I told her, finishing with, "I think the birds are out of whack because of the storm. I even saw an eagle a few times."

"And that's out of whack why?"

"They usually stay south, especially at this time of year."

"I don't like the sound of that. Let me do a little checking on eagle shifters."

I opened my mouth, shut it again. What could it hurt?

"Next time you see any bizarre animal behavior, call me first," Elise said. "Don't make me hear it through the grapevine. That always pisses me off."

"And I do live to please you," I muttered, but she'd already hung up.

I was wide-awake now. No chance of going back to sleep. Usually I hit the snooze three times before rolling out of bed, but today I was so far ahead of schedule, I not only made coffee and toast, but also read the paper while I enjoyed them.

Since our last newspaper editor was still listed as a missing person—though Claire and I knew better—we had a new one who was doing a very nice job. Balthazar Monihan had treated the *Gazette* like a small-town *Tattler*, printing all the gossip and running embarrassing photos of the citizens, which is probably why no one made much of an effort to find him. Not that they would have.

I turned the page, planning to glance over the smattering of obituaries published weekly, and paused.

An entire section was taken up with names, dates, and survived bys. Mostly elderly, a few terminally ill, nothing odd in the least—except for the large number.

I knew that during storms maternity wards were packed, with deliveries taking place in the hall, the elevator, the lobby. I blamed the barometer.

So if there were more births during a storm, maybe there were also more deaths. I'd just never noticed it before. All of these people *had* died of natural causes. If there'd been a hint of anything hinky, I should have been called to the scene. Nevertheless, I made a mental note to speak with the funeral director.

Since I was up so early, I stopped at the clinic. The doctor was in. Where else would he be?

"Grace." Ian's smile was full of the memories of the last time we'd met. Though I'd like nothing better than to step inside and have a repeat, I couldn't let myself be distracted. I had far too much to do.

Especially if I wanted to be ready for our date tonight—if he'd actually been serious. From the expression in his eyes, he had been. Very.

"Would you make a house call?"

His smile widened as he reached for me. "Anytime."

I stepped back, laughing. "Not that kind of house call. A real one, to a friend of my great-grandmother's."

"Oh." The hand that had been extended toward my waist lifted to push his hair out of his face. "Sure. I thought—" He stopped. "Well, you know what I thought."

"Yeah." I couldn't say that I wasn't tempted, but if I was going to take Ian to Quatie's, then get to work on time, I couldn't allow the temptation to become reality.

"Be right back."

He disappeared into the clinic, returning a minute later with a doctor's bag that looked like something straight out of a seventies TV show–*Marcus Welby, M.D.,* or maybe *Medical Center.* My brother Gene had always watched the reruns. He'd wanted to be a doctor, but he hadn't had the grades or the money. Last I heard, he was a paramedic in Cleveland.

Ian and I piled into my truck—if I had time, I'd check

on my new squad later—and I pulled a U-turn, then headed for Quatie's.

"You want to fill me in on this friend of your great-grandmother's?" he asked.

I did, giving him what facts I knew, which weren't many—an approximate age, no real knowledge of her medical history, my armchair diagnosis of age and arthritis.

"I've got more balm in my bag."

Only a few days ago I'd have rolled my eyes, snorted, or laughed out loud at the idea of herbal balm healing anything. But my nose didn't hurt and the skin around my eyes was fading from green to yellow already. I had to admit, I'd become a believer.

At Quatie's, we found her sitting on the porch as if waiting for us. When we climbed out of the vehicle, she frowned in my direction. "You didn't have to come, too, Gracie. You're busy."

I stifled a wince. Was that a dig?

No. Not Quatie. She just didn't want to burden me.

Right now, I wanted to be burdened. Maybe coming here often enough would ease my lingering guilt; I hoped it would send the spirit wolf back where she had come from.

"I brought Dr. Walker," I said.

"You didn't have to rush." Quatie moved to the steps and began to descend, slowly, painfully.

Ian sprinted forward. "Don't bother, ma'am. I'll come up."

Her round face became even rounder as she smiled. "Sweet boy. I'm so glad to see you."

Ian took her arm, and she leaned on him, patting it as he led her toward the door. But she sat in the chair she'd just vacated with a heavy sigh, her smile fading, her face strained.

I stood in the yard uncertain if I should return to the truck. Was this a case of doctor/patient privilege?

Ian glanced my way. "Could you grab my bag?"

He'd dropped it when he leaped to help her, so I scooped it up and climbed the stairs as he knelt at Quatie's feet.

"If you could stay and give me a hand." He looked at Quatie. "All right with you?"

She seemed to hesitate, and I couldn't blame her. Illness was private. But then she met my eyes and nodded. "Of course. I have no secrets from Gracie."

Ian got to work with his stethoscope. Asking soft questions. "Where does it hurt?" "How do you feel?"

Making quiet demands. "Take a deep breath." "Say 'ah.'"

Now and then he'd ask me to fetch him something from his bag—a small rubber hammer to check her reflexes, an instrument to look in her ears, eyes, nose, and mouth. As he continued to poke and pry, she began to question him.

"Where are you from?"

"Who are your people?"

"What clan is your mother?"

"Who taught you the old ways?"

"Why did you come here?"

"Do you plan to stay?"

And last but certainly not the least embarrassing: "Are you married?"

Ian answered every query with jovial patience. However, by the end of the inquisition, my patience was frayed. Quatie was obviously checking him out to see if he was good enough for me.

At last the exam, and the interrogation, was finished. Ian straightened and stepped back, leaning over his bag and pulling out a jar of balm that matched the one he'd given me.

"Use this for your aches, ma'am. I think it will help."

She screwed off the cap, took a whiff, then nodded in approval. "Rattlesnake oil. I'd run short."

I couldn't help but smile at that before asking, "How is she?"

"I'm wearing out," Quatie said, and shot me a glare when I began to protest. "Truth is truth. The body wears down. The only way to completely cure what ails me would be to get another."

"Barring that," Ian said, "use the balm. Take aspirin. Alternate ice and heat. Rest. Eat well. Exercise as much, but as carefully, as you can."

"Thank you, Doctor." She reached for his hand, then sandwiched it between hers, peering at him as if he were a long-lost grandson. "I'd love to talk to you more about the old ways."

He patted her shoulder with his free hand. "I'd be happy to."

"Now?" she asked.

Ian glanced at me.

"I . . . uh—" I had to get to work, but I didn't want to take him away when she was so clearly enjoying him.

"I'm afraid I have appointments." Ian tried to remove his hand, but Quatie held on, and he let her. "Contractors. Painters. But I'll come another day."

Quatie nodded and released him.

We left her on the porch enjoying the sun and returned to Lake Bluff.

"Sorry about that," I said.

"What?"

"The third degree. She was my great-grandmother's best friend and—" I broke off.

"She wants to make sure my intentions are honorable. I understand."

I kept my eyes on the road; I couldn't look at him.

"She doesn't want you hurt," he continued softly. "Neither do I."

I glanced over. There was something in his voice I couldn't read. But his face was open and honest. I wasn't sure what to say, so I said nothing.

A short while later I pulled up in front of the clinic. "I'll see you tonight," he said, then leaned over and kissed me. Before I could respond, he was gone.

I thought back over the last hour's happenings. I hadn't seen Quatie in nearly a year—my own fault— but despite my neglect, she'd stepped right into my great-grandmother's role. That she had made me a little choked up.

Though I didn't need anyone to protect me, it was nice when someone tried.

14

I WENT TO work, meaning to check in, then head to the funeral home as planned, except the day got away from me—extensive cleanup after the storm, electricity still out in several places, dogs gone missing. We'd had a bit of looting, too.

And the Chuck Norris bandit was back.

Today's chuckle went like this: *MacGyver can build an airplane out of gum and paper clips, but Chuck Norris can kill him and take it.*

"I never liked *MacGyver*," Cal said. "That wasn't realistic."

"And *Walker, Texas Ranger* is?" Jordan asked.

Cal scowled at her as if she were nuts. "Of course!"

There was really no talking to him.

I handed the joke to Jordan. She was keeping a file, not so much for investigative purposes as for the employees. Whenever anyone needed a laugh, they pulled out the Chuck Norris file. Cal didn't know. He'd have a cow.

Jordan went back to the switchboard. A tiny thing, despite her father's bulk, Jordan reminded me of a pixie with attitude. Maybe it was the way she kept her dark hair cropped close to her head. Could be the sharp edge to her chin or the spark in her blue eyes. Maybe it was just the collection of killer spike heels. But I liked her, and while she was the best dispatcher I'd ever had, I still hoped she earned her college money soon so she could live out her dream.

I glanced at my watch. Only an hour until change of shift. I needed to walk across the parking lot to the funeral home.

"Cal, can you take over here?"

He nodded, staring morosely at his desk. Were the jokes making him sad or was his inability to nab the culprit making him crazy? Perhaps a little of both.

Five minutes later I let myself into Farrel and Sons Funeral Home. Strangely, none of the viewing rooms were open for business. With the number of deaths, you'd think they'd be stacked like cordwood. I winced at the image.

A shuffle of a shoe against carpet announced Grant Farrel even before his Lurch-like bass murmured, "May I help you, Sheriff?"

Grant might have sounded like the butler of *Addams Family* fame, but he didn't look like him, being short, round, and sweet in both face and nature. I'd never understood how anyone could be a mortician, but I guess someone had to. I'd heard many people say that Grant's gentle and discreet manner had eased their grief. The man had a gift.

I gestured at the empty rooms. "What gives?"

His nearly invisible white eyebrows lifted toward his receding baby-fine silver hair. "Excuse me?"

"I saw in the paper that we'd had a rash of visits from the Grim Reaper. So where are the bodies?"

Grant's round gray eyes widened. Why I felt the need to be flippant whenever I entered this place I had no idea. Must be my way of coping with the uncopeable.

I cleared my throat and tried to be a good girl. "Mr. Farrel, considering the number of obituaries published in the *Gazette* today, and taking into account you're the only game in town—" He frowned and I rephrased. "You're the only funeral establishment in Lake Bluff, I'd think you'd have several services tonight."

"Oh no, Sheriff, not a one, considering. Was there someone in particular you were interested in? I could arrange for a private visit."

It took me a minute to realize he was offering to show me a corpse. "Uh, thanks. Maybe some other time. Let's get back to the lack of funerals. Why isn't there even one?" I lifted my hands and made quotation marks in the air. "Considering."

"Ah, I see what you mean. A layperson such as yourself wouldn't know."

"Know *what*?" Grant's discreet nature was starting to get on my nerves.

"In many of these cases the deceased was quite cl-derly. Most of their friends have already passed and some of their family members as well."

"Cut to the part where there's no funeral."

Grant's well-manicured hand fluttered up to his chest, and he cleared his throat. "The families, or sometimes the deceased, will make arrangements for a graveside service only."

"Straight from hospital to cemetery in one easy pay-ment?"

He winced. "It is cheaper, no doubt."

"So everyone who's died lately has been on the 'do not pass go, do not stop for a funeral' plan?"

"Not everyone. There is one service tomorrow for the family of an Alzheimer's victim."

He lowered his voice on the last two words, as if afraid that just by speaking them aloud he'd give the disease the power to rise up and grab him.

"There was nothing unusual about any of these deaths?" I asked.

"Unusual? In what way?"

I shrugged. "Seems strange to have so many."

"It happens that way sometimes, Sheriff."

"I guess you'd know."

Grant beamed. "Been in the business for forty years. Be sure and come to see us when you're ready to plan ahead."

I don't care what anyone said, Grant Farrel was ghouly.

I thanked him for his time, and as I headed for the door, Grant's phone rang.

"Hello?" He paused, listening. "Another one?" I turned. Farrel's eyes met mine and he nodded. "All right. Send him over."

The most recently deceased citizen of Lake Bluff was an octogenarian by the name of Abraham Nesersheim. There hadn't been a thing wrong with him until he'd come down with a summer cold that had turned to bronchitis.

His doctor, not Ian Walker, had ordered amoxicillin and rest. The next day Abraham's niece had found him in his bed after a long night of eternal rest. She'd called

911 and his doctor. In a replay of Ms. G.'s death, the doctor had pronounced the body and the EMTs had contacted the funeral home for direct delivery. I gave in to temptation and called the medical examiner, Dr. William Cavet.

Grant was beside himself. "Can you just order an autopsy, Sheriff, without even consulting the family?"

"When there's suspicion of foul play, yes."

"What foul play? You didn't even see the body."

"I'm afraid I can't tell you that," I said in my best cop voice.

"Of course." Grant practically bowed as he back-pedaled. "Police business. I'll just get the embalming room ready. Doc Bill has used it several times before."

I don't know that it had been several. We didn't have a lot of suspicious deaths in Lake Bluff—until last summer anyway—which is why we shared a medical examiner with the nearest town, Bradleyville.

Still, I supposed Doc Bill had used the room enough to feel comfortable there. I doubted I ever would. Not that I fainted at the sight of blood. Far from it. But I'd never been thrilled at observing an autopsy.

Looked like I didn't have much choice in this case. I wanted it done, I'd have to suck it up and watch. Twenty minutes later, the door opened and Doc Bill walked in.

He'd been a doctor for over fifty years, beginning as a GP, then becoming the ME. The man knew more about the human body than anyone I'd ever met. He also knew more about werewolves than anyone in town, even Malachi.

According to Doc Bill, Adolf Hitler had ordered his favorite Doctor Death, aka Mengele, to create a were-wolf army. Doc had been there when that army had been unleashed, just after the Allied landing. The fruits of that experiment were still running around causing havoc at every opportunity.

"Sheriff." His eyes met mine, and he lifted his bushy white eyebrows.

I knew what he was asking without the words, and I shook my head. "Not this time."

"Then what's the rush?"

"That's what I want you to tell me. Am I nuts or is something weird going on?"

"Better be more specific."

Quickly I told him about the strange increase in mortality since the Thunder Moon.

"No wolves?"

I hesitated, then decided to keep Granny to myself. She wasn't relevant.

"Not this time," I said. "No wounds on the body. No visible signs of death."

"You're pushing it, Grace."

"Humor me."

"You're the sheriff," he said, and headed for the embalming room.

The place smelled of chemicals that I really didn't want to put a name to. Everything was sparkling clean, though I didn't see the point of sanitization for the dead.

Grant had decamped after leaving the shrouded body next to a stainless-steel table covered with instruments and bowls, a scale, and a saw.

"You going to watch?" Doc Bill washed his hands and put on a gown, cap, gloves, and paper boots. I nodded. "You'll need to gown up. Don't want any of your hair or skin cells finding their way into a specimen."

I did as he asked, then stood as far away as I could get and still see.

Doc Bill turned back the shroud, revealing a marble-pale Abraham Nesersheim. I started at the expression on his face, which was very similar to the one I'd observed on Ms. G. after her death.

"Is that common?" I asked.

Doc, who'd been scribbling on a clipboard, paused. "Is what common?"

"He seems frightened to death."

Doc Bill stepped back, tilted his head, contemplated Abraham. "Not common, no. But not necessarily unusual."

He returned to work. Since there was no convenient X-ray machine at the morgue, he skipped that step and moved on to describing the outer appearance of the victim, then weighing the body.

Next, Doc sliced Abraham's chest open with what I knew to be a solid-silver scalpel. If Abraham were a werewolf, we'd already know about it.

But nothing happened. No smoke, no flames, no explosion. No shouts, no screams, no getting up and running off. Abraham was definitely dead.

Doc Bill worked with painstaking efficiency. As he did, he spoke of his findings into a tiny mike he'd pinned to his collar.

The smell of chemicals was beginning to make me light-headed when suddenly Doc froze, making a strangled, garbled sound of surprise.

I took a step forward, hand already on my gun, expecting Abraham to sit up, despite the hole in his chest, grab Doc Bill, and snap his neck like a twig. However, the corpse lay there, as a good corpse should.

"What is it?" I drew my gun. No point in being unprepared.

"Impossible," Doc managed, his voice hoarse and thin.

"What's impossible?"

His hand shook as he directed my attention to the chest cavity.

I'd never been a whiz at anatomy, but I knew what a heart looked like.

Abraham didn't have one.

15

A HUMAN BEING can't survive without a heart," I
said.

"Precisely."

"So what is he?"

Doc lifted his hand to rub at his face, saw his blood-
ied glove, and lowered it again. "I don't know."

My mind ran in several directions at once, searching
for an explanation.

"The heart wasn't removed after death?" I asked.
Anything could have happened between the time Abraham had died and Grant had been called.

Doc shook his head. "No scar."

"So what kind of monster looks human but doesn't
have a heart?"

"A woman?"

I gave Doc a quick glance. "Sorry," he said. "I make
jokes when I'm nervous."

"You and me both." Unfortunately, I couldn't think
of a single one, not even about Chuck Norris.

"He's not a werewolf," Doc mused.

"You're sure."

He lifted the silver scalpel. "As I can be."

Problem was, according to the *Jäger-Suchers,* there were more supernatural beings out there than either they or anyone else knew about.

I glanced at Abraham. *Obviously.*

"What else was Mengele making?" I wondered.

Just because Hitler had ordered a werewolf army didn't mean he hadn't ordered a whole lot more. He'd been a greedy bastard. Start with the Jews, why not toss in the Gypsies? Create a werewolf? Well, hell, let's see what else we can come up with.

"I don't know," Doc repeated. "I was just a kid, dropped behind enemy lines, fighting my way back home. We dealt with the werewolves, but I didn't see anything else."

"Did you hear of anything else?"

"No. For years when people brought up the war, I didn't listen. I didn't want to know."

"What walks like a man, talks like a man, but isn't made like a man?"

Doc spread his hands. "Zombie? Ghoul? Vampire?"

I rubbed my forehead. "Hell."

"On earth," he agreed.

Mengele's monstrosities weren't the only beings we had to consider. Many of the legends that had come down through the ages, terror-inducing tales told around campfires in every culture, were real. Which just meant I had no idea what we were facing or any hint where to begin looking for clues.

"Finish the autopsy," I ordered. "Let me know if any other crucial body parts are missing. Then get going on the others."

"Others?"

"Abraham isn't the only one who's died around here since the storm."

"You want an autopsy on every one of them?"

"Yep."

"Some of them were buried already."

"Dig them up."

"Grace—"

"Do it, Doc."

I only hoped they were still there.

⚭

I headed straight for Claire's office. She needed to know what we were up against. Too bad I didn't.

On a typical day there would be several constituents waiting in the outer office for a moment of her time. Today there weren't any, which should have struck me as strange, but I was on a mission.

"Grace!" Claire's assistant, Joyce Flaherty, jumped between me and the office door. "She's in a meeting."

"Not anymore." I moved to the right. So did Joyce.

I narrowed my eyes, trying to decide if I could take her. Probably not.

Joyce was at least six feet tall and built like the lumberjack her father had been. Though her hair was as dark as the day she'd been born, most estimates put her between prehistoric and antique.

She'd been a high school phys ed teacher before she'd become assistant to the mayor, Claire's father. Joyce had mothered both Claire and me for most of our lives, and she wasn't about to start taking shit off of either one of us now.

"It's an emergency." I moved to the left.

So did Joyce. "Can't it wait?"

"What is it about 'emergency' that you don't understand?"

"Do you really want to be sarcastic with me, Grace?" she said with deceptive gentleness.

I gulped. "No, ma'am."

"I didn't think so. Now sit down and wait until Claire's done."

I turned away. Joyce went to her desk; I turned right back and opened the office door. Then I shut it again. I should have caught a clue when I noticed that all the shades on the outer windows were drawn.

"Told you so," Joyce murmured with gleeful satisfaction.

"My eyes." I shaded them with my palm. "I've been struck blind."

"Karma." Joyce began to hit the keys on her computer in a *rat-a-tat-tat* rhythm that only made my brand-new headache worse.

The door to Claire's office opened. She scowled as she buttoned her blouse and motioned me inside.

"You missed one." I pointed to a gaping hole in the center of her chest, which revealed she'd forgotten to put on her bra. Or maybe she'd just lost it.

I used one finger to lift the lacy white garment from under the visitor's chair. Claire snatched it out of my hand and shoved it into a drawer.

Malachi lounged against the wall completely dressed except for his feet—bare. He lifted a brow and shrugged. I couldn't help but smile.

Claire was on the floor picking up papers and pencils, which appeared to have been swept from the desk by a whirlwind, or maybe just an arm.

I stifled a sigh. I wished I had a husband who'd

come to my office for a nooner—even when it was long past noon.

The thought made me straighten. I had more important things to worry about than my love life, even if it had taken a turn from loserville toward exceptional.

"Next time lock the door," I said.

"Next time keep your ass out unless you're invited in," Claire snapped, her fair Scottish skin beet red.

"Where's the baby?"

Mal pointed toward the car seat, which had been hidden by the desk.

I gasped. "Won't that cause irreparable psychological damage?"

"He's asleep, Grace."

"Oh." I knew nothing about babies. Only that I wanted some.

"What's so important that you had to interrupt the only alone time we've had in weeks?"

"Sorry," I said, then went silent.

"You want me to go?" Mal asked.

"No. You'd better stay. We've got . . ." I paused. What did we have?

Claire glanced up from putting her desk in order. "Werewolves?"

"No."

She frowned. "Something worse?"

"I don't know."

"Is this twenty questions? Because I'm really bad at games, Grace, and my patience right now is shot."

I told her everything, from last night, when I'd seen the messenger wolf on my porch, until ten minutes ago, when I'd seen a gaping hole where Abraham's heart should have been. I purposely started the tale after I'd had sex with Ian. Just because I'd walked in on

Claire and Mal didn't mean they got to walk in on me, even in their imaginations.

Besides, I knew what Claire would say. The same thing I'd said to her when I found out she'd kissed an itinerant Gypsy horse trainer.

He's out of your league.

I hadn't said it to hurt her but rather to keep her from getting hurt. Mal had looked like a player—a love 'em and leave 'em kind of guy. How could he not be when he'd once performed in a different town every week? What I hadn't known then was that he'd been searching for Claire for centuries.

In the same way, Ian was out of my league. He might not leave town at the end of every week, but he was just as emotionally unavailable. The man was still in love with his dead wife.

Boy, could I pick 'em.

At any rate, I didn't want Claire worrying about my love life any more than I needed to worry about it right now. We needed to focus on what was ripping apart our town.

"You talked to Doc Bill?" Claire asked.

"He only knows about werewolves."

"And the *Jäger-Suchers*?" Mal put in.

"Elise called this morning."

"Figures," he muttered.

"That must have been a pleasant conversation," Claire said.

"It wasn't bad, considering."

"What did she have to say after the two of you got done with your pissing contest?"

Claire knew me so well.

"She was going to check into eagle shifters."

"Huh?" Claire's face went blank. I guess I hadn't told her everything.

"Grace has seen an eagle a few times," Mal explained. "According to her, they're rare around here in the summer."

"They are." Claire bit her lip and studied me. "I hear the new doctor wears an eagle feather in his hair."

"He does. Though if he were the shifter, do you think he'd be that dumb?"

"Maybe not so much dumb as arrogant, which a lot of supernatural creatures are. With good reason."

"I doubt an eagle's our problem."

"Because?"

"The heart wasn't ripped out of the victim's chest by a bird beak; it was just gone. Or maybe never there in the first place."

"So you're thinking the *victim* is a supernatural being?" I nodded. "But if that's the case, then what killed him?"

"And why?" Mal added.

I sighed. "So many questions, so little time."

"Let's get cracking." Claire pushed her intercom. "Joyce, cancel all my appointments."

"Already done."

My eyes met Claire's and we shared a smile. Joyce could be downright supernatural herself sometimes.

"We need to call Elise."

"Your turn," I said quickly.

"Fine. Mal, any ideas about what we could be dealing with?"

His forehead creased. "I only know Gypsy legends. The *chovhani,* the witch."

We'd already dealt with the effects of one of those.

"Any bird legends?"

"Crows are good luck." I opened my mouth, but he beat me to the answer before I got out the question. "Ravens, too. The hoot of an owl is a harbinger of death, as is the howl of a dog."

"No shape-shifting birds?"

"No. The leading supernaturals for Gypsies are the werewolf and the vampire."

"I don't suppose the Gypsy vampire has no heart?" I asked.

"I haven't heard that, although one of my uncles told of a *mulo*—a vampire—literally one who is dead, that returned without a finger, and another who was marked by the tail of a dog."

I made a face; so did Claire.

"But for the most part, the *mulo* look like every other person on earth."

"Except they were dead and buried, which could be a little noticeable to the ones who buried them."

"Giving rise to that popular invention, the torch-carrying mob," Claire said.

Malachi gave her an exasperated glance. "I've met a few torch-carrying mobs in my time, and they aren't anything to joke about."

"Sorry."

Sometimes it was easy to forget that Mal had been born in a world completely different from our own.

"My people believe that the dead are angry at being dead and come back as vampires. Most often the *mulo* is someone who died by accident or design, and returned for vengeance."

"Doesn't really fit," Claire said. "The victims are dead, right? None have come back?"

"Not that I know of, though I'm having Doc do autopsies on the ones who've died since the storm."

"How do you kill a *mulo*?" Claire asked.

"The Rom use a *dhampir*—part human, part vampire—the only being capable of hunting down the undead and ending their existence."

"A Gypsy vampire killer?" I asked, and Mal nodded. "Know any?"

"As a matter of fact, I do. However, there's no need to call one."

"Because?"

"None of the victims are Gypsies."

"We did gloss over that one very important point," Claire murmured. "Any other ideas?"

"If we're going with the notion that the victims are the ones with the powers, maybe we need to research Scotch-Irish legends."

Claire nodded. "And what about the one who's killing them?"

"Once we know what they are, it should be easier to figure out what or who's after them," I said. "But first, let's make sure it isn't a *Jäger-Sucher*."

Claire frowned. "Wouldn't Elise have mentioned that?"

"You'd think, wouldn't you?" I motioned to the phone.

Claire sighed and made the call.

16

F IVE MINUTES LATER, Claire hung up.
"Elise insists there are no *Jäger-Suchers* in town."

"I don't trust her."

"She'd have no reason to lie, especially since we already figured out there's something rotten in Lake Bluff."

"I suppose she's sending an agent to take over for us idjuts and save the day."

"Not so much," Claire said. "According to her, all their agents are otherwise engaged. The last full moon was a doozy."

I didn't like the sound of that. From both Claire's and Malachi's expressions, they didn't, either. If supernaturals were acting up all over the place, that more than likely meant they were acting up here, and we were on our own.

Nothing we hadn't been before.

"Any advice from the great werewolf in the impenetrable fortress to the north?"

"Sounds like a fantasy novel," Claire murmured.

"Never sell," I said. "Too unrealistic."

"Got that right. Elise thought we were doing all that we should—exhuming the bodies, ordering the autopsies, checking the legends."

"Damn, we're good."

Claire shot me a glare, and I shut up.

"She hadn't uncovered any eagle shifter information, but suggested we check local Native American traditions, as they've been having a few problems in that direction."

"She mentioned witchie wolves." At Claire's lifted brow, I elaborated. "Ojibwe. Not from here."

"Doesn't mean they couldn't catch a plane, train, or automobile."

"Most Native American legends are tied to the land of their people, the way those people are part of the land they love."

"Like you and these mountains."

"Exactly."

"So we should be checking Cherokee legends," Claire mused. "You do that. I'll take the Scottish ones and Mal can take the Irish."

"Unless he already knows them."

Malachi shook his head. "We lived in Ireland, but we weren't truly Irish. We were Gypsies, remaining outside of every society we lived among, only trusting of ourselves."

His gaze went to Claire and softened. He'd been trusting of no one but other Gypsies until her.

I cleared my throat; they stopped mooning at each other and returned their attention to me. "We're going to have to tell the populace something once they get wind of the autopsies and the exhumations."

"Something that won't cause a panic," Mal murmured. "Mobs come in all shapes, sizes, and centuries."

People did get up in arms very easily, and around here that would mean a lot of guns in the streets—a cop's nightmare.

"What about a virus?" Claire proposed.

"Maybe." Better to have people staying at home, wearing masks to the store, rather than running around in the forest with their weaponry. "I'll talk to Doc. I'm sure he'll have an idea."

"Good." Claire tapped her keyboard, and her computer came to life. "Let's meet tomorrow."

"Same bat time?" I asked.

"Same bat channel," Claire answered.

We'd watched a lot of classic TV as kids—my brothers' favorite way to shut us up so they could do whatever it was older brothers did when forced to babysit.

As I closed the door behind me, Mal asked, "What's a bat channel?"

I glanced at my watch. My shift had ended over an hour ago. A quick call to Jordan revealed there were no pressing emergencies that required my attention.

"I'm headed home," I said. I could do my research in the office, but I'd learned it was better to do anything funky on my personal computer.

All I needed was to be under investigation for blowing up a citizen with a silver bullet and have the investigators discover I'd been researching werewolves during my on-duty hours.

I checked in with Doc Bill on my cell as I drove out of town. He was on top of things—having already done the paperwork for the additional autopsies and the exhumations. The lack of a heart in Abraham had freaked Doc Bill out as much as it had me.

"What are you going to tell the relatives?" I asked.

"As little as possible."

"Seriously, Doc, we should get our stories straight."

His sigh sounded tired, and I felt kind of bad. The man was at least eighty and should have retired years ago. But his wife had died, and he'd kept working. He'd always seemed happy about it, until now. Can't say that I blamed him, but I needed Doc on the job. I certainly couldn't explain this mess to someone who wasn't already with the program.

However, when he spoke again, he seemed stronger. Doc knew what was at stake; he wouldn't fail me.

"I'll tell anyone who insists on an explanation that we're doing a study for the Centers for Disease Control."

"Okay."

"I can make it sound official. Government ordered. Hush-hush. Blah-blah-blah."

"And when they panic about the Ebola virus?"

"I'll swear whatever this is, it isn't contagious."

"In other words, you'll lie your ass off."

"Without a qualm, Sheriff. We don't know what we're dealing with, and a panic won't help anyone."

"I like how you think, Doc."

"That's because I think like you."

"And smart, too. You're my kind of co-conspirator."

He chuckled. "I'll get back to you," he said, then hung up.

Another thing I liked about the man—he didn't bother with niceties. He got the job done. I only hoped he'd get *this* job done before we had more bodies on our hands.

I turned into my long dirt drive, holding tightly to the steering wheel as my dad's truck jerked over the muddy ruts left by the storm. I hadn't had a chance to ask Claire about my new squad car, but since the truck worked so well on the still-saturated side roads, that was probably for the best.

The wheels bounced over a particularly large hump and rolled down the other side, sliding into my front yard and nearly slamming into the car already parked there.

"Crap." I'd forgotten about my date.

Ian Walker wasn't in his car. He wasn't on the front porch. I glanced toward the trees, wondering if he'd gone to the creek, hoping to find me there as he had last night. How mortifying that he might think I'd actually wait for him at the water for more of the same . . . although it wasn't a half-bad idea.

I had to remind myself that this was an affair, nothing more. Even though I'd broken my self-imposed rule on sleeping with a resident of Lake Bluff, that didn't mean this was going to be anything more than a short interlude that would end badly.

If that's all this was, then where lay the harm in going directly to bed? After the day I'd had, I could use a little comfort, a chance to forget for a few moments everything that was whirling in my head.

I climbed the porch steps and opened the door. Ian sat at my kitchen table.

I looked at the door, then at him. How had he gotten in?

"The door was open," he said.

Which wasn't like me. Of course I had been distracted lately—hot doctor, messenger wolf, ravens, crows, eagles, dead people.

"I forgot," I said. "There was—" I stopped. I couldn't tell him even if I knew.

"It's all right." He got to his feet, hovering by the table as if uncertain.

"It isn't. I didn't think. I'm not good at—" I waved a hand.

"Talking?"

"No, that I'm good at. I suck at dating."

"Then we're two of a kind. I haven't dated since . . ."

His voice trailed off, and he glanced down, his braid and the feather swinging across his face. I'd reminded him again of his dead wife. Maybe I wasn't as good at talking as I'd thought.

"I wrecked everything. I'm—"

His head came up. "Don't say you're sorry. I'm glad you forgot."

My eyebrows lifted. "Glad?"

"Grace, I'm a doctor. I'm going to forget a lot of things. Dates. Birthdays. There'll be times I'm so wrapped up in something, I might forget your name." My eyebrows lowered, and he laughed. "Kidding."

"You aren't mad?"

"Of course not." He brushed his hair out of his face. "There was something we didn't discuss the other night."

Discussion hadn't been on my list of options, but I had a pretty good idea of where this was headed.

"Protection," I said. We hadn't used any.

"Yes. I . . . well—I didn't think."

That made two of us.

"I'm on the pill," I said. Had been for years. I wanted children, but a surprise pregnancy was not the way I planned to get them. "And I've never had unprotected sex."

"Never?"

"Until you."

That admission made me look away from his intent gaze. It felt like more than it was. It felt like some kind of promise.

"I haven't either," he murmured.

I looked up. Was he serious? From his expression, very. I wasn't sure if I should believe him, but what reason would he have to lie? Besides, that milk had already been spilled, so to speak. No sense crying over it now.

I smiled and his shoulders relaxed. He was as glad to have that conversation out of the way as I was.

"What was so engaging that you didn't get home until nearly nightfall?" he asked.

"The usual."

"Which is?"

He seemed awfully interested, but maybe it was just the natural curiosity of a non-cop for a cop's life. I'd fielded such questions a hundred times before, but I really didn't want to now.

"Cats up trees, dogs in the garbage. Such is the life of a small-town cop." Most of the time—just not lately.

"Hear anything from Quatie?"

"No." I tensed. "Did you? Is there something wrong?"

"Not that I know of." He spread his hands. "I was just making conversation."

"Oh. Right." I shuffled my feet. "Thanks again for seeing her."

"My job and my pleasure. She's a neat old lady." I warmed at the description. She was. "Did you still want to go out to dinner?"

He seemed so out of place wearing a suit and tie in my eighties-style peach and teal kitchen. I'd run out of remodeling money a long time ago.

His ring reflected the overhead light, flashing silver

even though it was gold. His feet were bare; he'd kicked his sandals off at the door.

I think it was the feet that got me—long, slim, tan. They made me want to take off my shoes, too, along with everything else. I crossed the room and kissed him.

I needed to get to work, but right now I needed this more. From the way he kissed me back, he did, too.

My fingers tangled in his hair, the sweep of the strands, the braid, the feather over my wrists made me shudder in anticipation. What would that feather feel like drifting over my breasts, my stomach, my thighs? I intended to find out.

I backed away; he reached out, then stopped, clenched his fingers, and let his arms fall slowly to his sides. "I'll go. You're tired."

"Do I look tired?"

"No." He moved closer, his gaze wandering over my face, staring at me as if I were fascinating. "You look . . . amazing." I smiled. "That balm really worked."

My smile faded, but he didn't notice.

"I wasn't sure it would." He began to pat his jacket, his pants pockets. "I have to make a note. Check Quatie in the next few days and see if the results are the same."

I saw now why he'd warned me about forgetting things. Give him a medical miracle and he was in another world. I couldn't blame him, but now was not the time.

Taking his hand, I led him toward the stairs.

17

H E HAD THE good sense to keep quiet as we climbed to the second floor and entered my room. Once there I pulled off my gun belt, unloaded my Glock, and shoved everything into a drawer.

I turned, expecting him to be stripped to the skin. Instead he stood in the doorway staring. Well, I had used most of my remodeling money here.

We'd walked into a forest—or at least that was the impression I'd wanted to convey. The walls, the bedspread, the heavy curtains were green, with detailing that made them seem like long, swaying blades of grass. The carpet held the blue of a mountain lake reflecting a sunlit sky. I'd bought sheets and pillowcases in a muted violet, the same shade as a lily pad. A miniature fountain in the corner spread the peaceful sound of running water.

"You must sleep right through the night in a place like this."

The way Ian said it, the way he stared, made me think he didn't sleep through the night often. Some people didn't. My dad had been one.

He'd wandered the house at all hours, making it extremely difficult for me or any of my brothers to sneak out. When we were kids we'd thought he did it on purpose, but now I realized he'd been troubled—by my mother's desertion, the stress of raising five kids on his own, the job, probably all three.

Then, just when he and I were starting to get along, bonding over the job in a way we'd never bonded over anything else, he'd died on me. Massive coronary, just like Claire's father. My dad had been older than hers by at least twelve years, me being the youngest and Claire being the only. However, Dad had shared with Jeremiah Kennedy not only a close friendship but also a deep love for booze, cigarettes, and red meat.

However, I didn't want to think about my father, or anything else, right now.

"Shut the door," I said.

When the door closed, this room became an island, filled with the sight and sound and scent of serenity. I pulled candles out of the nightstand, fumbled a bit for a match. A soft glow swirled through the room—the forest beneath a murky moon.

Ian took a deep breath. "Grass, water." He frowned and breathed in again. "The air right after a thunderstorm. Where did you get those candles?"

"My great-grandmother made them."

Another thing I couldn't do if I couldn't read her papers. She'd always made the most amazing candles that gave off scents no one in the world could duplicate. She'd lived on the proceeds from the ones she sold to a gift shop in town. Every time I went past the place, the owner begged me to tell her how Grandmother had done it, but I didn't know.

"These are the last of them." I peered into the flames, mesmerized.

I felt him come up behind me. "Thank you."

That he understood what the candles meant, and what it meant to use them, made my stomach flutter. When he kissed the back of my neck, my stomach dropped toward my toes.

His hands slid around my waist, his palms resting on my belly as if he knew the turmoil going on beneath my skin. I leaned back, absorbing his heat, enjoying the pressure of him against my spine. Arching, I rubbed myself along his hardness, and the hands that had been gentle were gentle no longer.

He gripped my hips, pulling me more tightly against him, then running his palms up my ribs, cupping my breasts through the heavy material of the ugly sheriff's uniform. I had to get it off; I had to feel all of him against all of me.

Buttons opened under my busy fingers. His were occupied releasing my pants.

"Wait," he whispered as I began to shrug out of the shirt, his breath tickling the moistness left on my neck by his mouth and making me shiver. "Let me touch you like this."

Before I could ask or even wonder what he meant, he spun us around so that we were facing the mirror above my dresser. The candles gave off just enough light so I could see everything.

My uniform blouse gaped open, my lacy white bra peeking from beneath. My pants unbuttoned, unzipped, the silken V of my panties revealed, as well as the swirling, curling darkness that lay beneath.

His hand stark against my belly, his skin lighter than mine, our hair the same shade of ebony. Him wearing a suit, all buttoned up and stiff. Me in my uniform, unbuttoned and loose. We looked like an ad in *Hustler*.

His fingers slid beneath the tan waistband; then lower still, they crept beneath the white silk, one finger unerringly finding the center and stroking.

I arched, my shirt parting as my breasts thrust upward, seeming to strain at the soft white cups of my bra.

He nuzzled my ear; his teeth worried the lobe, as his finger continued to stroke. I was so interested in that finger, I didn't notice his hand releasing the catch on my bra until the pressure eased and his palm swept over the tingling peaks.

My eyes remained open, watching him, watching me, watching us. I couldn't see what he was doing beneath the cover of the bra still hanging over my shoulders, shrouding my breasts; I couldn't see what his finger was doing beneath the white silk of my panties, which only made what I felt more exquisite.

His thumb rolled my nipple, then joined with the forefinger to pluck me in a rhythm equaled by the strokes between my legs. His tongue swirled into my ear with a similar beat as my blood pulsed in time with the throbbing of his penis pressed to the curve of my spine.

One more hard thrust of his finger and I cried out, riding the wave, riding his hand as he drew out the orgasm. Lights flashed in front of my open eyes so brightly I was forced to close them, even though I wanted nothing more than to watch the two halves of myself—the woman and the warrior—cry out as one.

When it was over, he turned me around and kissed me. He was still hard against my stomach. I wanted to touch him as he'd touched me.

My fingers worked at his belt, his buttons, the zipper. He began to protest and I bit his lip, just a nip, one I could soothe with my tongue.

As he'd done, I slid my palm down his stomach, enjoying the flutter of the muscles beneath his skin; then my fingers slipped beneath the waistband of his briefs, immediately encountering the smooth, hard length of him.

I took him in my hand, rubbed my thumb over his tip, then worked him until his tongue was darting in and out of my mouth and his hips were pumping in time to the flick of my wrist. When he was so close I didn't dare go any further, I shrugged out of my shirt, my bra, then stepped out of my boots, my slacks, my socks. Holding his gaze, I dipped my thumbs into my underpants and lost them, too.

His eyes flowed over me like water over rocks; smooth and cool they caressed. When he reached for his tie, his fingers shook, and I took pity on him.

"Let me." I undid the knot, tossed the length of silk aside. Made short work of his buttons, revealing his beautiful smooth chest inch by glorious inch.

Shoving the jacket and the shirt from his shoulders, I couldn't help but pause to taste him; then I became distracted by the slope of his collarbone, the flat, dark disc of his nipple, and the spike of his ribs and hips.

"Grace," he muttered. "You're killing me."

Lifting my head, I smiled. "Not yet."

I stripped him of the rest, admiring the way his penis sprang out of his underwear ready for anything.

Then I inched him backward until his legs met the bed, and gave him a little shove.

He fell, bouncing once and laughing. The sound was so light, so uncommon coming from him, that I paused just to listen. But when I didn't join in, he began to sit up, so I straddled him.

I didn't think I could be ready again so soon, but I couldn't wait; I didn't want to, and from the way he cursed when I pressed my damp curls against him, he didn't want to, either.

Lifting myself, I took him in, my breath coming faster as he filled me, stretched me, took me. His palms cupped my hips, pulling me down as he pressed up, and I began to move.

"Wait," he managed, voice hoarse, the desperation at its edge a contrast to the word. He tightened his fingers, stilling me.

"Are you crazy?" I asked, fighting against his hold, needing to move as much as I needed to breathe.

"Shh," he murmured, then yanked the band off the end of my braid. "Shake it out."

I did, my hair flying, sliding across his chest, flicking his face, cascading over my shoulders, my breasts, rippling all the way past my hips.

"Now," he said, and I clenched my thighs, ready to ride.

But he flipped me onto my back, the movement so sudden, so unexpected, all I could do was fall.

I landed with an *oomph,* and I had no time to recover as he slid into my body once more. We were both on the edge, so close we shook with it. I lifted my legs, crossing my ankles at his spine, the movement pressing us together just so.

The lights went off in front of my eyes again, even

though this time they were closed. He pulsed inside of me, his sigh in tandem with mine. He buried his face in my hair, kissed my neck, then my cheek, then my mouth.

He grew heavy, lax with satisfaction and languor. I had the same problem. All I wanted to do was sleep, but I wanted to breathe, too. I shoved at his shoulder, and he tumbled onto his back. As he did, his eagle feather brushed my skin and heat trailed in its wake.

I rolled onto my side, fingered the feather. "I was wondering how this would feel against my—"

He turned his head, lifted a brow. "Your what?"

"Use your imagination."

He lay back and closed his eyes. "All right."

I hadn't meant "use your imagination" literally; then again, round three was beyond me right now. I'd just hold that thought, or maybe dream a little dream.

From the smile on Ian's face, he was already doing just that.

18

I AWOKE TO complete darkness, disoriented. I'd forgotten the candles.

Panicked, I turned in that direction and bumped into
someone. The sense of dread increased momentarily
before everything came flooding back.

Ian. The date that wasn't. The sex that was.

I relaxed, allowing my thigh to press against his.
This was nice, though I didn't dare get used to it. Once
I did, he'd be gone. I knew that as surely as I knew he
was going to break my heart if not sooner, then definitely later.

Now I couldn't sleep.

I glanced at the clock. Four A.M. I might as well get
up and do the work I was supposed to have done last
night. When I met with Claire and Mal I certainly
didn't want to do so empty-handed. They'd wheedle
out of me why, and I really didn't want to say.

I slid from the bed, snagged my robe from the closet,

and slipped out the door without Ian ever moving. He seemed to be sleeping well, and I was glad.

I'd left my laptop downstairs, so I padded in that direction rather than to my office. I'd installed wireless Internet the week after I'd buried my dad.

In the same way that Claire's father had sneered at air-conditioning, calling it a sinful waste of money, mine had refused to allow the Internet in his house. Anything that needed to be done in that direction could be done at work or at school.

Personally I'd thought he was scared of computers. I never had seen him use one when he could get someone else to use one for him. He'd called it delegating; I'd made chicken noises when his back was turned.

At any rate, I now had wireless Internet and Claire had central air. The times they were a-changing.

In the living room, I curled up in the recliner, tucking my bare feet beneath the hem of my robe. It might be summer, but the nights often turned cool, especially this close to the mountains. Right now the windows had fogged over with the mist that would shroud everything until the sun burned it off.

The computer connected, the cursor blinking, waiting for me to proceed. I bit my lip. It was kind of hard to look up creepy crawly things when I didn't know which creepy crawly things I wanted to look up.

I typed in *supernatural creature without a heart*. I got back nothing useful.

I tried *heartless,* which was worthless, as were any other combinations of "creature," "paranormal," "supernatural," and "heart."

Next I tried *Cherokee myths*. I didn't discover anything I didn't already know—legends of creation, stories that explained the sun, the moon, the thunder. Tales of the little people and the immortals, beings who were often invisible until they wished to be seen. The rabbit as trickster, the hummingbird that brought us tobacco before tobacco was common.

No mention of eagle shifters, although there was the belief that a great warrior could change his shape at will, and I found it quite interesting that the symbol of a great warrior was the eagle. Still, none of these stories gave any clue as to why Abraham had no heart.

I searched my mind for some other possibility. In desperation I typed *ghoul.*

A monster from Arabia or Persia, I read. *Appears in graveyards. A desert-dwelling, shape-shifting demon that can take the guise of a hyena.*

That wasn't very helpful, either.

Lures unwary travelers into the desert and devours them. Robs graves. Eats the dead.

Well, there wasn't a desert anywhere near here. Still, a ghoul might have eaten Abraham's heart, although how that could have been accomplished without tearing open the chest, and in the small window of time between his dying and his being found, I wasn't sure.

No matter which way I sliced this, it came back to the heart being missing without a single scar. Which to me meant the heart had been missing all along, and that in turn meant the dead person wasn't a person at all.

I sighed and rubbed my face just as a board creaked upstairs. I didn't want to explain any of this to Ian, so I shut down and went back to my room.

He wasn't there.

I checked the bathroom, the next bedroom, and the next. Another creak, from the third floor, had me scowling and climbing the last flight of stairs to the office that had once been my father's and was now my own.

I'd re-done that room, too, at first using it to attempt some of the spells and cures my great-grandmother had shown me. But the time between when she'd died and my father had was a period of several years, during which Dad had forbidden any hoodoo, and I'd been too busy learning to be a cop to care. The problem was, when I went back to it, I couldn't remember enough to do anything right.

I reached the open door; Ian stood at the window. The bulb had burned out in here long ago, and I hadn't replaced it, preferring instead to use candles as *E-li-si* always had. With the moon falling down and the sun not yet up, the room was cast in navy blue shadows.

Books and beakers, a few test tubes, and the toad. The amphibian had been dead a long time. Grandmother had kept it in an aquarium, so I did, too. She'd told me she was waiting for it to turn to dust, then the powder could be used for a very powerful spell. Unfortunately, I didn't know what spell that was.

I'd brought everything she'd left me here. Crystals lay scattered about; dream catchers hung from the ceiling. E-li-si had enjoyed all things magical, trappings from every culture. The room had a fantastical air, especially in candlelight. I loved spending time here.

Alone.

My gaze went to Ian. The slump of his shoulders took away any annoyance at his intrusion. Yes, this was my private place, but since he'd pretty much been in all my other private places, what difference did it make?

He hadn't bothered to put on any clothes, and for an instant I wondered if he was sleepwalking; then he spoke. "I didn't realize this was where you kept your great-grandmother's things. I intruded."

I opened my mouth to deny it, then said instead, "Why did you?"

"Where I lived in Oklahoma, everything was flat."

I blinked at the randomness of his statement, then gave a mental shrug. "I thought all of Oklahoma was flat."

"A lot of people do. But we have mountains, though nothing like these; canyons, rivers, plains. Oklahoma is the most geographically diverse state in the union. We're proud of that. Though I was born there, I never felt like I belonged. I never felt like I belonged anywhere until . . ." He pointed toward the Blue Ridge. "I saw those. I wanted to be closer to them."

As a kid I'd often snuck up here for the same reason, even though my father had warned me to keep out. I would stare out this highest window, and I would know that there was somewhere that I belonged.

"Sah-ka-na-ga," he murmured.

I crossed the room and looked past him at the horizon. "The Great Blue Hills of God."

"I heard about them all my life, but I didn't believe anything could be so beautiful." He reached out and touched his fingertips to the window. "I was wrong."

His eagle tattoo caught my gaze. Reaching out myself, I touched it. The muscle jerked beneath his skin, and I froze, hand hovering in the air.

Slowly he turned, his eyes dark when I knew they were light, his face shadowed.

"I've never seen a tattoo like that," I said.

He didn't answer, just kept his gaze on mine, waiting. "What does it mean?"

He turned away, stared out the window again as if he couldn't bear not to see the mountains for a moment longer. "Only warriors can wear the eagle."

"The feather?"

"Yes. But feathers can be lost, stolen, ruined. I got the tattoo so I would have a reminder to be a warrior always. Warriors do what must be done no matter the cost to themselves or anyone else."

Something in his voice, a starkness, a desperation, made me move so I could see his face. What I'd heard I saw reflected there, and it made me shiver. Despite his calm demeanor, his vow to harm none, I recognized a ruthlessness in this man; I sensed secrets and danger, and I was enthralled.

"Come back to bed," I murmured.

He followed me downstairs, where he trailed that eagle feather all over me. I shuddered and writhed; I begged and then I came, clutching his shoulders, holding him close. Sated, we slept, only to be awoken by the doorbell.

Shoving my tangled hair from my face, I stared at the clock. "Nine? Hell."

I was late. So why hadn't Jordan or Cal called?

Ian turned over; I became distracted by the way the sheet twined across his waist, the outline of his legs, how his skin shone in the small ray of sunlight that strayed past a slight gap at the side of the heavy green drapes.

"I'll have to go right to the office," he said.

"Sorry."

He looked up, and in his eyes I saw a reflection of our memories. "Don't be."

I threw on my robe. "Use the shower, whatever you want."

As I ran down the steps, the doorbell chimed again. I threw open the door and discovered why my deputy and dispatcher hadn't called.

They were here.

Cal stood on the porch; Jordan leaned against a brand-new squad car. A second was parked behind it. The mist that so often swirled in from the mountains shrouded my yard. Beyond the cars lay the trees; I just couldn't see them.

"You sick?" Cal strode past me without being invited.

"Not yet. What's the matter? The Chuck Norris joke of the day too good to wait?"

"Huh?" Cal appeared preoccupied. "Oh, well, there was a joke, but it wasn't good." He reached into his pocket and handed me a crumpled sheet of paper, which I smoothed, then read.

There is no theory of evolution. Just a list of animals Chuck Norris allows to live. I thought it was pretty good. But— "You came to show me this?"

"Of course not. Claire dropped off the keys for your new squad car. We figured we'd bring it out so you could drive it in."

"Thanks."

Cal moved to the door. I followed, thinking he meant to leave. Instead, he shut the door and turned with a serious expression, even for him. "There's something I wanted to tell you, but not at the office."

He was acting strangely. Showing up at my house. Not noticing there was an extra car in my yard and asking about it. Bringing me the squad without calling first. Not commenting that I'd left the shower running upstairs.

Cal seemed . . . well, my great-grandmother would have called him "out of sorts." Something had gotten him worked up, and today it wasn't Chuck Norris.

"What is it?" I asked.

Ducking his head, he began to pace, and I caught a clue. Cal must have observed something supernatural, and being Cal, tip-top, tough Marine, he didn't know what to do about it. Anything that didn't make sense could not be true. Poor guy. I was surprised his head hadn't exploded in confusion.

"Cal, I—"

"I found out more about the doctor."

My mouth snapped shut so fast I narrowly missed biting my tongue.

"The doctor?"

"Ian Walker. You wanted me to check on him."

"His credentials, which you did."

"I kept digging." He shrugged. "Figured it wouldn't hurt."

From the expression on his face, he was wrong. This *was* going to hurt.

"He has a wife."

"Had. He *had* a wife. She died."

The fine lines that had been etched around Cal's mouth and eyes by the sun and the wind in countries I never wanted to visit, deepened. "She didn't die, Grace. She disappeared. There one day, gone the next. Not a trace of her anywhere, ever."

"How long?"

"Five years."

"He was a suspect?"

Cal tilted his head, his eyes sympathetic.

Of course Ian had been a suspect. In cases of spousal

death or disappearance, the husband or wife is *always* a suspect.

"They could never pin anything on him," Cal continued. "No evidence of foul play."

"Alibi?"

"Squat."

"Where's he been in the five years since?"

"Not in the town where she disappeared. He left as soon as the cops said he could."

"Odd," I murmured.

"Especially since I've had a hard time tracing exactly where he went, but I will."

"What made you suspicious? Why'd you keep checking?"

Cal glanced away, then quickly back. "I saw you go into his store that first day, and I waited until you came out."

I thought back. I'd gone into what I'd thought was an abandoned building, ended up kissing a stranger. Cal had called my cell phone. He'd been checking up on me.

I could imagine what I'd looked like when I emerged onto the street. I hadn't been kissed in a very long time, and I hadn't been kissed like that in . . . forever.

"You need to stay away from this guy, Grace."

Into the silence dropped the sound of a door closing. The shower had stopped running. I had no idea when.

Cal frowned and glanced up, then back at me. Understanding dawned in his eyes even before Ian Walker came down the staircase.

His hair was wet; his shirt wasn't buttoned; his tie was looped around his neck and his jacket over his arm. His feet were bare. From where I stood, I could see his sandals near the back door.

"Jeez, Grace," Cal muttered.

"I didn't know."

"Know what?" Ian asked, pausing five steps from the bottom.

Cal opened his mouth, and I elbowed him in the stomach. He didn't react—his gut was a brick—but he did shut up.

"Thanks for bringing me the new squad," I said, my eyes on Ian. "I'll see you at the office."

Cal hesitated; then after giving Ian an evil glare, he opened the front door and slammed it behind him, which was probably the most emotion I'd ever seen from Cal—unless you counted his reaction to the joke bandit.

Ian came the rest of the way down the steps. "What's wrong?"

I peered into his face, searching for something, I'm not sure what. A scarlet *M* didn't magically appear on the foreheads of murderers. More's the pity. It would make law enforcement so much easier.

"Did you think we wouldn't find out?" I asked.

He frowned. "Find out what?"

"That your wife isn't dead, Ian!"

He jerked as if I'd slapped him. "You ran a check on me?"

"You told me to."

"My credentials."

I shrugged. "Two for the price of one."

"It isn't what you think."

"You mean I haven't slept with another woman's husband?" I hadn't realized when I'd quipped that I wasn't sick *yet* just how prophetic my words would be.

Nausea rolled through me. I'd seen enough domestic

disputes, enough ruined families, to swear I'd never be a part of that. But here I was.

"I haven't been a husband for five years. I know she's dead."

I glanced up, suspicious. "How can you know?"

"She was gone without a trace. She didn't come back; she didn't write; she didn't call. People don't drop off the face of the earth like that anymore, Grace."

"You'd be surprised," I murmured.

The *Jäger-Suchers* were experts at making people disappear. I wondered if Ian's wife had been the victim of some kind of monster. Another question for the great and powerful Dr. Hanover.

"I thought you were mourning her. That—" My voice broke; I was horrified. I'd thought he was coming back to life because of me. I'd known this man was going to hurt me, but I hadn't expected it so soon.

"I was," he said. "I am. I loved her and she—" He stopped, cursed, shoved his hand through his still-damp hair. "She left me. She didn't love me enough. Do you know how that feels?"

I did. My mother had left. She hadn't loved me enough. I still looked for her in every dark-haired, green-eyed woman who passed through Lake Bluff.

I clenched my hands into fists against the twinge of sympathy that swirled through my chest. Just because I understood his anguish didn't mean I could, or should, forgive him. He'd lied, or at least misled me over what "gone" meant. I guess I could have asked more questions, but wasn't that considered rude when dealing with a dead wife, even when she wasn't dead? The lines on rude had always been a little unclear to me.

"Get out," I said. I knew *that* was rude, but I didn't care.

"Grace—"

I narrowed my eyes, and he clamped his lips shut, then walked to the back door, slid his feet into his sandals, and left.

I felt a twinge when his car started, when I heard his tires crunch on gravel. There'd been something between us, something that could have become a whole lot more.

If he hadn't had a wife.

I kicked the door. I was late for work. What else was new?

I ran upstairs, tore the covers off the bed, and tossed them into the clothes chute. I couldn't sleep on sheets that smelled of him. Even now the minty fragrance lingered. I'd have to burn candles in here for an hour before I could bear to lie down and rest.

I showered, soaping up twice for the same reason, then dressed in a fresh, crisp uniform, strapped on my weapon, braided my hair. I stared at myself in the mirror.

My nose was back to normal; the only remnant of my two black eyes was a slight yellow shading across one brow bone. I could use Ian's balm, but I didn't want to. For all I knew, the stuff was an aphrodisiac or some kind of lust potion, which would explain my hopping into bed with him so easily.

"It couldn't just be that you were horny and he's hot?" I asked the woman in the mirror.

She gave me the finger.

My boots made a satisfying thunder against the wood as I ran downstairs. I concentrated on the rhythmic thud and not the pain in my chest.

The best way to forget all of this was to throw myself

into my work; it wasn't as if I didn't have plenty to do. I had a dead citizen minus one heart, and a lot of relatives to interview.

I opened the front door and stepped onto the porch.

"Déjà vu," I muttered.

The wolf was back.

19

THE ANIMAL STOOD on the hood of my brand-new squad car. If I hadn't known she was a messenger, I might have been worried about the paint job. Those claws appeared awfully sharp for a spirit wolf.

"Now what?" I asked.

The beast tilted her head.

"I got the message. Watch over Quatie. I'll go there later today. You don't have to keep coming back, Grandmother."

The wolf growled and jumped off the hood. The car bucked up and then down as if something heavy had just been removed.

"What the—?" I took one step forward. The wolf turned and ran. I followed, but by the time I reached the trees, she was gone.

The mist was lifting; the sun shone through, sparking brightly off the droplets of moisture on the grass, the branches, my shiny new car. Come to think of it, the spirit wolf had looked a little wet, too.

"Damn." Too much was going on this morning. Far too much had been going on all night. I sat on the hood and put my head in my hands.

"What's done is done," I murmured. "If the wife ever turns up, I'll apologize. Let her pop me in the nose."

I probed my recently healed appendage. It was only fair.

"Until then," I continued, "leave him alone and you're good." Or at least as good as I was going to get.

Standing, I peered at the smooth finish of the car. Not a mark on it. I hadn't expected there to be.

I peered in the direction the wolf had gone. North, just like last time. I hadn't figured to see the wolf again since I'd gotten the message, but either I'd gotten the wrong message or there was a new message.

I wished I could ask Ian about this, but I was going to have to make do with my own investigative skills from here on out.

Inside I found a book I'd bought on Cherokee traditions—sad that I had to get a book off of Amazon for something I should already know, but I didn't have much choice.

I turned to a section on directions. As Ian had said, to the west lay the Darkening Land, a place of thunder, its color black. In the east was the land of the sun, triumph, power, the color red. The south held Wahala, the white mountain where peace and good health were found. To the north waited the Frigid Land, a site of sadness and trouble, its color blue.

The wolf had materialized each time either before Ian had shown up or after he'd left, then run north. Was she trying to tell me that Ian was trouble?

As if in answer, a sharp, insistent howl rose from the

distant hills. I'd never heard a wolf howl in the day-time. Hell, I'd never heard a wolf howl at all until last summer. As previously stated, we didn't have them.

If the messenger wanted me to help Quatie, I would. If the wolf wanted me to be careful of Ian, I'd already figured that out for myself. And if she came back?

I almost wished the thing *were* a werewolf, because then I could shoot it.

◯◯◯

I didn't bother to go to the office. I didn't want to see Cal or Jordan. I called in, said I was going on patrol. I could do whatever I wanted. I was the boss.

Pulling out the obituary section, I headed for the first house on the list. Before I got there, my cell phone buzzed. I nearly let it go to voice mail, figuring the caller was Cal or, worse, Ian. But I was too respon-sible to ignore what could be an emergency, so I glanced at the display, then I jerked my car to the side of the road, nearly dropping the phone under my seat in my haste to answer.

"Doc?"

"Freaking caller ID," he muttered. "I hate progress."

"Tell me you've made some."

His exasperated sigh came over the line. "Have you ever known me to dawdle? I've performed autopsies on two of the bodies still at the funeral home. No hearts."

I sat there, uncertain what to say. I'd suspected as much, but now what?

"Don't you want to know what killed them?" Doc asked.

"Not the lack of a vital organ?"

"No."

Which led me to believe that my initial diagnosis was correct: The victims weren't people, but creatures we hadn't identified yet, and there was someone in town who knew not only how to recognize them, but also how to kill them.

"Okay," I asked when Doc didn't elaborate, "how did they die?"

"From the exact cause you'd expect in the particular circumstance of each victim."

"Which makes no sense."

"And human beings without hearts do?"

"I'm not so sure they were human."

"I didn't find any indication of that," he took a deep breath, then let it out, "except for the pesky tin-man syndrome."

"I don't understand how this wasn't discovered before now," I said.

"In the case of these victims, I'm not surprised."

"Why not? I'd think that a dead . . ." I paused, not wanting to use the word "person" but being unable to think of a better one, since we had no idea what they were. I gave up and moved on. "They come into the funeral home with a gaping hole in their chest cavity and no one notices?"

"The chests were unmarred, so the lack of a heart would only be found during an autopsy, and there wouldn't be an autopsy ordered in any of these cases. Nothing suspicious."

"What about during the embalming process?"

"None of them were embalmed."

"But isn't that required?"

"Embalming's only used to preserve the body for the

funeral. If there's a quick, planned, small ceremony, no ceremony, or a cremation without a viewing, no embalming."

Since I'd already had a variation of this conversation with Grant, I nodded.

If the dead were some kind of supernatural creature, then how could they be dying from a human ailment?

Maybe they hadn't been, but the "hunter" was able to kill them so it looked as if they were, or perhaps infect them, somehow, someway, so that they died in a manner that wouldn't begin a rash of autopsies.

Which was pretty far-fetched, but I wouldn't put it past the *Jäger-Suchers*.

Except Elise insisted none of them were here. I wasn't sure I believed her; however, plenty of people in the world had seen strange things and might have decided to kill them. Neither me, Mal, Claire, nor Doc was a *J-S* agent, but we all kept silver weapons close at hand.

"None of the deceased showed any signs of waking up and walking around?" I asked.

"Not when I was through with them." I grimaced at the image of what had been done. "You're thinking zombie? Vampire?"

"I have no idea."

"Huh," Doc said, as if we were discussing the new special at the Good Eatin' Café. "I saw no evidence of movement or reanimation. If they were capable of it, I'd think they'd do so before I—" He stopped before elaborating, and I was glad. "But who knows? I've scheduled an exhumation for this afternoon. Three o'clock."

"That was fast."

In most places, exhumation of bodies is a long, drawn-out, expensive process. Here we did things with a bit less fanfare.

"You need to come," Doc continued. "If we open up the grave and there's no one home, you could be on to something."

◍

I agreed to meet Doc at a quarter to three; then I continued on my way to the house of Barbara O'Reily, daughter of Peggy, who'd passed away the morning after the Thunder Moon from complications of Alzheimer's and whom Doc Bill had just sliced up like a Thanksgiving turkey. How was I going to explain that?

Barbara opened the door wearing a black dress and heels. Today must be the day of the small ceremony. Could I have picked a worse time?

"Grace."

Those of my father's generation or older continued to call me Grace instead of Sheriff, and I didn't mind.

"I'm sorry about your mother," I said.

"Thank you." She stepped back, inviting me in. "It's nice of you to come by."

I followed Barbara into the living room, accepting her offer of a seat before I disabused her of the notion that this was a condolence call.

"Ms. O'Reily—"

"Call me Barbara. I've known you since you were four."

Which would be a good reason for me to continue to call her Ms., but I smiled and said, "Thank you, Barbara. I need to ask you a few questions."

Her distracted, artificial smile faded. "Questions?"

"About your mother."

I decided to leave the autopsy news until last. Some people tended to get pissy when you ordered knives and saws applied to their relatives. In case Barbara was one of them, I wanted my questions out of the way first.

"All right." She glanced at the clock on the mantel. "I've got a little time before I have to meet my sister at Farrel's."

The O'Reily sisters were twins. Betty had married and moved to Atlanta. Barbara had stayed home with her mother. Since Betty's husband had already died and she'd never had any children, that would make for the small ceremony that seemed to be a requirement of this strange rash of deaths.

"I can't imagine what you'd want to ask," Barbara continued.

I wasn't quite sure myself. "Can you tell me how she died?"

Barbara frowned. "Alzheimer's."

"I know. I mean *how*? Was she conscious? Did she say anything? Did she seem—" I remembered Ms. G. "Afraid?"

Barbara's eyes widened. "How did you know?"

Bingo.

"What happened?"

She hesitated, as if she didn't want to speak of it, and I couldn't blame her.

"Where are my manners? Would you like some coffee? Tea? A soft drink?"

"No thank you," I said politely, though I wanted to snap, *Get on with it.* I patted her hand awkwardly. "Just tell me."

I *had* learned to be a little less short and sharp with people since being elected.

Barbara bit her lip, nodded, and began. "Mom was in a home. I couldn't keep her here anymore. She'd take off in the night. She was always looking for Dad. Didn't remember he'd been dead for a decade." Her lips trembled.

I made noises of commiseration. At least my dad had gone quickly. There was something to be said for a massive coronary.

"I'd gone to see her after work. I always did."

"Was she any better, or worse, than usual?"

"That was the strange thing—she was better. The doctor thought she'd last a few more weeks. I wasn't sure how I felt about that. Her going was really a blessing."

I nodded. She was right.

"So I sat with her longer than usual, but she got agitated. Said there was someone in the room."

I stiffened as an icy finger seemed to trace my neck. "Who?"

"She was paranoid, a symptom of her disease. I didn't think anything of it until she screamed and began to thrash, clawing at her throat like she was fighting for breath."

"How strange."

"The doctor had warned me. Some of them forget how to eat, how to swallow, and literally starve to death. Some forget to breathe and—" She lifted one shoulder. "Struggling for breath sent her heart into overdrive, and it just couldn't handle the stress. She died of a heart attack."

We seemed to be having a rash of those, too.

Barbara took several deep, slow breaths. "Her face when she died . . . She was so afraid."

"Not being able to breathe would scare the crap out of me," I agreed.

Barbara gave a wan smile. "I don't like to believe that in her last moments she thought someone meant to hurt her. I'd hoped that when she went, she'd do so peacefully. I guess that was too much to ask."

I didn't think so. Unfortunately, no one had asked me.

"Was there anything else about the night that struck you as odd?"

She cast me another quick, suspicious glance. If I weren't careful, people would be whispering that I had the sight. Too bad I didn't, because it would make interrogations a whole lot easier.

"There was a scream," she said. "It didn't sound—" She broke off, then dropped her gaze to her lap, where she began to pick imaginary bits of lint from the black material.

"It didn't sound what, Barbara?"

"Human."

I blinked. *Uh-oh.*

"Screams probably sound a whole lot different than a person's voice," I managed, "and if your mom was scared—"

"Maybe. I was in the hall, and then there was this horrible, blood-curdling shriek. I thought someone was in there with her, even though I knew no one could be."

"You didn't see her scream?"

"I was talking to the nurse, and—" She made a vague motion with one hand. "We both froze for a second, then ran in. Mom was gasping, choking, struggling."

"But she was alone?"

Barbara nodded. "I was right outside the door. No one went in or out."

"The windows?"

Barbara's gaze met mine. "She's an Alzheimer's patient, Grace. There were no windows."

20

"WHY ARE YOU questioning me about my mother's death?" Barbara asked. "It was pretty cut-and-dried."

Except for the scream, the choking, the mask of fear upon dying, and the lack of a heart, but I decided to keep that to myself.

One thing I couldn't keep to myself, no matter how much I might want to, was the autopsy I'd ordered.

"There've been more than the usual number of deaths in town over the past few days. Doc Bill has been asked by the CDC—" At her blank stare I elaborated. "The Centers for Disease Control want him to do some tests."

"Why?"

"Hard to say. But I authorized an autopsy on your mom as well as the others."

Her eyes widened. "You didn't ask me."

"It had to be done right away."

"Is there some kind of epidemic?" Her hand fluttered up to rest, trembling, at the base of her throat.

How had I known that would be the first question? Maybe I *was* psychic.

"Doc assures me nothing's contagious. Just a precaution. Tests." I spread my arms, trying for the good-old-boy grin my father had used so well. "You know how those folks from Atlanta are."

Barbara nodded. To the citizens of Lake Bluff, Atlanta was a strange and foreign land, a place of crime and dirt, one that dazzled the youth of our town into absconding down the mountain, then spit them back out when they were ruined.

Claire had come home from Atlanta a ghost of her former self. If it weren't for Mal, I wasn't sure she'd have been able to get over what had happened to her there.

At any rate, playing the Atlanta card usually worked to bring people into an "us against them" partnership. I just wasn't sure how many times I'd be able to get away with using it today.

"Did Doc find anything?" she asked.

"I'm going to have to get back to you on that."

"What? But—"

"It's an ongoing investigation." I stood. "Until we've come to some kind of conclusion, I won't be able to give you any answers."

"Well, as soon as you know anything—"

"Of course." I headed for the door. "One more question—was there anything different about your mother lately?"

"Besides her thinking I meant to kill her every time I walked in the room? Or the charming way she started to keep her shoes in the refrigerator and the milk under her bed?"

"Sorry," I said. "We're just looking for a pattern."

"To what?" Barbara threw up her hands.

"I—"

"Can't tell me. Right. Never mind." She patted her hair. "I need to go."

"Thanks for your time."

When I left, Barbara shut the door a little harder than necessary. I headed for the residence of the next name on the obituary list.

The interviews were all eerily similar. Walking down Center Street after the last one, I was cataloging those similarities in my trusty notebook when I bumped into someone.

A sharp, horrified gasp, followed by, "Oh no!" made me glance up as a glass jar of something sped toward the ground. I snatched it out of the air before it smashed into the pavement.

"Grace." Katrine Dixon set her perfectly manicured hand against her great big breasts. "You always were the quickest gal in these mountains."

I handed her the jar, which appeared to be a jelly container full of swirling liquid the shade of skim milk. I glanced at the nearest storefront. "Did you come out of there?" I nodded at Ian's clinic.

"Have you met him? I think he might be able to help me."

Lake Bluff being what it was, I already knew that Katrine didn't need any help. There wasn't a thing wrong with her that a good, swift kick in the ass wouldn't cure. Katrine liked attention, hence the balloon breasts and itty-bitty skirt.

"What did he give you?" I demanded.

She blinked at my tone. "A natural cure. Suzanne Somers used natural cures on her breast cancer, and it went all away."

"You don't have breast cancer, Katrine." What Katrine had was a raging case of hypochondria.

She sniffed and stuck her suddenly pert nose in the air. Hell, had she had that fixed, too?

"Ian takes me seriously. He gave me a *complete* physical." She drew one bloodred nail over her left breast. I half-expected the pointy tip to pop the silicone like a balloon. I took a step back just in case. An explosion like that could put out an eye.

"He gives great physical," she purred.

I narrowed my eyes. I could imagine.

Katrine had once been a knobby-kneed, flat-chested, stringy-haired whiner. But she'd left Lake Bluff after high school—no one knew for where—and come home a completely different person, except for the whining.

I eyed the short white skirt and the tight red top, which showed off the body she'd returned with to perfection. I wondered how many plastic surgeons she'd had to blow to get those breasts. I wondered how she planned on paying Dr. Walker for his exam. Despite the shiny new exterior, Katrine was *poor* white *trash*—emphasis on "poor," double emphasis on "trash"—and she always would be.

She worked at the Watering Hole—a local tavern, located as far away from Center Street as it could get and still actually be *in* town—as a bartender. The place was rough. I'd been there half a dozen times in the last month on disturbance calls, and I usually worked the day shift.

The door to Ian's clinic opened and another woman stepped out, in her hand a similar jar, although the liquid inside held a greenish tint. I recognized Merry Gray, and I left Katrine behind without so much as a good-bye.

"Well, ain't that just like you, Grace McDaniel,"

Katrine shouted after me. "You always did have the manners of a savage."

Since I didn't particularly care if I did or I didn't, and I certainly didn't care if Katrine thought so, I kept right on going.

The clinic had improved a lot since I'd been there last. The lower floor had been cleaned and painted a calming pale blue. Someone had thrown up drywall, creating a separation between the waiting room and the receptionist's desk, although there wasn't any receptionist. Past that, three exam rooms had been roughed in. A fourth appeared to be done, since Ian walked out of it wearing the traditional white coat over a pair of khaki slacks, a mint green shirt, and a tan tie.

He stopped dead at the sight of me. "Grace, I—"

"How did you get all this done?" I blurted. He'd only been in town a few days, and a lot of that time had been spent with me.

"You'd be amazed at what you can accomplish if you're willing to pay for it."

"What did you give Mrs. Gray?"

He stiffened as if I'd jabbed him in the butt with a stick, which wasn't a half-bad idea. "That's none of your business, Sheriff."

"It is if you're selling her lime-flavored water and calling it a miracle. She's dying."

"Then I doubt lime-flavored water would hurt her." His voice and posture gentled.

The entire town knew Merry Gray had endured every cure available to modern science in an attempt to kill the tumors raging inside of her. Instead of growing smaller, the cancer seemed to feed on the chemo and the radiation, multiplying out of control and making her sicker and sicker.

"I don't want her hopes up," I said.

"Why not?"

"You give her green water and tell her it'll heal her, then it doesn't? That's criminal, Doctor."

"I'd say what's happening to her is criminal. I've given her nothing that will hurt, and I have every reason to believe it could help. She's exhausted all other avenues of treatment."

"I don't want her disappointed."

"It's been proven that a person's attitude can mean as much or more to their health than the actual medicine."

"Did you give her a placebo?"

"I'm not telling you what I gave her."

"What about Katrine? There's nothing wrong with her."

"I know." His lips quirked. I had a strong feeling that Katrine was the one with the placebo.

"The way you do business doesn't sit right with me." The way he did a lot of things no longer sat quite right.

"Let's make an agreement, Sheriff. You don't tell me how to deal with my patients, and I won't tell you how to beat a confession out of a subject."

"I don't do that."

"And I wouldn't give people anything I didn't think could help them. When I take an oath, I live by it."

" 'Do no harm,' " I murmured.

"Among others." I opened my mouth to ask, *What others?* and he stepped in, quick and close, startling me so much any questions I'd been about to ask got caught in my throat.

"The balm I gave you worked." His long, slightly rough fingers brushed my cheek, and my eyelids fluttered closed.

The scent of him brought back the feel of his body

in mine. His breath stirred my temple. I wanted so badly to touch him, to have him touch me.

"You should trust me," he whispered.

My eyes shot open; my chin came up. His face was so close our lips nearly brushed before I backed away. "You haven't exactly been trustworthy so far."

"You took me to see Quatie; you had to have trusted me then."

Which only made the loss of trust in him now hurt worse. "If you lie about one thing, you'll lie about everything."

His mouth tightened, as if he were trying to hold his temper. But when he spoke his voice was so calm I wanted to shriek. "You're not mad about my business; you're mad about my wife."

"I'm pretty sure I'm mad about both. I don't trust you. For all I know you could be doling out poison."

A surprised bark of laughter escaped him, more convincing than any denial would have been. "Why would I do that?"

"Why would you tell me your wife was dead when she'd disappeared?"

"I never said she was dead."

"You never said she was alive, either."

He sighed. "This is getting us nowhere."

"Where did you want to go?"

The look he sent me left no room for misunderstanding. He wanted to go back to bed—immediately.

My body reacted as if he'd run his beautiful hands all over me. I longed for him, and I hated myself for it.

"Put that right out of your head," I snapped. "We won't be going there. Not ever again."

"You're overreacting."

"Marriage means something, Ian." I thought of my mother. "Or at least it should. And lying—" I stopped.

Why did it bother me so much? Probably because so many men had told me what I wanted to hear, then walked out on me.

You're beautiful, Grace.

I love you, Grace.

I'll never leave you, Grace.

My wife is gone, Grace.

So I'd started saying good-bye to them before they could say good-bye to me. It was the only way I could keep from getting hurt. I'd waited too long this time.

"This was crazy from the beginning," I said. "We met three nights ago. Two nights ago we went to the water and—"

"Had sex," he finished.

"It was too much, too fast. I thought—"

I broke off, unable to finish. He took a step forward, and I narrowed my eyes, daring him to come any closer. His fingers curled against the legs of his slacks, the scritch of his fingernails loud in the sudden silence.

"Thought what?" he asked softly.

I'd thought it had meant something. I should have known better. Just because he was Cherokee didn't make him any less of a man.

21

I WALKED OUT, and Ian let me. I hadn't really expected anything else. It wasn't as if he loved me. It wasn't as if I loved him.

No time to weep and wail—as if I would. I had an appointment at the cemetery.

Luckily, all of the churches still buried their dead outside of town. We'd have fewer gawkers that way. Not that word of what we were doing wouldn't get around, but the longer it took, the better.

I turned my car in the opposite direction of Lunar Lake. In the old days it was common practice to construct burial plots as far away from the populace as possible, mostly to keep the roving bands of wild animals from dragging a stray leg or arm under your porch.

As time went on and Lake Bluff grew, there wasn't room for a cemetery in the town proper, but there was plenty of space to expand out where the dead had already been established.

I turned into the gate of Mountain View, saw Doc

Bill's car parked near what must be the grave we were interested in, and pulled up behind him.

Doc was already giving instructions to the man standing next to the machinery. Since he'd only been buried yesterday, no grass covered the grave of Alec Renard, just dirt. According to his obituary, Alec had expired from a stroke.

However, according to Alec's granddaughter, whom I'd spoken with fourth on my happy hit parade of interrogation, Granddad had been as healthy as a horse.

Until he died.

Doc finished speaking with the worker and headed toward me across the lush green carpet that covered the majority of Mountain View.

There truly was a mountain view here, not that any of the residents would benefit by it. Or maybe they would. What did I know?

This would have been a nice place for my father, except he'd been cremated per his instructions. I'd wanted to keep his ashes with me in the town and the home he'd loved, but he'd specified that all five of his children would take turns. You'd be amazed at some of the stuff people put in their last will and testament. Sheriff McDaniel, senior, had been no exception.

Grandmother had been buried like a true Cherokee on the slope of a forest-clad mountain. Illegal as hell, but by the time I'd told Dad about it, the deed was done.

He hadn't been happy. My father was the law here, and even if he hadn't disliked Grandmother with an intensity rivaled only by her dislike for him, he would have put a stop to her being buried as she'd wanted to be. To him, the law was the law and human remains were not to be put into the earth without observation of the required legalities.

I glanced at the white stone markers. It would have been nice to have her closer, in a place like this where I could visit. Although, according to Quatie, Grandmother wasn't available for visits since she was running around on great, big wolf paws trying to tell me something.

I choked back inappropriate laughter just as Doc Bill joined me.

"You okay?" He thumped me between the shoulder blades, just in case.

"Yes. Thanks." I stepped out of his reach. He might be old, but he still packed quite a punch. "Everything set?"

I indicated the grave, where the man fiddled with a machine as if he were dealing with a recalcitrant child. I even heard the distant murmur of his voice, cajoling, praising. As I watched, he started the engine, then patted the metal monstrosity gratefully.

"He's going to dig up the vault, remove the top, then leave it to us to open the casket." Doc cast me a sidelong glance. "In case the thing's empty."

Which would be a little hard to explain.

"I doubt that'll happen," I said.

"No?"

"I've been interviewing the relatives."

"Do tell."

I motioned for Doc to follow me farther away from the grave site, since talking for any length of time where we stood would have necessitated shouting over the sound of the machinery.

I told him everything. When I was through, Doc asked, "Conclusions?"

I pulled out the notebook I'd been scribbling in when I ran into Katrine. "The deceased were either old or ill. They were expected to die, though, in most cases, not quite yet. They all passed on in the night, seeming to gasp for breath in their last moments."

"But none of them died from asphyxiation," Doc murmured. "Or with any signs that they'd been deprived of oxygen or any bruises that would match strangulation."

He'd answered my next question before I'd even voiced it. I liked that in a doctor.

"Those who could speak," I continued, "and had a nurse or family member present to hear them, believed there was someone or something in the room, though no one else saw or heard anything."

"Could easily have been the presence of a loved one who'd gone before."

I lifted my eyebrows. "Seriously?"

"You think only evil entities come back from beyond?"

"I hadn't thought of anything coming back from beyond." I scowled. "But now I will. Thanks."

He quirked a bushy white brow and shrugged in lieu of apology. "I've been in attendance at enough deaths to know that there's something waiting on the other side. Sometimes, the other side comes over and gets us."

His face took on an appearance of rapture at odds with the slightly cranky Doc Bill I knew and loved. I wasn't sure how to deal with him, except to move on.

"Since all of our victims died with an expression of surprise, perhaps shock, or even fear on their faces, maybe every one of them was visited by a loved one they'd hoped never to see again."

Doc shook his head. "Everyone I've ever observed in that situation dies at peace. It's made me believe in the afterlife along with the ghosts and goblins, witches, warlocks, and werewolves."

Since I knew he wasn't kidding about the werewolves,

I had to figure he wasn't kidding about the other entities, either, but right now I really didn't want to know.

"So you think our victims aren't getting a glimpse of the great beyond," I continued, "they're getting a glimpse of their killer—invisible as he or she might be?"

"Perhaps," Doc said slowly. "Don't forget, the lack of a heart has made us conclude that the victims themselves could be supernatural."

"That doesn't preclude them being frightened of whatever's killing them." Doc frowned. "What?"

"I was just imagining what might frighten a being that has no heart. I don't think I want to meet it."

I didn't, either, but I had a hunch I was going to.

The sudden cessation of sound had us both glancing toward the grave site. A coffin-shaped vault now rested aboveground rather than below. The worker indicated with a wave of one gloved hand that Doc and I could return.

"One more thing," I said as we headed across the grass in that direction. "In several of my interviews, relatives or friends who were either with or near the deceased reported hearing an unearthly shrieking right before the victim began to gasp for breath."

"Shrieking from the victim?"

"Some didn't know, but the ones who did said it definitely didn't come from the victim. The scream was so loud it seemed to come from the air itself. A few saw bright sparkling lights as well."

"So the killer, whatever it is, announces itself with a shriek and some sparks?" Doc contemplated my face. "What else?"

"I heard a shriek and saw a trail of sparks fall from the sky on the night of the Thunder Moon."

"The what?"

"The full moon in July is known as the Thunder Moon. After that, people started to die."

"That was the night of the big storm."

"According to Cherokee legend, when thunder arrives on that night, magic happens."

We reached the grave site. Doc nodded to the worker, and he strolled off to have a cigarette under a tree at the edge of the last line of stones. The top of the vault rested against the side, leaving the rectangular container open.

"You think we've got an alien?" Doc asked.

I gaped. "What?"

"Falls from the sky in a shower of sparks, then invisibly starts to kill people—or perhaps unpeople—definitely heartless people, literally, which cannot by any stretch of the anatomy *be* people. What do you think?"

"I think you've been watching a little too much *Predator,* pal."

Although now that I thought about it, there had been that weird crater Cal and I had found after those sparks tumbled from the sky.

"*Predator?*" Doc asked. "Is that some new reality show?"

"Arnold, Doc. He commandos in to some bizarre jungle and fights a monster from another planet." At his continued blank stare, I gave him one more clue. "Schwarzenegger?"

"The governator? I never much cared for him. Too puffy." He made a fierce face and brought his scrawny arms into a muscleman pose in front of his body. "*Errrr!*" he growled.

I had to laugh, though I sobered quickly enough as I stared at the vault in front of us. "You really think we've got aliens in Lake Bluff?"

"We had werewolves."

The man made an excellent point.

"What if we have aliens in town, then an alien hunter arrives on a sparkling trail of stars?" Doc murmured. "And when he—she—it kills the aliens he—she —it screeches, like a battle cry."

"If that's the case," I said, "then where did the original aliens come from?"

"Pods?" Doc slid a glance my way. "*Invasion of the Body Snatchers.* That one I know." He jerked a thumb toward the vault. "Shall we?"

We stepped forward until we could see the casket ensconced within. A lot of people don't know that you need to purchase not only a casket for the deceased but also a vault for both to go into before the burial. Even if the loved one is cremated, a casket is still required. The item is just burned with them. Death is both a huge and a strange business.

Doc leaned over and went to work removing the top of the casket. Of its own accord, my hand went to the butt of my gun. Unfortunately, a bullet, silver or lead, could do nothing to eliminate the smell.

"Why?" I asked, putting my other palm to my nose.

"No embalming, Sheriff, and it's July in Georgia. What did you expect?"

I wasn't sure. More action from the corpse, less smell than we had. Wrong on both counts.

"Although . . ." Doc paused. "For an alien, this corpse is behaving pretty human."

"Whatever he is," I said, "he's here." Which took care of any vampire, zombie, ghoul theories, not that I'd been all that wild about them. "Now what?"

"Now I open him up and see what made him tick,

unless he didn't tick, which seems to be the case with everyone I've opened up lately."

Doc's gaze went past me. He lifted a hand, and I turned. A hearse bounced toward us over the rutted dirt path.

"What's that for?"

"You didn't think I was going to crack his chest right here in front of God and the cemetery guy, did you?"

I hadn't really thought of it at all.

I was trying not to.

22

AFTER MAKING DOC promise to call me as soon as he had news, as if he wouldn't, I left him to deal with the hearse and the body. I went to meet Claire and Mal.

As I drove back to Lake Bluff, I considered Doc's "alien" theory. I didn't buy it; however, if it were true, then these people had to have become "other" sometime in their lifetime. They couldn't have been born that way.

Lack of a heart would have been revealed, if not when they were a baby, then somewhere along the line. People didn't go through an entire lifetime without having a chest X-ray.

Well, one person might, but not several. At some point, they must have had bronchitis, pneumonia, or—

Wait, Ms. G. must have had a chest X-ray. Since she'd been diagnosed with congestive heart failure, she'd definitely had a heart to congest somewhere along the line. So when had the thing gone poof?

I pulled up in front of town hall and hailed Joyce, who was just leaving, as I got out of the squad.

"You've lived here since the dawn of time, right?" I asked.

She lifted her black brows. "Do you *want* me to smack you?"

My lips twitched. Joyce always cracked me up. "Anyone in town strike you as different?"

"Different how?"

Yeah, how? "I don't know, just weird. Not like everyone else."

"No one's like anyone else, Grace."

"Okay, let's try it this way. Did anyone leave Lake Bluff and come back later acting strangely? Or maybe disappear without a word for a few days and come back without ever saying where they'd gone?"

"Do you have a fever?" She reached over before I could stop her and placed a palm against my forehead.

"Stop that!" I stepped out of her reach.

Joyce narrowed her eyes. "The only one acting weird is you. What's going on around here this time?"

We'd kept what had happened last summer under wraps. The only people who knew the truth were me, Mal, Claire, and Doc, but Joyce wasn't dumb. She knew something bizarre had gone down, but so far we'd been able to put her off the scent by ignoring her questions.

As long as we stuck together, she'd never find out, because the *Jäger-Suchers* had, as usual, done a bang-up job of lying their asses off to explain away any out-of-the-ordinary weirdness.

"We got another rabid wolf in the woods?" she asked.

J-S doublespeak for werewolf.

"Not this time."

"Then what?"

"Nothing, Joyce." Or at least nothing I could put a name to.

Yet.

She opened her mouth, and I jumped in first. "Gotta go. You know how Claire is when I'm late."

Her teeth came together with an annoyed click. "Oh yeah, she's a regular slave driver."

"Mmm," I said, and fled.

If Joyce set her mind to discovering what was going on, I'd cave. The woman had been like a mother to me—hell, she'd *been* a mother to me and to Claire. The only reason we'd kept the truth from her so far was because she'd let us. And she'd probably let us because she understood, on the level that all great mothers have, that she really didn't want to know.

Six o'clock and town hall was deserted. My steps echoed in the cavernous marble foyer. They didn't build places like this anymore. Between the labor, the materials, and the slashing of municipal budgets, they couldn't afford to.

Claire, Mal, and Noah reclined on the floor of Claire's office, Claire making fart noises by placing her mouth against her son's stomach and blowing. He thought it was hysterical. Typical man.

I stopped in the doorway and watched them for a second. Noah kicked his legs, wiggling with joy. Claire's expression was full of a happiness I'd feared I would never see on her face again. And Mal—

His eyes were full of love and wonder. I had to glance away. I wanted someone to look at me like that so badly I ached with it.

"I see you're bringing him up right." I flopped into

the nearest chair. "Can't start too early teaching them how funny farts are."

"Boys will be boys." Claire lowered her head and blew one last, loud raspberry on Noah's baby belly.

God, I wanted one just like him.

Claire got to her feet. Noah made a squeak of protest and Mal scooped him up.

"Who wants to go first?" Claire asked as she rummaged in the bag on her desk, then tossed a bottle to her husband.

Mal caught it with one hand, flipped the top with a thumb, and popped the nipple into Noah's mouth. "That'll be me," he said. "The only vampirelike creature in Irish legend was the Dearg-dul, or red blood sucker— an unhappy maiden forced to marry not for love, but by arrangement, and so commits suicide. Then she walks the night luring first her husband, then her father, to their doom. Ever after, she leaves her grave several times a year to prey on any young man she sees."

"I don't think we're dealing with a vampire," I said.

"She's also a shape-shifter," he added, "turning into a lovely bat-winged creature as soon as her victim is in her clutches. The other Irish shape-shifters are the Children of Lir, who became swans, and a host of others who turn into various creatures, including insects, as a result of a curse or magic."

"I don't think we're dealing with any of those, either."

"Don't you now?" Mal murmured softly as Noah's eyes fluttered closed. "What, then?"

"Hey," Claire interrupted, "don't you want to hear what I scrounged up on Scottish shape-shifters?"

"If we must," I said.

"Well, I did spend a lot of time searching. Apparently the Scots aren't big on shape-shifting. I found only one."

"Which is?"

"Selkies—seal shifters. Since we're not anywhere near the sea, I'm not feeling the magic on that one. So there goes our theory that the victim is the supernatural."

"Not necessarily," I said.

The two of them exchanged a glance, then sat back in their chairs. "Get to it," Claire ordered.

I told them all I'd discovered, and they didn't laugh, though Claire did roll her eyes at the "alien" theory.

"You got any better ideas?" I asked.

She glanced at Mal and together they shrugged.

"We're at a dead end. I'm not sure what to do next." I hated to admit that. I always knew what to do. That's why I was the sheriff in these parts.

"We'll keep searching for a connection," Claire said. "Sooner or later something's going to pop, and then we'll be on whatever demon or monster or alien like white on rice."

I never had understood the "white on rice" adage, but now didn't seem the time to bring that up.

"Maybe one of us should check in with Elise," Claire said.

"I will."

"*You* will? No way."

Since I wanted to ask about Ian's disappearing wife, I didn't have a problem calling the wise and furry doctor, but I wasn't going to tell Claire that. I didn't want her sympathy about another doomed affair, especially one she hadn't even known I was having.

"I'm a professional." I lifted my chin. "If she knows anything worth knowing, I'll get back to you later."

"Okay," Claire said, though she stared at me suspiciously. I got out of there before she pulled out the thumbscrews.

Since I hadn't been to the office all day, I stopped before I went home. Both Jordan's and Cal's shift had ended hours ago. Cal had left a note on my desk—or at least I thought he had. When I picked it up, I saw it was merely another Chuck Norris chuckle.

When Chuck Norris crosses the street, the cars better look both ways.

With a smile, I set the sheet aside to give to Jordan tomorrow.

Several other messages lay beneath Cal's, people who had called during the day but not been urgent enough to contact me about.

I shuffled through them. All were from citizens, wanting to know why I was ordering autopsies and digging up corpses. Well, I wasn't going to tell them. I'd already met with the next of kin and shared what I could.

I tossed the messages into the trash. I was certain citizens would accost me on the street if given a chance, so I'd do my best not to give them one.

I snuck out the back door and slid into my brand-new squad car. At home I changed out of my uniform into jeans, a red tank top, and sandals. Then I headed upstairs to the third-floor office to call Elise.

Like Ian, I was drawn to that room. The view of the mountains from the window soothed me. I sat at the desk facing them as I dialed the super-secret phone number of the *Jäger-Suchers*.

"What now?" Elise asked without benefit of "hello." The longer I knew her, the more like her grandfather she became.

Edward Mandenauer had founded the *Jäger-Suchers*

over sixty years ago. From what I'd seen of him in the short time he'd been in town, he wasn't much on "hello" and "good-bye," either. Edward liked to shoot first, ask if you were human later. It saved time.

"Caller ID is wrecking polite conversation as we know it," I said.

"If I know who's calling, why waste time making nicey-nice?"

See what I mean? Edward junior.

Well, two could play at this, and I didn't want to chitchat with wolf girl any more than she wanted to chitchat with me.

"We've got a new kid in town, and I was wondering if you had any info on him in your handy-dandy 'Big Brother is watching you pee' database."

"You'll be glad we've got that database if he's in there."

I didn't argue.

"Name?"

"Ian Walker."

"What do you think he is?"

"If I knew that, I wouldn't be calling you."

"Nothing here," she said, and started to hang up.

"Wait!" I shouted. "I was actually more interested in his wife."

"Oh, really? Why's that?"

"Because she disappeared without a trace, which sounds suspiciously like your work."

"Doesn't it though? Except it wasn't."

"You know that off the top of your head?"

"If we'd disappeared her, we'd have a record of that right next to any record on her husband, which there isn't. We like to keep our lies straight, and the only way to do that is to keep track of them."

"Well, when it comes to lying, I guess you'd know."

"Got that right." She sounded proud, and maybe she was. Her lies, and those of her colleagues and underlings, were what allowed the world to continue turning on its merry axis, secure in the false knowledge that monsters were not crawling all over the place.

I opened my mouth to thank her, but Elise was already gone.

23

As I ended the call on my side, something howled out there in the night. Spirit wolf or real wolf, didn't matter. The sound reminded me that I needed to check on Quatie. I got to my feet and headed for the door.

The rush of air from my movement caused something to swoosh out from under a bookcase against the front wall. Whatever it was, it was as light as a—

"Feather," I murmured, and snatched it up.

I'd never had a feather in here that I could recall, except for Ian's, and this wasn't his. Not only had I seen the eagle feather in place in his hair earlier today, but the one I held in my hand wasn't from an eagle.

Big and black without a hint of white, I had no idea what kind it was or how it had gotten here. Feathers this big didn't appear out of nowhere. Or maybe they did in this new world evolving every day in Lake Bluff. I put the feather into the top desk drawer for later perusal.

Aaaewww!

I jumped. The howl seemed to come from right outside my window.

"Coming," I muttered as I ran down two flights of stairs.

However, when I went outside, the wolf wasn't there, and she had gone as silent as the ghost she no doubt was. I jumped into my dad's pickup and headed north.

Quatie sat on her porch. As I got out, she stood, moving a lot easier than the last time I'd visited. That balm of Ian's really needed to be bottled and sold.

Seeing her get around so much better, I was relieved. I'd brought Ian to Quatie—at her request, true, but I never would have forgiven myself if his cure had harmed rather than helped.

Several sticks lay on the ground in front of the house. Kindling, most likely. I scooped them into my arms, frowning when I saw the ends had been honed to points.

"I whittle," Quatie said without my asking. "Not very good at it."

If she'd been trying to make a mammal or a bird, she wasn't. If she'd been aiming at poking out someone's eye, I'd have to change my mind. Physicians recommended handiwork to soothe arthritis, the movement working out the kinks. Quatie must have taken up whittling for just that reason.

I wondered if Ian had been back to visit without me and had suggested it, but I wasn't going to ask. The subject of Ian Walker was still a little raw.

She'd shoved one into the ground at the corner of the house; the pointy end stuck straight up.

"A little dangerous." I indicated the stick.

"For squirrels," she said.

I wasn't sure if they were meant to keep the squirrels

away, entertain them, or skewer them, and I had no chance to ask since she turned and went into the house.

As I followed, I marveled again at how much her gait had improved. Even with the miracle balm, the progress was amazing. Then I saw a probable reason why on the table and forgot all about pointy sticks and squirrels.

"Moonshine's illegal," I said.

"You going to turn me in, Gracie?" She squinted through cataract-murky eyes. "This settles the pain in my old bones."

It would probably eat her old bones if she drank too much. I was concerned it might eat right through her stomach lining, too, but she slammed back a shot, licked her lips, and smiled with more teeth than I recalled her having. She must have gotten dentures. I only hoped the moonshine didn't ruin them.

I shook my head when she offered me a shot. I spent a lot of time chasing stills in these mountains. Theoretically, moonshine was dangerous. Too much alcohol and a person could go blind. In truth, the old folks who made it had been brewing the stuff for decades and they knew what they were doing.

I could tell by the jar and the shade of the brew that Quatie had gotten hers from Granny McGinty, the biggest moonshiner in the county because she made good hooch for a reasonable price.

Since Quatie appeared a lot better now than she had the last time I'd seen her, I wasn't going to complain. In the old days, people doctored quite a few things with moonshine—rheumatism, arthritis, toothache. They managed with what they had. I couldn't fault Quatie for doing the same.

"I wanted to see how you were doing." I took a seat.

"Better." She took another gulp. "You don't need to

keep checking on me, child. I've been alone a long time."

"Is your great-great-granddaughter still coming to visit?"

"Soon." She laughed with such pure joy I had to smile.

"Where's she coming from?"

"Not far. Enough about me. How's your young man?"

He wasn't my young man. But the eagerness on her face, her genuine fondness for Ian—I couldn't tell her he was a lying, married weasel. At least not today.

"He's fine, Quatie."

"Very fine." She winked and took another sip of moonshine.

I frowned. "You aren't going to take a walk later, are you?"

"No. No walking tonight." She didn't seem affected by the alcohol at all. I suppose familiarity bred resistance. "Have you read your great-grandmother's papers yet, Gracie?"

"No, ma'am."

"Mmm." She seemed to think about that. "That's probably for the best."

"Why?"

She got up from the table and walked without a wobble to her couch, where she lay down. "They'll just make you sad." She closed her eyes.

The silence that settled over the room was so thick I began to get nervous. She hadn't died, had she?

"Quatie?" I called softly.

My only answer was a snore.

I went home. I didn't have much else to do.
    Heading down the highway, I let my mind wander.

I'd driven these roads a thousand times; I knew how they twisted and turned. I considered ignoring my house and returning to work or maybe going to Claire's or even—

The wolf appeared as if from nowhere, right in front of my truck. I slammed on the brakes, but it was too late. I braced for the impact, but the truck passed right through the animal and came out the other side.

I looked in the rearview mirror. The wolf stood behind me, not a mark on it. I got out of the vehicle.

A flurry of movement, the scrabble of claws against pavement, and the animal ran through me again. Cold wind, a heavy rain, I felt thick and full, then thin and empty. I had a mental image of my body and the wolf's melding, stretching, coming together, then suddenly flying apart.

I swayed, and when I could see clearly once more, the beast had stopped several yards ahead. She glanced back, then ran a few feet.

"If you wanted me to go in that direction, all you had to do was wait," I said. "I was already doing it."

The wolf snorted and I remembered. I'd been thinking of going anywhere but home.

"You can read my mind?"

I wasn't sure how I felt about that. It wasn't as if the wolf could tell anyone my thoughts, but they were *my* thoughts, and I preferred to keep them that way.

I scowled at the furry beast. "What difference could it possibly make if I go home or not?"

As if in answer, the air seemed to shriek. I put my hands over my ears and glanced up just in time to see a shower of sparks falling from the sky.

The wolf whined. I would think a noise like that

would hurt her ears worse than mine, even if they were spirit ears.

The animal ran south again, then turned, waited. South, the direction of peace and good health—the direction of home.

I peered at the area of the sky where the sparks had disappeared. Just like last time, orange glowed against the night.

Cursing, I jumped into my truck, fumbling for my cell phone even as I thrust the vehicle into gear and drove over the messenger wolf. The animal didn't seem to mind, catching up in seconds and loping alongside, oblivious to the trunks of trees that lined the road. The wolf just ran right through them.

I reached the fire department and gave them the approximate location of the blaze; then I called Cal.

"Remember when the sparks came down and started the fire that wasn't?"

"Where is it this time?"

"I think it's my house."

"I'll be right there."

I continued to drive as fast as I could on the narrow, winding roads, praying that this fire was as much a myth as the last one. The wolf ran beside me until I turned down my long, rutted driveway; then she disappeared.

The orange glow had only brightened as I approached. I knew even before I shot out of the trees and into my yard that my house was toast.

The fire department had arrived ahead of me, as had Cal. A scuffle was going on near my front porch. Cal and the fire chief held on to someone who seemed to be fighting to get inside.

"What's going on?" I called.

The three men stopped struggling and turned. One of them was Ian.

"You're okay," he said.

"Not really. My damn house is on fire."

"I told him you weren't in there, but he didn't want to listen," Cal said.

Ian had been trying to run into a burning building to save me? I couldn't help but be touched. Because I was, I turned away to look at my house. I almost wished I hadn't.

The roof was completely engulfed. There wasn't much I could do except watch the fire department do their thing and wonder what in hell had fallen from the sky onto my house. Whatever it had been, it wasn't there any longer.

Ian and Cal joined me, staring at the flames, too.

"What are you doing here?" I asked Ian. Cal took one look at my face and walked off.

"I wanted to talk to you."

"Was the house on fire when you arrived?"

"Yes."

"So you didn't see what started it?"

He frowned. "You're thinking arson?"

I hadn't said that, but I found it interesting that he'd heard it.

"I'm a cop," I said. "I think a lot of things. What did you see?"

"I drove up, and the roof was on fire. I thought you were inside. The place was locked. I pounded on the door, shouted for you; then those guys grabbed me."

"I appreciate your concern, but I'm fine. You may as well go."

"I'm not leaving you."

His voice was too loud, and I winced, then glanced

over my shoulder toward Cal, who, from his scowl, had heard. He took a step in our direction, and I shook my head. I didn't need my deputy to step in when I had man trouble.

I faced Ian. "I'm a big girl, Doctor. I can take care of myself."

"Where are you going to sleep?"

"Certainly not with you," I snapped.

"That wasn't what I meant."

Too bad, I thought. Despite all my protestations to the contrary, I wanted to sleep with him, to hold him and have him hold me. If I'd lived in another town, one that wasn't so small, so conservative, so judgmental . . . No, that wouldn't matter.

If I'd been a different person, one who didn't care about what was real or true or right, I'd have agreed with him that a missing wife was as good as a dead wife. But I wasn't and I didn't. However, that didn't keep me from wanting what I couldn't have.

"Thanks," I said softly. "But I can't."

"Grace, you have to listen to me—"

I held up my hand. "Not now. Please."

He pressed his lips together, then gave a sharp nod. "It's just that I came over here with my speech all prepared and then—"

"My house was on fire."

"Yeah."

"Grace?"

I turned as the fire chief, Sam Makelway, strode up. He'd taken over recently from Joe Cantrell, who'd been the fire chief as long as my dad had been the sheriff. Sam was more than qualified since he'd joined the department right out of high school.

A few years older than me, Sam was broad and tall,

with short red hair and a round, pale face that got ruddier and ruddier the closer he got to a fire and the longer he had to stay there. Right now his facial barometer hovered between salmon and rose, and I let out a relieved breath. Couldn't be too bad.

Sam had been in the same class as my brother Gene. They hadn't been pals—my brothers had been pals only with one another—but they'd been friendly enough. I liked Sam. He knew his job, which made mine so much easier.

"We've got it under control." He waved at the roof, which was only smoking now, no longer shooting spiky tendrils of flame toward the slightly lopsided silver moon. "Looks like just the top room is ruined."

"Well, I guess that's better than—" I stopped as I realized what that meant.

"Grace?" Ian took my arm, shook it a little. "You need to breathe."

I not only couldn't breathe, I couldn't stand, so I sat with a thud on the ground at Ian's feet.

Both men went to their knees next to me, Sam bellowing for Cal to call the paramedics.

"No," I managed, then drew in a huge, loud, gulping breath. "I'm okay."

I wasn't, but I didn't need a paramedic. No one, nothing, could fix this.

Grandmother's papers had been in that third-floor room, and now they were gone.

It was as if I'd lost her all over again.

24

IAN'S LONG FINGERS wrapped around my wrist as he took my pulse. From the expression on his face, he didn't like what he'd found.

"You need to calm down," he murmured.

Cal hovered; so did Sam. They weren't used to seeing me sitting down on the job. The way I'd hit the ground, they probably thought I'd fainted. How would that appear to the general public? *Lake Bluff sheriff faints at the sight of her house on fire.*

Not that I wouldn't have every reason to, but people liked their sheriffs tough. Can't say that I blamed them. I forced myself to my feet.

"I'm good." I yanked my wrist out of Ian's grasp, even though his fingers felt pleasantly warm and dry against my cold, clammy skin. "I just thought of all I kept in that room. Things that can't be replaced."

"You can't be replaced," Ian said, and I cut my gaze to his. What I saw there made me look away.

"What do you think started the fire, Sam?"

Sam stared at me for several beats, decided I wasn't going to swoon, and got on with it. "Hard to say. I'll have the investigator over here first thing tomorrow. You better not stay tonight. Even though the lower floors weren't burned, there's going to be water damage and the smell—" He spread his huge, hard hands. "You'll have to hire a professional cleaning company."

"Ka-ching."

Sam grinned at the evidence I was back to my old self. "Yeah. But you've got insurance, right?"

"Of course."

My dad had been big on insurance. We'd had a couple of crosses burned on our lawn back in the old days—which weren't all that old.

When Dad had taken over as the first Cherokee sheriff in Lake Bluff history, there'd been some who hadn't been as happy about it as we were. We'd never been quite sure if it had been the Cherokee sheriff part they objected to or the African-American part. Maybe both.

If it hadn't been for the sparks I'd seen tumbling from the sky, accompanied by the supernatural shrieking, I'd have figured someone who wasn't happy about a female Cherokee, African-American, Scotch-Irish sheriff had lit up my roof to express their point of view. From the expression on Sam's face, he'd had the same thought.

"I'll take care of it from here," I said.

Sam nodded and returned to his men.

I considered going inside, maybe grabbing some clothes, but I knew from past experience with other fires that everything I owned would smell like wet charcoal. I was going to have to live with what I had until I could buy new underwear and enough casual clothes to last me a few days. Luckily I kept some spare uniforms at the office.

I hated to knock on Claire's door this late and scare the crap out of her, so I decided to rent a hotel room. We had plenty in town, and since the Full Moon Festival was still several weeks away, there should be a lot of vacancies.

"Stay with me," Ian murmured.

I didn't even dignify that with a glance, let alone an answer.

Instead I strode to where Cal was talking into his car radio. I meant to tell him where I'd be and get gone, but as I approached, his words made me pause and listen.

"She's dead?" he asked. "They're sure?"

"Dad," Jordan said with a scorn that made me want to reach through the radio and strangle her, "I think people know what dead looks like."

"Not as often as you'd think," Cal muttered. "I'm on my way."

He glanced at me. "You heard?"

I nodded. The sound of a car starting made me glance over my shoulder. Ian had at last taken the hint and left.

"Who's dead this time?" I asked.

"Merry Gray."

"But—" I stopped before I blurted something I'd have to explain later. I guess Merry *did* fit the profile. She was dying.

"But what?" Cal asked.

As far as Cal knew, we'd only had a rash of deaths. I wasn't going to tell him about the supernatural questions. He was a straight shooter, an eternal Marine. He'd never believe in aliens, or anything else out of the ordinary for that matter, and I didn't have time to convince him.

"I'll take the call," I said.

"I'll go with you."

"No." I was going to have Doc go with me. "I need you to hang around here. I—" I forced my voice to break. It wasn't that hard. "I can't do it."

Sympathy washed over Cal's face. "Of course. I'll stay."

He tried to pat my shoulder, fumbling the gesture and smacking me in both the chin and the neck. I stepped out of his reach. "Where'd they find Merry?"

"Died in her bed, I hope in her sleep. Poor woman."

"Yeah," I agreed. It would be nice if we had a plain old death for a change, but I doubted it. "I'll see you tomorrow. I'm going to stay in town. You can raise me on my cell."

Cal lifted a hand in good-bye and took off with long, sure strides toward the huddle of firefighters on my lawn.

In the past few days, Doc had moved up on my speed dial to the number-one position. He answered on the second ring, and I gave him directions.

"I'm getting real sick of seeing your number on my caller ID," he said.

"Be honest, Doc: Did you ever really like it?"

I reached Merry's house, which stood on one of the many side streets in Lake Bluff. Despite the hour, the place was lit up like the Fourth of July. Merry's husband, Ted, opened the door before I even knocked.

His face was pale and tear-streaked. He tried to speak and choked, then turned and walked into the living room, leaving the door open.

I'd dealt with hysterical relatives before, but they were usually women. Ted was six-four and weighed about three hundred pounds. He was a mason, and his hands were as big as bricks. I guess size didn't matter when it came to heartbreak. Still, Merry had been sick a long time and, according to all the gossips, there'd been no hope. I don't know why I'd thought he'd be ready for the inevitable by now, but I had.

"Ted." I crept into the room, not wanting to disturb him but needing to ask questions. I was going to try to finagle an autopsy out of this man—it wouldn't hurt to actually have permission from the family member on record—but I couldn't do it if he was incoherent.

"Grace." He paused, trying to breathe, but his chest kept hitching like a child who's sobbed too long and too hard.

"Take your time." I perched on the edge of the couch. He stood by the window.

"She—she—she—"

"I know," I said gently.

"She wasn't supposed to die."

I stilled. "What?"

"She went to the doctor yesterday. She was in remission. It was a miracle."

"Miracle," I murmured, wondering what in hell Walker had put in that jar. I meant to find out.

"What, exactly, did her doctor say?"

"Just that. Remission. She had more time."

"How much?"

"He wouldn't say, but then—" He lifted his huge hands and let them fall back to his sides, helpless.

"Tell me what happened."

"She went to bed early; she always did. I watched the news, then Leno. I heard this horrible noise." He winced and put his palms over his ears. "So I went up and she was—" He choked, dropped his arms, and began to sob again.

I wanted to check on her, but I didn't want to leave him. Thankfully, Doc arrived.

"Stay with him," I said, and before Doc could protest, I hustled up the steps.

Merry lay on her bed. If it weren't for the expression on her face, I'd have thought her sleeping. Her body was in repose, thin hands folded over a concave stomach. But her eyes were wide open, her mouth twisted in pain or fear.

I pulled the sheet over her face and went back downstairs, jerking my head at Doc, who joined me in the hall. Ted still stared out the window, shoulders shaking.

"Same as all the others," I said. "Her face, the shrieking before she died. Except, according to Ted, she'd just gone into remission."

"She wasn't dying?"

"Not today."

"I told him I needed to do an autopsy," Doc murmured, and I stifled an inappropriate hoot of happiness that I wouldn't be the one who had to ask. "He was agreeable. I'll do it right away. Maybe this isn't even related."

"Maybe," I agreed, but I didn't think so.

I called Ted's sister to come and sit with him, then left Doc to deal with Merry. I headed for Ian Walker's place; I didn't even take my vehicle, just stalked downhill toward Center Street.

His building was dark except for a tiny glow on the second floor. I pounded on the back door loud enough to wake everyone on the street. Luckily, all of the establishments nearby were retail. Walker was the only person I knew who lived above his business.

He opened the door and smiled. "I'm so glad you—"

I put my palm in the center of his chest and shoved. He stumbled back a few steps and I followed, kicking the door shut behind me. "What did you give her?"

He lifted one hand and rubbed at his sternum. "Who?"

"Merry Gray."

"We already had this conversation, Sheriff. I'm not going to tell you."

I began to walk forward, my steps echoing on the wood floor. He stood his ground, chin lifting, the smooth silver light of the moon through the windows glancing off his cheekbones and nose, sparkling in his dark hair, and playing hide-and-seek with his eagle feather.

Why was it that in the darkness he looked like a warrior and in the daylight he just looked like a man? Without the feather, no one would ever mistake him for Cherokee between nine and five. After midnight, he could be mistaken for nothing else.

"You think you can take me?" he murmured.

I stopped with the toes of my sandals just brushing his bare feet. He'd removed his jacket and tie, loosened the buttons at his throat, rolled up his cuffs. His skin gleamed in the half-light. Taking him took on a whole new meaning, one I was tempted to explore—until the moon's glow glanced off of his wedding ring.

"I don't have to take you," I said. "I can get a warrant."

"Good luck with that."

I wanted to scream. He made me so mad.

I took several breaths and tried a different tactic. "What's the big secret? She went into remission. I'd think you'd want everyone to know what a great doctor you are."

"Remission?" His brow creased. "Really?"

"You seem surprised."

"I am. What I gave her—" I perked up, but he paused, shrugged. "I'm glad she's better, but I had nothing to do with it."

"She not so much better as dead."

"But you just said—"

"Yeah, things change fast around here." I headed for the door. He wasn't going to be of any help, and if I stayed I'd only want to jump him, which just made me madder at both him and myself.

I slammed the door, then stood in the silvery light trying to think of what to do. I wasn't trained for paranormal investigation; I was getting nowhere and people were dying.

If they were people. The committee was still out on that.

Regardless, beings that inhabited my town were turning up dead, sans hearts, and I had no idea why. Pretty soon someone besides me was going to notice the epidemic, and then there'd be real trouble.

Inside I heard the faint mumble of Ian's voice. Either he was talking to himself or he'd called someone. I inched closer to the door, noticing that I'd shut it so hard, the latch hadn't caught, and now it stood open a few inches.

"A woman in remission died tonight."

I frowned. Who could he possibly be calling about that?

"I gave her one of my healing potions. Herbs, vitamins. Nothing major. Believe me, if I could cure cancer, I'd be doing it."

My lips curved. Wouldn't that be something?

"I know it doesn't make sense. The Kâlanû Ahyeli'-skǐ steals the lives of the dying."

I froze.

The *what*?

25

W HILE I WANTED to bust right in and demand answers to a whole lot of questions, I forced myself to remain where I was and listen.

"No one's reacted to the feather."

His feather? I'd reacted to it, though I certainly hoped he wasn't sharing how.

"Buzzard," he continued, "just like the legends said."

Buzzard feather? I flashed on the huge black feather I'd found in my office at home—the office that was now toast. What in hell was Ian Walker up to? Who in hell was he? And who was he working for?

"I'll keep looking." His voice faded, and the stairs creaked as he went up them. I leaned back as his shadow passed in front of the second-story window. Before I confronted him, I needed some answers. Namely, what did a buzzard feather repel and what in hell was a Kâlanû Ahyeli'-skĭ?

Leaving the door ajar—I'd definitely be back—I headed for the sheriff's department.

The place was quiet at this time of night. My third-shift dispatcher, a semi-retired lawyer by the name of Catfish Waller, manned the phones. Catfish was the only lawyer left in Lake Bluff. Since we didn't have much need for a lawyer, that worked out well.

Catfish had come to work for me when his insomnia had gotten so bad he never slept a wink between midnight and 9:00 A.M. He not only was responsible, but he also knew the law. If I could only get him to stop writing his memoirs during his shift. Not that there was all that much else to do, but he had a bad habit of reading them to anyone who would listen. There'd been complaints.

"Grace!" he greeted. "Chapter seventeen, where I lose my virginity."

Oh, God.

"Sorry, Catfish, gotta hit the Internet. Maybe later." I made a dash for my office.

"Real sorry about your house," he called.

"Thanks!" I waved as I escaped inside, then locked the door behind me and pulled down the shades. I didn't want Catfish deciding he really needed my opinion any more than I wanted him seeing what I was researching on the Internet.

I also wanted to change my clothes, which reeked of the fire, so I stripped and donned one of the extra uniforms in the closet, exchanging my sandals for sneakers, then made my way to the computer and typed in *buzzard feathers.*

I got back a whole lot of ways to use them for decorating or arts and crafts. Did people have lives? Who spent their time thinking up this stuff? Psychotic Martha Stewart clones?

Native American legends, buzzard feathers, I pecked out next.

That got me a hit right away.

The Cherokees believed that by placing a buzzard feather at the entrance of any dwelling, a witch would be unable to cross the threshold.

"Oookay."

I'd overheard Ian say that no one had reacted to the feather, which led me to believe he was looking for a witch, and I wasn't the only one he was looking at.

My heart pounded in my throat, not with fear so much as excitement. I'd been at a dead end. I'd had nowhere else to turn for answers, and suddenly answers were falling into my lap. I just didn't know the question.

The Internet had been of no use to me before, but I hadn't had enough information. Now I had a name.

"Kâlanû Ahyeli'-skǐ," I murmured as I typed, then hit *enter* with a flourish.

Of all the Cherokee witches

"Well, that explains the buzzard feather," I murmured.

the most feared is the Kâlanû Ahyeli'-skǐ or the Raven Mocker.

"Could also explain the sudden increase in ravens." I frowned. "Maybe."

The Raven Mocker robs the dying of life. Flying through the night with arms outstretched trailing sparks, the witch announces its approach with a horrible shriek.

The Raven Mocker eats the victim's heart, stealing whatever days the person has left on the earth. Because the Raven Mocker is a witch, it is able to remove the hearts without leaving a scar.

Well, at least that took care of our theory of alien invasion. I can't say I was sorry to see it go.

Now I knew what we were dealing with, kind of. I had no idea what this thing looked like, how it worked, a way to kill it, but I had a pretty good idea who did.

⬭⬭⬭

Since the door was still partway open, I walked right into the clinic. Out of curiosity I glanced up. A buzzard feather had been tacked to the wall directly over the entrance at both the back door and the front. Obviously not taking any chances, Ian had placed one over each window as well.

I'd already broken in, so I took off my shoes, snuck up the stairs, and headed for the only room where a light remained burning. No one was there.

I allowed my gaze to wander over the area. Desk, books, papers—his office, not his bedroom. He'd probably gone to bed and forgotten to shut off the light. Before I woke him up and questioned him mercilessly, I'd take a look around.

I wasn't worried any longer about a warrant. No court in the land was going to believe any of this anyway.

Medical texts. Medical journals. Tiny bottles of oil.

Colored liquids. Bowls of herbs. A bag of what appeared to be grass. I opened it and took a whiff, determining it was the kind that cows ate, before setting it down.

I made my way to the desk where several loose sheets of paper lay on the blotter. The words were in Cherokee. I couldn't read them, but there was something familiar about them.

I threw a quick glance over my shoulder; I'm not sure why. The place was as quiet now as it had been when I'd walked in.

Ian stood right behind me.

I let out a pathetic squeak and stepped back, stumbling over a stack of books next to the desk.

He reached out, quick as a snake, and snatched me by the forearms, hauling me against him. His eyes caught the golden glow of the lamp, flickering topaz, even as the pupils dilated so large they nearly obscured the lighter shade of his irises.

"What are you doing here?"

I opened my mouth to answer, or maybe to question, and he kissed me. That seemed to be his prelude to everything.

I tasted desperation on his tongue, lust, desire, need, on his lips. My body responded; I couldn't make it stop. I felt all those things, too, even though my mind knew better.

But right now my mind seemed to have gone on vacation. Something nagged at the corner, but I couldn't quite grasp it with him kissing me like this. Then he was touching me, too, and I couldn't do anything but respond.

My thighs hit the edge of the desk, and I sat abruptly. He stepped between my legs, nudging them farther apart. Looming over me, his shadow blotted out the light. His hair sifted over my face, creating a curtain between us and the world.

"Grace," he whispered, as his lips trailed across my jaw, down my neck. My head fell back; to keep my balance I wrapped my legs around his, hooking my ankles.

His fingers popped the buttons on my uniform seconds ahead of his mouth. He traced his tongue across my collarbone, then dipped it into the valley between my breasts and up and over the swell. One tug and he bared me to the night air, then his mouth closed over a peak, and he suckled.

Somehow my shirt came off, my bra, too. I was naked from the waist up, clothed from the waist down, but wrapped around him, center to center; his erection rode me right where I needed it to. My gun belt thwapped against the desk in an enticing rhythm, which only added fuel to the arousal.

He lifted his head, reached behind me, and flung the papers and pencils and books off the desk in a single sweep of his arm. For an instant I was stunned and excited; then I saw again those papers, the writing, and I remembered where I'd seen it before. I shoved him away and drew my weapon.

His gaze shifted slowly from my bare breasts to the Glock. "You have an odd idea of foreplay."

"Then you're really not going to like the climax." I lowered the barrel until it was pointed at his crotch. He took a step backward. "Don't move."

I got off the desk, ignoring the sudden chill as the air drifted over my skin. I wasn't going to give him the satisfaction of covering myself. It wasn't anything he hadn't seen before.

Keeping my eyes and my gun on him, I bent and retrieved one of the papers he'd swept so grandly to the floor. I would have known sooner if I hadn't believed they'd been burnt to cinders in the fire at my house earlier that night.

Straightening, I held up a paper covered in my great-grandmother's handwriting.

"Who in hell are you?" I asked.

26

You know who I am."

"I may know your name but not *who* you are. Not why you're really here." I set the paper on the desk, then leaned my hip against it. "Tell me more about the Raven Mocker."

His eyes widened. "I should have known you'd figure it out."

I didn't bother to tell him I'd only figured it out because I'd been eavesdropping.

"You left a buzzard feather at my house?" He lifted one shoulder, lowered it. "You thought I was a witch?"

"Someone is."

"Why me?"

"You were out in the forest the night of the Thunder Moon."

"So were you."

"I was looking for the Raven Mocker, and there you were."

"You knew it was here?"

"I knew it was coming."

"How?"

He tilted his head. "You wanna stow the gun, maybe put on a shirt so I can think straight?"

"No."

"Grace, I won't hurt you. If I planned to, I could have a hundred times already."

"Well, that makes me all warm and fuzzy," I muttered, my stomach rolling.

I'd believed he wanted me for me, just as I'd wanted him. But like so many others, he'd wanted something *from* me—to get close so he could see if I was evil and then steal my great-grandmother's medicine.

I stared at him, uncertain what to do. Scream, shout, shoot? None was a good idea, so I put up my gun and reached for my shirt, keeping my eye on him the whole time.

"Talk," I ordered as I buttoned the last button.

"I'm a member of an ancient society."

I sighed. "I am going to kick Elise Hanover's ass."

"You know about the *Jäger-Suchers*?"

"They were here last summer."

He frowned. "Werewolf troubles?"

"Like you wouldn't believe."

"I hadn't heard. I run into a *Jäger-Sucher* here and there on various assignments. It's hard not to since we're both hunting supernatural creatures, but I'm a member of the Nighthawk Keetoowahs. You've heard of them?"

I nodded. I'd learned about the Keetoowahs in school. They'd been formed in the eighteenth century for the express purpose of keeping Cherokee history and language alive.

"So you're a member of a Cherokee society devoted to preserving the traditional ways," I said. "Big deal."

"That's what the Nighthawks are on the outside, but on the inside we're sworn to track down and eliminate evil supernatural entities, like the Raven Mocker."

"If you know about the *Jäger-Suchers,* then it would follow that they know about you." Especially since they seemed to know about everything.

"Sometimes we make use of the others' resources."

I wondered momentarily if Edward had used his influence to get Walker's medical license approved so fast or if perhaps the Nighthawks had their own Edward on staff.

"I asked Hanover about you, and she said she'd never heard of you."

He smiled. "She lies."

"No shit."

"You don't like her?"

"No," I said shortly. "We rub each other the wrong way."

"Wolf and panther." He was suddenly right next to me. "I can understand why you would."

"Back up." I shoved at his chest. I couldn't think when he was so close. He smelled too good and his body lined up with mine just right. Damn him. "I'm not a panther."

"You are." He reached out and drew one finger between my breasts. "Here. Just like I'm an eagle." He pointed at himself. "In my heart."

"Speaking of hearts, I have a sudden rash of missing ones, which I hear is the fault of the Raven Mocker."

"Yes."

"But no one's seen this thing."

"It's invisible."

I *had* suspected that.

"Though not all the time. It's a person and a raven. Witch and shape-shifter. The Raven Mocker enters the rooms of the dying by becoming invisible."

"The shrieking?"

"Frightens the victim to death."

I remembered the terror-stricken faces of the dead, and I wanted the witch to die as frightened as all of its victims had been.

A little vindictive? Sue me.

"How do we find it?" I asked.

"That's the problem. I don't know."

"I thought finding these . . . things was what you did."

"If it was that simple, everyone would do it."

I narrowed my eyes. I was in no mood for jokes. "Why isn't it simple?"

"Do you know what a witch looks like?"

"Bad teeth, warts, long, gray scraggly hair?"

"Could be. Could also be you, me," he spread his arms wide, "everybody."

"How do we figure out who it is before someone else dies?"

He jerked his chin, indicating the desk. "That's why I'm translating your great-grandmother's papers."

"I thought those were cures."

"Cures can have more than one meaning—medicinal cures for human ailments and supernatural cures for monstrous entities. Most of the papers of great medicine men and women also contain legends that were passed down through the generations. Stories of beings from ancient times—both good and bad."

"Why do you think my great-grandmother's papers

contain information about the Raven Mocker?" I paused as another thought occurred to me. "Wait. You were already here when the storm arrived on the night of the Thunder Moon. You said you knew the witch was coming, but how?"

"I'm A ni wo di."

"A paint clan medicine man. I know."

"Paint clan are more than medicine men; some of us are sorcerers."

I waited to see if he'd laugh, but he didn't. "You've been reading way too much Harry Potter."

His lips curved. "While I do enjoy Harry and clan, I was a sorcerer long before he showed up. Besides, I think he's a wizard."

"Wizard, witch." I threw up my hands. "What's the difference?"

"I've never met a wizard, so I'm inclined to believe they don't exist, but I could be wrong. A witch can be either good or bad, depending on the witch. And a sorcerer, in the world of the Nighthawks, is a medicine man with a little something extra."

"What?"

"Magic."

"Right," I said. "You bet."

"You don't believe me?"

I hesitated. I'd seen magic, both as a child and as an adult. I'd shoved aside the memories of my great-grandmother's gifts, refusing to believe what my eyes had seen. Then last summer I'd had no choice but to believe when I'd witnessed men and women turn into beasts and back again.

"What kind of magic are you talking about?" I asked.

Ian didn't answer, at least with words. He closed his eyes and began to chant in Cherokee. The air thickened, shimmered, changed, and when he opened his eyes, they weren't human anymore.

"Eagle eyes," I murmured. "You're a shape-shifter?"

"Not completely. After years of practice, I can draw the essence of my spirit animal, take on some of its powers."

I thought of the eagle that had been seen soaring over the mountains. "Can you fly?"

He smiled. "Not yet."

"There's been an eagle spotted near town."

"I'm sure it's just drawn to the . . . ," he shrugged, "vibes. When I call on my eagle spirit, something must go out into the air."

"Okay." That could explain the sudden influx of ravens, too. If this witch was a raven shape-shifter, that would put "something" into the air as well and perhaps draw them in. "If you can't fly, what can you do?"

"I see."

"Me, too, pal, and I'm not even magic."

"You're a descendant of Rose Scott, one of the most powerful medicine women in recent history. With some training, you could easily do what I can and more."

"No thanks. I'm not much of a bird lover."

He gave me a knowing look. I *had* been a bird lover, several times.

"You're A ni sa ho ni," he said, letting me off the hook without comment. "Clan of blue. The panther. You have powers beyond your wildest dreams. If you study, if you practice, there's nothing you can't do."

I'm not saying it wasn't tempting. The long-ago childhood dream of actually *becoming* a panther, of course it called to me. But I was no longer a child, and I'd had to put away childish things. Like my panther collection.

"You're starting to make me think more of a snake in the garden than an eagle in the medical clinic."

He tilted his head with a birdlike flick that kind of gave me the willies. "What do you mean?"

"You're tempting me, Ian. I've seen what werewolves can do, and I want no part of that, regardless of how powerful I might become."

"What do werewolves have to do with anything?"

"Shape-shifters are shape-shifters. Just because I'd be a panther wouldn't make me any less . . ." I waved my hand. "Evil."

"Why would you be evil? I'm not evil."

"That remains to be seen."

"You've got this all wrong, Grace. I was born to be a sorcerer, a Nighthawk, and a warrior. Accessing the eagle spirit is part of who I am, just as your panther is part of who you are. Elise sensed it in you, just like you sensed the wolf in her. You think if she believed you were evil she wouldn't have shot you in the head the first chance that she got?"

He had a point. I had no doubt Elise Hanover would have blown my brains out gladly if she sensed any threat to humanity. I might not like much about her, but I did like that.

"Tell me more about what you can do."

"I have the eyes of the eagle, so I can see farther, better. At times I can see the future. Which is how I knew to come here before the Raven Mocker appeared."

"If you can see so damn well, why can't you see who it is?"

"The Raven Mocker has powers, too. We just need to find a way to be more powerful."

"Yeah, that oughta work."

He ignored my sarcasm and continued. "He or she is

invisible when stealing lives and probably too visible when not stealing them."

"Too visible?"

"The witch blends right in."

"How does the Raven Mocker thing work?" At his puzzled frown, I elaborated. "Is it, *shazam,* there's a new person in town, and he or she is a witch?"

He was already shaking his head. "The Raven Mocker is born during a storm on the night of the Thunder Moon. You saw the sparks trail down to the Di'tatlaski'yi?"

"English," I ordered.

"The place where it rains fire."

"Yes," I said slowly. "Twice. Once on the night of the Thunder Moon, and once when my house almost burnt down."

"You saw the sparks that night?"

"Didn't you?"

"No, but that doesn't mean they didn't happen before I got there."

"I also had reports of sparks before the shrieking, though no other fires," I said.

"The legends say the Raven Mocker arrives in a shower of sparks. I'd thought that just meant original arrival, but I guess not."

"On the night of the Thunder Moon I saw the sparks, heard the shriek, saw what seemed to be a fire, but when we got there all we found was a crater."

"Where the Raven Mocker was born."

"The crater was empty."

"You think it would wait around to be captured or killed?"

"What *was* it?"

"An evil spirit."

"Which is so easy to capture and kill. Where did it go?"

"If we knew that, we'd know who it was."

"You said the Raven Mocker wasn't a new person."

"No. Someone called on the Ani'-Hyûñ'tĭkwǎlâ' skĭ."

I just stared at him until he translated.

"The thunder beings. They released the Raven Mocker from the sky vault. The spirit rode in on the lightning, then possessed the one who called it."

"You're saying someone in my town is possessed by a shape-shifting witch who eats the hearts of the dying and steals their lives?"

"That about sums it up."

27

WHERE DO WE go from here?" I asked.
Ian stared at me intently with his all-topaz eyes.

"Can you put those back the way you found them?" I waved vaguely at his head.

He murmured an indecipherable Cherokee word, gave one slow blink, and voilà, his eyes were light brown again, surrounded by normal, human white.

He flicked a finger at the papers all over the floor. "I need to translate those and hope I find something that will help us."

"For instance?"

"How we identify a Raven Mocker, how we kill one once we do."

"And why would you think my great-grandmother knew this?"

"I saw her before I came here. She showed me her papers, told me where I could find them."

"You know she's been dead for seven years?"

"So?"

"Was she a wolf when you saw her?"

His brows lifted. "Should she have been?"

"Hell if I know."

"The wolf you saw at the pond . . . You think that was your great-grandmother?"

"She's not a real wolf. Thing ran right through me." I shuddered at the memory of the sensation. "Ran through a couple of trees, too. They didn't even slow her down."

"Messenger wolf."

"That was my vote."

"What did she want to tell you?"

"She wasn't inclined to chat." If it had even been my great-grandmother. Who knew? "I thought she wanted me to keep an eye on Quatie, which I have been. But then she kept appearing and running north."

"Sadness and trouble," he murmured.

"She showed up quite a few times either before or after you did."

"Me? What'd I do?"

"Seduced me? Stole my papers?" I scowled. "Seduced me *to* steal my papers?"

He didn't deny it.

"If I hadn't stolen them, they'd be incinerated."

"That doesn't excuse it."

"No?"

"No!"

"I've learned in my business that the end justifies the means."

"You *should* be working for the *Jäger-Suchers*," I muttered. They were mavens of the "end justifies the means" philosophy. "And while I'm on the subject, why *aren't* you working for them? They've got government funding up the wazoo. You're both looking for supernatural entities; why split your force? Isn't that how Custer got his ass kicked?"

"So I hear," Ian drawled. "We don't join forces for several reasons. First of all, the Nighthawks began hunting in the eighteenth century. The *Jäger-Suchers* are a little kill-them-come-lately. They can join *us* if they like, but why should we join them?"

I opened my mouth, though I wasn't sure what I meant to say, but Ian continued without pausing. "Second, pardon us if we don't trust the government. They don't have the best record when it comes to Indian affairs."

"Don't you think it's time we got over that?"

"No," he said succinctly. "Third, we specialize in Cherokee spirits, though we have branched out into the spirits of other tribes, and we aren't averse to putting any old evil entity to rest if we happen to run across it. You can ask Dr. Hanover, but I don't think they have the best luck with Native American spirits."

"She said something about witchie wolves. Ojibwe. Considering how she likes to howl at the full moon, I was surprised at how little she cared for them."

"Just because they're wolves doesn't make them pals. Same goes for the Nighthawks and the *Jäger-Suchers*. We might both be monster hunters, but that doesn't mean we'd work together very well. I've talked with Edward. He was perfectly agreeable to our continuing in our way and the *Jäger-Suchers* in theirs. Many of the Cherokee spirits require someone with knowledge of the language to understand what they are and how to get rid of them."

"Hence your assignment to my fair town." He dipped

his chin. "So the Raven Mocker has possessed a Chero-kee?"

"Not necessarily. Anyone in possession of the spell can call the Raven Mocker, and since it's an ancient legend, there are no doubt a lot of old ones who know it. Although the Raven Mocker is a Cherokee spirit and therefore the incantation must be spoken in Cherokee, if someone read the words—"

"My great-grandmother always said a spell would only work if the caster spoke the Cherokee with true understanding."

"Understanding would only require a translation, which is easy enough to get if you really want to. Even if the Raven Mocker does need to be of Cherokee de-scent, around here that could be anyone."

He was right. There were very few full-blood Chero-kee left, but just about everyone could claim at least one ancestor who had a drop or two of Aniyvwiya blood. Basically, we were screwed.

However, I didn't plan to just lie down and let every-one in town get their hearts ripped out by an invisible raven witch.

Try saying that five times fast.

"I guess you'd better get cracking on that transla-tion," I said.

"I guess I'd better."

"I'm going to find a hotel."

Ian had already knelt and started gathering the tum-bled sheets, but at my words he glanced up. "You don't have to."

"Yes, I do."

He stood, hands full of paper. "I'm going to work all night. You can sleep in my bed." My lips tightened, but he didn't notice. He'd already turned away and begun shuffling the mess into some semblance of order. "As soon as I find something, I'll come and get you. It'd be easier if you were already here."

Since he had a point and I was tired, I gave in. He'd slept with me to get Grandmother's papers. Now he had them, so I doubted he'd be crawling between the sheets with me any time soon.

I don't know why that bothered me. I should be glad I wouldn't have to keep fending him off. I should be happy it had ended before someone—me—got really hurt. I should remember that he had a wife. Somewhere. But all I wanted was to take him by the hand and lead him to his own bed.

And because I wanted that, I turned and left.

⊙⊙

"Grace!" Someone shook me.

I'd fallen asleep easily, deeply, the scent of Ian's sheets, of him, more soothing than it should have been.

My eyes snapped open. Papers rustled; a switch clicked. As shards of light pierced my brain, I moaned, then flipped the covers over my head.

Ian tugged them right back down. "I found something."

That woke me quicker than a cold shower and a hot cup of coffee. "What?"

He scooted next to me on the bed as he laid the papers on my lap and pointed. In the jumble of words I recognized one.

" 'Kâlanû Ahyeli'-skĭ,' " I said. "Raven Mocker."

"Yes. The word actually means 'killer witch.'" He shrugged, and his shoulder rubbed against mine. "Same difference."

I'd removed my uniform and stolen a T-shirt from his drawer to sleep in. Beneath the sheet my bare legs tingled with goose bumps. I gritted my teeth and willed them to go away.

"So my great-grandmother's papers did contain the legend."

"Better than that," he said. "She included a way to banish it."

The goose bumps, which had at last been fading, came back. "How?"

He leaned closer, and his feather brushed my cheek. Was he trying to drive me crazy? "Here." His long finger tapped the papers that lay at the juncture of my thighs. The vibration started goose bumps somewhere else. "If a sorcerer of great power sees the Raven Mocker in its raven form, the witch will die."

I shifted on the bed. My hip bumped his. We both froze. I picked up the papers and handed them back without meeting his eyes. "How are you going to accomplish that when the thing's invisible?"

"Your great-grandmother included a revealing spell."

"Nice of her."

"I thought so." He stood, and I was able to breathe again. "Get dressed."

My gaze flew to his. Was he kicking me out?

He smiled gently. "I know you're tired, but I'd like you to go with me. I'll put together what I need for this spell, and then we'll destroy a Raven Mocker."

"How will we find it?"

"The witch feeds on the lives of the dying, and I've

got a patient who's doing just that. If we sit with him we should be able to end this. If not tonight, then tomorrow night, or the night after."

"Why would it choose your patient over anyone else?"

"In a town of this size, there aren't a lot of people who fit the profile, especially when the Raven Mocker's already sucked the life out of so many."

"Eventually it'll run out of the ill and the elderly," I murmured.

"Then it'll move on."

I imagined a trail of towns with dozens of fresh graves. And what happened when the Raven Mocker reached a big town like Atlanta? The carnage would be mind-boggling.

"We need to kill it before that happens." I threw the covers off, forgetting I wore only a T-shirt that ended at mid-thigh and a pair of white nylon panties.

When Ian didn't answer, I glanced over my shoulder and found his gaze on my legs. The goose bumps sprang up again, making me shiver. I shoved my feet into my uniform trousers and covered myself, turning so that I couldn't see the heat in his eyes that called to the chill in my soul.

When I faced him again, he was gone. My phone beeped with a message, so I checked it while Ian rustled around first in his office upstairs and then in the clinic downstairs.

"You have one new voice message."

"I locked up the house," Cal said. "The fire investigator should be there at eight A.M. Sam will get you a report as soon as he has one. Don't bother to come in tomorrow if you aren't up to it. I can take care of things. Oh, and we found the man who hit you."

I blinked. The accident now seemed so long ago, I'd nearly forgotten all about it.

"Guy in Bradleyville. Was probably drunk and that's why he ran, but we'll never prove it now. Sheriff over there said the guy's always been a model citizen, so he gave him a ticket and a stern talking-to. You can call him if you want."

I turned off my phone and tucked it into my pocket. I had bigger problems right now than some guy from Bradleyville.

"Ready?" I jumped as Ian spoke from the hall. I hadn't even heard him come back upstairs.

"Are you sure it's okay if I come along? I can't see how a dying man would want an audience."

"Better an audience than the Raven Mocker."

Though I still felt uncomfortable, I followed him through the clinic and out the front door.

"Who's your patient?" I asked.

"Jack Malone. You know him?"

"Of course." I'd arrested Jack a dozen times since I'd become sheriff. He had a little drinking problem.

"Advanced cirrhosis," Ian murmured.

I wasn't surprised. "How did you get his case so quickly?"

His gaze slid to mine, then away.

"No one else wanted him," I guessed. Jack was a mean drunk. "He doesn't really like me."

"I don't think he likes anyone, but that won't matter. He's close to the end. I doubt he'll even know we're there."

Jack's sister—the only one who could stand him, and I'd never figured out why unless he'd been a much better boy than he was a man; it wouldn't have been hard—let us in, nodded when Ian asked if we could sit with him, and disappeared.

I followed Ian into the room, and he sprinkled whatever he'd brought along in a brown paper sack in a circle around the bed, chanting in Cherokee; then he set a buzzard feather on Jack's pillow and we sat in two folding chairs near the door.

"If the Raven Mocker goes near the bed, the spell should make it visible, and then—" He spread his hands.

We both stared at Jack. He appeared more peaceful now than I'd ever seen him before.

"Don't the buzzard feathers have to be at the entrance of a home to work?"

"Just being near one should do it."

I glanced at my watch. Four A.M. We didn't have long until dawn. I had my doubts the Raven Mocker would show up here tonight, but one could always hope.

Since we couldn't really talk or risk waking Jack—that was something neither one of us wanted—time passed slowly. The room was warm. I was tired. My head would dip toward my chest; then I'd jerk awake and stare bleary-eyed at Malone, who hadn't moved but still breathed.

Ian took my hand. "You can sleep."

I shook my head. I didn't want to be awakened by that unearthly shrieking. I'd have a heart attack myself.

Ian's fingers clenched on mine so tightly my bones crunched. I glanced at him and froze. He stared upward as if he'd heard something; then his gaze lowered. I couldn't look away as he jibber-jabbered words in Cherokee I didn't understand.

"Repeat that," he ordered.

I did, mangling it so badly he said it again, his voice, his face, urgent. This time I got it right.

"What was that?" I asked.

"A charm of protection." His head tilted. "Something's coming."

The air felt close, as if a storm approached. In the distance, I could have sworn I heard the call of a great black bird. My gaze switched to Jack, but he slept on undisturbed and I was glad. As much as I disliked him, I didn't want him to die afraid.

Thunder rumbled from a clear sky. Both Ian and I came to our feet. He whispered in Cherokee, blinked once, and his eyes went eagle. His gaze swept the room.

"Nothing," he muttered, and the shrieking began.

I slapped my hands over my ears. Ian flinched, the movement alien and birdlike. Through a slice in the curtain, lightning flashed. He crossed the room and threw back the drapes. Sparks flickered. Slowly I lowered my hands and watched the sparks fall.

28

THE SHRIEKING STOPPED; the sparks faded away, but we could see the house over which they'd tumbled. The roof still glittered as if the sky had rained diamonds, but not a flicker of flame rose toward the star-studded sky.

"Fitzhughs," I said. "Ben and Nora. Young couple in their twenties. No children. Run the ice-cream shop on Center." As far as I knew, neither one of them was sick, let alone dying.

Ian dropped my hand and ran. I was right behind him.

Two blocks down and on the other side of the street, Ian went to the front door and turned the knob.

"Hey!" I put my hand on his shoulder. "You can't—"

He shook me off and went in anyway. Years of training and a cop for a dad made me hesitate. But when I heard the crying and the shouting, I followed. With those kinds of noises, I could easily claim probable cause.

I found Ian tossing his herbs around the room again. Nora was crying and pointing at both him and what appeared to be her dead husband. I already knew, even before I saw his fear-frozen face, what had happened.

"What-what-what's wrong with his eyes?" she sobbed.

I looked at Ben, whose eyes were a little bugged out. But Nora shouted, "Him!" and jabbed a shaking finger at Ian.

He still had eagle eyes. Hell. How was I going to explain that?

I put myself between them and murmured, "Ian. Your eyes."

"I don't see anything," he said. "I think it's gone."

"Put them back before she strokes out."

"Huh?" He glanced at me, and I gave an exaggerated blink. "Oh." He did as I asked.

When I turned to Nora, she sat on the bed. "Ben?" She patted his face, his hand, his chest. "It's okay. Wake up."

I doubted she'd remember any of this in a few hours. I knew shock when I saw it.

I yanked a handmade afghan off the recliner in the corner and draped it around her shoulders. "Nora?"

She didn't answer. I opened my mouth to say her name louder, and Ian murmured, "Shhh."

The tiny shushing sound fell into a silence broken only by Nora's murmurs and pats. Ian stared upward, tense, alert.

Slowly I stood, feeling it, too, something hovering above us, peering back and forth, picking, choosing, who would die and who would not.

"Say the charm, Grace."

Ian didn't even glance my way, but his voice was so

sharp and intense, I began to recite the words as if my great-grandmother herself had ordered me.

Whatever was here with us drew a breath. Shock? Fear? I paused, listening, and something bitch-slapped me across the room.

I flew off my feet; my shoulders hit the wall. My head snapped back. I heard the sick crack, a thud as I fell, then nothing.

∞

G race?"
     I opened my eyes. I couldn't remember where I was. From the pain in my head, I was half-afraid I'd landed in the hospital, but then my senses came back one by one.

The soft sound of Nora weeping.

The hardwood floor beneath me.

The scent of Ian, the heat and strength of his hand in mine. His expression so worried, I got worried, too.

"Am I bleeding?"

His smile was strained. "No. Though not for lack of trying. What happened?"

"Your charm *sucked*!"

"Did you say it right?"

"Exactly the way you did."

"It's always worked for me."

"Saying the words without understanding them is worthless." I put my hand to the back of my head, wincing at the bump. "I guess Grandmother was right again." If we'd had more time, I might have remembered that.

Suddenly Ian leaned over and kissed me. I was so startled, I let him.

"This was my fault," he said.

"You didn't throw me across the room."

"I brought you into this situation; you weren't prepared. You could have died. Or worse."

"Worse?"

He looked away, his face haunted. There was more to this, which I'd get to the bottom of later.

I sat up, gritting my teeth against the pain. I had things to do and no time for a headache. Ian reached for me, hands gentle, and I shoved them away. "I'm fine."

I was able to get to my feet under my own power. Nora still sat on the bed with Ben, whispering to him as if he'd wake up sooner or later.

"I should probably call Doc," I muttered.

"I'm a doctor."

"He's the medical examiner. He can deal with Ben; you can deal with Nora. She's going to need sedation, but not before I talk to her."

"You might not get anything useful."

Maybe not, but I had to try. I inched closer and put my hand on her shoulder. "Nora?"

I half-expected her to keep whispering, lost in another world where Ben still answered, but instead she said, "Hey, Grace."

We'd gone to high school together, though she'd been a few years younger than me. However, in a town like this, everyone knew everyone else and most of their business, which made me wonder why I hadn't known her husband was sick.

"What was wrong with Ben?" I asked.

"Wrong?" Nora's forehead wrinkled. "I think he's dead."

"I meant when did he get sick? What did he have?"

"Ben's never been sick a day in his life. Hardly even a cold. He made me so mad."

I glanced at Ian, who shrugged. "You're sure he didn't see a doctor lately?"

"He hated doctors. No offense," she threw in Ian's direction.

"I'm not wild about most of them myself," he said, and Nora's lips curved just a little.

"Can you tell us what happened tonight?" I pressed.

Nora's smile faded, but she nodded. "I got up to get some water, and there was this awful noise. I ran back to bed, and he was gasping, clutching his throat." Her voice broke; she buried her face in her hands.

"Okay." I patted her, as clumsy with it as Cal had been, then moved to where Ian stood by the door.

"I've got a bad feeling," he said.

"I've had one for days. What's going on?"

"I can't be sure until we've got an autopsy report, but I think the Raven Mocker's figured out how to steal the lives of the living."

I got a sudden chill, even though the room was July-in-Georgia warm. "But that's not what the legend says."

Ian's eyes met mine. "Legends are made to be broken."

⦾

"Merry was as heartless as the rest of them," Doc said in lieu of "hello." He complained about caller ID, but he had it, too.

"I've got another one."

Doc sighed, sounding as exhausted as I felt. "Who is it this time?"

I'd moved out of the bedroom and into the hall, not wanting Nora to hear me call the medical examiner and order an autopsy. Ian had run back to the clinic to get his bag so he could sedate her if she didn't stop whispering to the dead. Before I'd called Doc, I'd called Nora's mother, who was on the way.

"Ben Fitzhugh," I answered.

"What the hell? He's maybe twenty-five."

"He doesn't fit the profile," I said, "but then, neither did Merry. At least when she died." An idea flickered. "I wonder if the Raven Mocker didn't know that until it was too late?"

"The what?"

Whoops. Doc was still under the impression we were dealing with aliens. I hated to burst his bubble, but quickly I filled him in.

"You think that makes more sense than alien invasion and pods in the basement?" he asked.

"You're kidding, right?"

"Not really," he muttered.

"All the evidence points to the killer being a Raven Mocker. The loud shrieking, the lack of a heart in the victims, lack of a scar from the removal, and the storm on the night of the Thunder Moon."

"Except the Raven Mocker steals the lives of the dying. So what about Merry and Ben? If Ben's actually a victim and not just a fluke. We won't know for sure until I crack his chest."

Sometimes Doc was too blunt even for me.

"Legends are made to be broken," I murmured.

"True. When dealing with the *super*natural, it's good to remember that anything can happen. You have a theory?"

"Yeah," I said slowly. "What if the Raven Mocker

didn't know Merry was in remission, killed her anyway and discovered it could, so it moved on to a completely healthy victim with Ben? In killing a person who has years left, the witch would gain so much more time than it's ever gained before."

"If that's the case, no one's safe."

I didn't bother to curse, even though I wanted to.

"I'll be there in ten," Doc said.

"Thanks." I hung up. Ian stood just inside the front door. "You heard?"

He nodded. "We'd better figure out how to identify this witch before the thing eats every heart in town."

"Works for me," I said. "Got any ideas?"

"Actually, I do."

29

IAN'S IDEA FOR identifying our culprit involved visiting every elderly man and woman in Lake Bluff and surrounding areas and gifting them with a buzzard feather.

According to him, the Raven Mocker should appear as a withered senior citizen—cronelike with the weight of the days it had stolen. Such an appearance for a witch seemed too cliché, but then, clichés became clichés for a reason.

Before we'd left on our odyssey, we'd stopped in town, where I'd bought enough underwear, jeans, and shirts to last me a week. Ian had bought postcards to run through his computer.

While I'd taken a shower and changed, he'd made up fairly professional-looking flyers for his new clinic, then attached a buzzard feather to each of them.

People didn't seem to think that was any odder than the sheriff, wearing jeans and a plain white T-shirt, escorting the new doctor, also in jeans and a black T-shirt, but wearing cowboy boots instead of sneakers, from door to door. No one had burst into flames or cried, "I'm melting!" Not one person had hesitated to take the buzzard feather at all.

"How many buzzards are now bald?" I asked.

Ian shrugged. "Buzzards are kind of bald anyway."

"Are you sure these things repel a witch? What's supposed to happen?"

"Extreme aversion to the feather."

"Cringe, cry, run away?"

"Maybe all three."

I narrowed my eyes. "How many witches have you dealt with?"

"Enough."

"Any Raven Mockers?"

"Not personally, no."

"Swell." Was it too much to ask that he'd be an expert in this field? Apparently.

We continued to visit the elderly. We continued to have no luck. We never ran out of feathers, though. I swear the basket was like the proverbial fish and bread for the masses; the more elderly there were, the more feathers we had.

I'd checked in and told Cal I was taking a personal day, which he assumed was because of the fire, and I let him. Once Claire got to work and heard about the incident, she called and made me promise to come to dinner.

Since I needed to update her on the latest in paranormal occurrences, I accepted. When she found out I was spending the day with Ian, she invited him, too. I felt weird about that, like it was a date, but the least I could do was provide him with dinner.

Later, Sam called. The investigator had ruled the fire

accidental. Even though the night had been clear, enough people had heard thunder and seen what they swore was lightning to blame just that for my torched roof. I knew better, but what could I say? A shape-shifting witch had thrown sparks out her ass onto my shingles? I'd get the insurance money regardless, so I kept my mouth shut.

We finished my list of old folks without having one person behave oddly. However, there were at least half a dozen on the list who hadn't been home, including Quatie, which disturbed me more than I liked. Where could she be? It wasn't as though she belonged to the local book club or women's society. She didn't even drive.

Ian must have sensed my unease. "We'll make Quatie's place our first stop tomorrow," he said.

Just as we had at every house where we hadn't been able to hand one to the resident directly, I tacked the buzzard feather to the front porch. If it didn't reveal the Raven Mocker, the feather could then protect the holder *from* the Raven Mocker. Ian's test became a charm.

We rang the doorbell at the Cartwrights' at 6:00 P.M. Ian had insisted on stopping at Goldman's Save U and buying a bottle of wine and some flowers for Claire. I brought the bright orange pacifier in the shape of a bas-ketball that I'd been unable to resist buying for Noah. Malachi would just have to be content with the plea-sure of our company.

The door flew open. Claire didn't even say hello be-fore she hugged me so hard I coughed.

"Hey. What's wrong with you?" She had me wor-ried. "Where's Noah? Mal!"

Malachi appeared in the hall with the baby, saw Claire mauling me, and shook his head. "Ye scared her half t' death, Grace." His Irish accent was more pronounced than I'd heard it in a long, long time.

"What'd I do?"

"She finds out your house was on fire and you didn't call, you didn't come to us?"

I leaned back, met Claire's eyes. "Sorry. I—"

Her gaze went to Ian and she smiled. "Dr. Walker, come in. Are these for me? Thank you."

Suddenly all mayoral, she turned and headed for the kitchen. Now that she'd hugged me and made sure I was in one piece, she was going to make me pay. I suppose I deserved it.

I should have called. I'd have been pissed if the situation were reversed. Hell, I'd given her a seriously hard time for taking off to Atlanta and leaving me behind, even though the only way she could have gotten me out of Lake Bluff would have been to shanghai me. We were best friends, and we were supposed to share everything, depend on each other. Just because she was married and I—

I glanced at Ian. Well, I wasn't. That didn't mean I shouldn't follow the best-friend rules. They were women law. Break them at your own risk.

I took Noah and offered him the new pacifier, which he promptly started drooling on as he laid his cheek against my chest.

Something bumped against my ankles, and I glanced down to see Oprah rubbing her head on me just like she used to. I went down on one knee and scratched behind her ears. She began to purr.

One of Noah's wildly waving hands smacked Oprah's tail. Before I could stop him, his fingers latched on and yanked. Instead of hissing, Oprah went still and let him tug. Definitely true love.

I pried Noah's fingers loose. They came away covered in cat hairs, which I began to pick off one by one.

"Come along and have a drink on the deck." Mal led the way through the kitchen.

Claire had opened the wine and put the flowers in water. She was messing with something on the stove that didn't appear to need messing with, but what did I know about cooking?

"Need help?" I asked. She snorted. "Guess not."

"Ah chroí," Mal murmured, and her shoulders raised and lowered on a sigh.

"I actually could use a hand bringing the drinks out. Does anyone want anything other than wine?"

We declined, so she began to pull out wineglasses. I turned to hand Noah to Mal, but he'd already stepped outside.

"Here." Ian held out his hands. I hesitated, and he tilted his head. "I'm a doctor, Grace. I've held quite a few babies. Haven't dropped one yet."

"Of course not." I handed Noah over, and he curled up on Ian's chest with as much trust as he'd cuddled against mine.

The men disappeared outside. Claire poured four glasses of wine, then handed me one and took a sip of her own.

"I screwed up," I said.

"Big-time. Don't let it happen again."

"Yes, Madame Mayor."

Her blue eyes narrowed. "I thought we were making up."

"We are. But sometimes I just can't shut my mouth."

"Most times," she muttered. "Now tell me what's going on around here, but first take the boys their drinks."

She handed me a bottle for Noah, which I tucked in

a pocket, then picked up the other two glasses of wine. Mal and Ian faced the trees that lined the property, watching the sun fall and chatting about—

"NASCAR?" I said incredulously.

Mal shrugged. "I like fast cars."

"And you?" I asked Ian.

"What's not to like?"

Noah spit his basketball pacifier directly into Ian's face. Ian caught the thing before it fell to the ground and laid it on the table. He really did seem to have a knack for kids.

I set the bottle between the two men, figuring Ian would turn Noah over to his dad for the feeding. But they continued to talk about drivers I'd never heard of. I couldn't stand car racing, probably because all of my brothers had watched it incessantly. Around and around and around. Crash, bang, explosion. Snore.

I reached the sliding glass doors that separated the deck from the kitchen and glanced back just in time to see Ian shift Noah into the crook of his arm and pop the bottle into his mouth as if he'd done the same thing a hundred times before.

My chest tightened; my eyes went hot, and I had to turn away before I embarrassed myself. The sight made me want him in ways that didn't involve being naked in the night. Ways that were far more dangerous.

I practically dived inside and nearly smacked into Claire, who was watching him, too. Her gaze met mine. "He could be a keeper."

"Too bad someone else is already keeping him."

"He's married?"

"That's the word on the street."

Claire looked at him again. "He doesn't seem married."

"How does someone seem married?"

"They just do." She handed me my wine, which she'd topped off to the brim in contrast to every Southern Belle Rule of Etiquette.

Claire and I had always done our best to break all those rules as often as we could. I took a swig instead of a dainty sip; she did the same and we clinked glasses, then leaned against the counter, as I filled her in on everything that had happened.

"Raven Mocker," she murmured. "That's a new one."

"So was werewolf, but we handled it."

She lifted her glass in a salute. "And now the thing's moved on to the young, the strong, the healthy."

"Yeah." I took another swig of wine.

Doc had tagged me by noon with the news I had dreaded. No heart in the chest of Ben Fitzhugh, either.

"Maybe we should call Elise again." Claire glanced toward the deck where the men continued to lounge. "At least see what she knows about this other secret society."

Since I did want to give the woman a piece of my mind, I dialed the number.

"What can you tell me about the Nighthawk Keetoowahs?" I asked as soon as she picked up. I could ignore "hello" as easily as she did.

"He told you," Elise murmured. "Interesting."

"You said you knew nothing about him."

"I said he wasn't in my database of paranormal baddies."

I wondered if she knew about his tendency to go eagle eyed, literally, then decided I wasn't going to be the one to tell her. Two could play at the secret game.

"I called you for help and you didn't give me any."

"Listen, Sheriff, there are quite a few ancient groups that were fighting evil long before the *Jäger-Suchers* showed up. We work with them sometimes, but against them never, which means I don't give away their identity to anyone who calls and asks."

"I'm not just anyone."

"The secret was his to share, which he did, so what are you whining about?"

God, she was annoying.

"We've discovered we have a Raven Mocker in Lake Bluff."

"I haven't heard that one before."

"Ian seemed familiar with it."

"Then you're lucky he's there."

"We could use a little help of the *J-S* variety."

"Can't do it. We've got . . ." She paused. "Issues."

"What kind of issues?"

"Creepy things are crawling all over the place. Like I told you before, I can't spare anyone, especially when you seem to have things under control."

"People are dying here!"

"People are dying everywhere, Sheriff, and at a lot higher rate than usual. I have confidence you and your people will prevail just as you did the last time you were visited by supernatural creatures."

In the background I heard phones ringing, people shouting, buzzers buzzing. Sounded as if all hell were breaking loose.

Elise hung up, or maybe the line went dead. I couldn't tell. I glanced at Claire, lifted a brow.

"I got the gist," she said. "They aren't coming."

I shrugged. "She annoys me anyway."

"What is it with you two?"

"Ian thinks her wolf smells my panther and the other way around."

Claire's eyes sharpened. "You been turning furry and not telling me about it?"

"No. But according to legend, my clan descended from panthers."

"Which kind of explains your collection obsession," she said. "You believe that?"

"I'm not sure. Stranger things have happened."

Claire tilted her head with an expression that said, *Got me there,* then finished her wine without further comment.

We ate dinner outside—grilled fish, garlic potatoes, steamed broccoli, and a lot more wine.

Noah sat in his swing and watched us, wide eyes on Ian all the time. I think he had a crush. Which just made two of us.

As darkness fell, we said good night. Though Claire had insisted I stay with them, I'd refused. I was going to get that hotel room tonight.

Really.

Ian and I could have walked from Claire's to his place and then I could have gone on to a hotel. Except I had my truck, and it was full of packages, and I'd need it in the morning, so I drove down the hill, slowing as we neared the clinic.

Someone stood outside. "Hell." Ian lay down, putting his head in my lap. "Keep driving."

Katrine leaned against the brick wall. The street-light spilled down, revealing her usual tight, low-cut blouse and short skirt. Her hair had been curled and teased into the trademark trailer trash big hair, and she wore a shade of lipstick that must be labeled Ruby Red Botox.

"Go to the hotel," Ian whispered, as if she could hear

him. "I'll help you check in and then walk back. Hopefully she'll be gone by then."

His breath puffed against my knee, warm and moist. I shifted in the seat as other places grew warm and moist. I wished I could forget the times he'd touched me, but I wasn't sure I ever would.

"She's been hitting on you?"

"A little."

Knowing Katrine, a little was more like a lot.

"You tell her you were married?"

"Yep."

"She didn't care?"

"Nope."

"I think you can sit up now."

I'd turned at the end of Center and wheeled onto the next block toward a decent bed-and-breakfast run by the Fosters, a retired couple from Ohio. They'd come to Lake Bluff for the Full Moon Festival five years ago and loved it so much, they'd snapped up the eighteenth-century hotel as soon as it had gone on the market. They were now as much a part of Lake Bluff as I was.

"That woman scares me." Ian lifted his head, tentatively checking the dark streets around us. "She's got more replacement parts than a Fiat."

"A Fiat?"

His smile was quick and sheepish. "I had one in college. You know what it stands for?" I shook my head. "Fix It Again Tomorrow."

I laughed.

"Wasn't funny then," he muttered, and got out of the car.

He grabbed my shopping bags and started up the walk, pausing at the porch and reaching into his pocket.

As I joined him, he handed me a bag and used his free hand to tack a feather on the underside of the handrail.

Jordan sat behind the desk. "What are you doing here?" we both said at the same time.

I glanced at Ian, and my cheeks heated, which was silly. Not only was Jordan twenty years old, but I was certain most of the town had figured out there was something going on between Ian and me.

"He's helping me with my things," I blurted.

Jordan just grinned.

"My house is trashed. I need a room. What are you doing here?" I repeated.

"Mrs. Foster hurt her back. Mr. Foster needs to sleep since he worked all day. I'm filling in."

Jordan filled in a lot around town. Everyone knew she needed every penny for Duke.

"Didn't you work the switchboard today?" I asked.

"Yeah. But I'm a night owl. I don't sleep much."

I recalled Cal saying she'd been a difficult child, only sleeping a few hours each night and then being up the rest of the twenty-four. She'd driven her mom nuts, and more often than not, Cal had been off in a war zone unable to help. Which kind of explained how Jordan had wound up an only child.

I handed her my credit card; she handed me a key, then offered her hand to Ian. "Jordan Striker."

"Sorry," I said. "I should have done that."

The two ignored me, shaking hands and making nice. When Ian snatched the key from me and turned toward the stairs, Jordan wiggled her eyebrows and made kissy noises in my direction.

What had I said about her being mature beyond her years? I took it back.

"He's just going to take up my bags," I said. Ian was already tramping up the steps.

"I don't care, Grace. This isn't an all-girl dorm in the 1950s."

She returned her attention to the notebook she'd been scribbling in when we arrived. I glanced at it and stilled.

Because my brothers had always tried to hide things from me, I'd become very good at ferreting out secrets. I'd learned how to read upside down at almost the same time I'd learned to read.

What I read this time was: *Hand sanitizers claim they can kill 99.9 percent of germs. Chuck Norris can kill 100 percent of whatever the fuck he wants.*

"You're the Chuck Norris bandit?"

Her eyes widened and she slapped the cover shut, but it was too late. I'd already read another: *Chuck Norris's calendar goes from March 31 directly to April 2. No one fools Chuck Norris.*

I bit my lip to keep from snickering. "Why do you want to make your dad crazy?"

"I don't. I write these jokes for a Web site. They pay me. Not a lot, but—" She shrugged. "The best jokes are always the ones that make him turn purple."

"You're a bad girl," I said, but I smiled.

"You aren't going to tell him, are you?"

"No, but he'll catch you sooner or later, and then you're on your own. How did you bypass the security cameras?"

"It wasn't hard. Your security is lame. Have you even updated it since your dad was king?"

"No."

"Of course, who'd want to break *in* to a cop shop?"

"Besides you?"

"I didn't break in."

"What *did* you do?"

I knew Jordan was smart. She'd have to be to have any prayer of going to Duke. But bypassing a security system—even a lame one? I wasn't going to tell her so, but I was impressed.

"A little computer mumbo-jumbo," she said. "A screwdriver here, a wrench there, and—" Jordan flipped her hands in a voilà gesture. "Just call me the Invisible Woman."

30

I HALF-EXPECTED TO meet Ian coming downstairs as I went up. How hard was it to drop shopping bags on the bed?

Apparently pretty hard. The door to my room was open and Ian stood at the window, staring at the night, the bags still in his hands.

"You okay?" I asked.

"There's something I have to tell you."

From the tone of his voice, this might take a while, so I stepped inside and shut the door.

The room was clean and quaint, with a carved wooden headboard and a homemade quilt for the queen-sized bed. An overstuffed flower-print love seat hugged one wall, and a thoroughly modern bathroom lay behind a recently refinished door. There was even a desk with a lamp, chair, and Internet connection.

I took the bags and set them on the floor, but Ian continued to stare out the window so intently he started to worry me. I laid my hand on his shoulder, tracing the material that covered his tattoo with one finger.

"When did you get this?" Maybe if he started talking about that, he'd segue into whatever it was he was having such a hard time telling me.

"All the Nighthawks have them."

"You said it was to remind you to be a warrior always."

"It is. The Nighthawks must be ready to fight against evil spirits at any time. The eagle is the bird of war. He gives us strength, sight, and power."

"Does every Nighthawk do the same thing with their eyes?"

"We can all do something."

"Like?"

He turned, and my hand was left hovering in the air where his shoulder had been. His fingers closed around my wrist, and he placed a kiss at the center of my palm. For just a minute I closed my eyes and let myself feel.

His mouth touched my nose, my cheekbones, my jaw. I bit my lip and tried to be strong, but I wasn't. When he kissed me, I kissed him back.

My palms framed his face, tilted his head so I could explore his mouth. Warm and hot, he tasted of wine and desire, or was that me?

I traced his shoulders, let my thumb rub beneath the sleeves of his T-shirt, learning the contours of his biceps and the smooth trail where his forearm became his elbow. I wanted to put my mouth there, lick his skin, feel his pulse beat against my tongue. Instead, I lifted my head, my hands, and stepped back.

"I can't, Ian. You're married."

"I'm not, Grace. I swear."

Into the silence fell the sound of sudden raindrops—*tink, tink, tink*—against the glass.

"Are you saying that was a lie? You never had a wife?"

"No." He shoved a hand through his hair. "I had a wife."

"And she disappeared?"

"Yes."

"So until you find her and get a divorce or—" I stopped, not wanting to put into words the other scenario, but he had no such problem.

"Until I have a body. Except I do, or I did. Or I would, if there was a body left to have."

"You'd better just tell me what in hell you mean."

"She was one of them."

"Them who?"

"The ones we fight."

"You married an evil spirit?"

"She wasn't evil when I married her; that came later."

"Is this a supernatural variation of 'my wife is an emasculating fiend'?"

His lips twitched, but his expression remained sad. "I loved her, Grace. She was a soft-spoken, sweet woman who lived just for me." I put my hand on his arm, but he pulled away. "It was because of me that she died. Because of what I do. I didn't protect her. They came, they took her, and they . . . infected her."

"Who's they?"

"The Anada' duntaski. The cannibals."

"Cannibals came and took your wife? And they infected her with what? Cannibalitis? You aren't making any sense."

" 'Anada' duntaski' translates to 'cannibals,' but what

they are is—" He broke off and bit his lip as if he suddenly didn't want to tell me.

"You've gone this far," I said. "You think after what I've seen in this town I'm not going to believe you?"

He let his lip go, and a tiny spot of blood bloomed where his teeth had torn the skin. My chest hurt at the pain I saw on his face. He reached for my hand, and I met his halfway.

"What are the Anada' duntaski?"

His eyes met mine. "Vampires."

I opened my mouth, shut it again. Looked away and then looked back. "Cherokee vampires?"

"Every culture has their own version of the vampire and the werewolf myth."

"There's a Cherokee werewolf?"

"In a way. When I was a boy, the old men told me of the war medicine. The ability of certain warriors to change their shape, becoming any animal they wished to triumph over their enemies. Many chose a wolf because he was brave and loyal and fierce."

I nodded. I'd heard about that, too. "And the vampire?"

He glanced down, though he continued to hold my hand. "The Anada' duntaski were called the roasters because they supposedly cooked the flesh of their enemies and ate it."

"Which makes them cannibal and not vampire." Not that either one was all that appealing.

"They began as men who did just that—killed their enemy and ate him. They were the most feared of warriors, even before they discovered that drinking the blood of the living made them live, too. Forever."

Okay, *that* was a vampire.

"The Anada' duntaski are day walkers," he continued.

"The sun doesn't hurt them. They live like any other man, except they must hunt the night. They drink the blood of the innocent, and they multiply."

"How do you kill them?"

"Cut off their heads."

He said it so calmly I got a chill. "You'd better be sure you've got the right man before you try that."

Ian's smile was completely without humor. When he smiled like that he no longer seemed like a healer, but a Nighthawk Keetoowah, scourge of supernatural creatures everywhere.

"What happened?" I asked.

"It was the first time I'd gone after an Anada' duntaski. I was young, foolish, flush with my own power, the secrets I knew that no one else did. I thought I was invincible. I found them; I killed them. But one of them got away, and he made my wife like him."

Which explained why Ian insisted he was no longer married. Undead was as good as a divorce.

"She became a spy," he continued. "Because of her, because of me, we lost a dozen Nighthawks in the next six months."

"That must have been horrible."

His haunted gaze met mine. " 'Horrible' doesn't begin to describe it."

"Do you want to describe it? Would you feel better if you talked about it?"

"I try to forget, as much as I can; otherwise I couldn't go on; I couldn't do my job. And even though I screwed up and people died, the only way to atone for that is to keep destroying the evil ones."

"It wouldn't help anyone for you to quit."

"I won't, but I want you to back off and let me handle this."

I gave one short, sharp bark of laughter. "Yeah, right. You bet."

"I'm serious, Grace. Look what happened last night."

"Another person died. That's as much my fault as yours."

"No." He grabbed me by the elbows and shook me a little. "You could have been killed. That thing threw you against the wall."

"If you think that would kill me, you obviously have a misguided view of me. My brothers did worse than that every day of the week."

His eyes flickered, topaz, then brown, war bird, then furious man. "I want to meet your brothers."

His face, his tone, his eyes—he wanted to do more than meet them; he wanted to beat the crap out of them. I should have been insulted; I wasn't a damsel in distress. Instead I was touched, and that was a more dangerous feeling than just wanting him.

Ian loved his wife; he still wasn't over her. She'd been gentle and sweet and soft-spoken—three more things I could never be.

"I survived," I said. "Being the only girl in a household of men made me stronger. Stronger than you seem to think I am. I'm the sheriff here, Ian. I can't just sit back and do my nails while you save the world. Not even my little corner."

"I can't protect you, Grace," he whispered. "Just like I couldn't protect her."

He moved past me, headed for the door, and I reached out, caught his hand, clung. "I'm not her, Ian. I don't need you to protect me. I don't want you to. I can take care of myself."

"Grace—" He tugged on his hand; I wouldn't let go.

"I know what's out there. I won't be surprised by it.

I'm not going to let this witch win. This is my home; I've protected it before, and I'll do it again."

He opened his mouth to argue, and I kissed him, the one way I knew to shut him up, shut him down.

I took charge, needing to show him my strength, convince him that he shouldn't worry. I was at his side in this, not hiding behind him, getting picked off like a weak link when he wasn't paying attention.

I experienced a moment of unease for thinking of his wife like that, but truth was truth. Ian had been wrong to keep her in the dark, so she hadn't known what she was facing and could then not be prepared for it. However, I couldn't help but think she'd been foolish, allowing some bloodsucking fiend to get the better of her.

That was uncharitable, downright mean. But the way he'd said her name, the way he mourned her, the way he described her, like a saint who'd loved him too much, made my stomach jitter with jealousy. I didn't like the feeling.

But I was here with him now, and from the beat of his erection pressing against my stomach, I was the only one who mattered.

I slipped my hands beneath his shirt, traced my palms across his flat abdomen, dipped my fingers below the waistband of his jeans, under the elastic of his boxers until I brushed his tip. He jerked, and I closed my fingers around him, slowly sliding them up and down in a rhythm to match the pace of my tongue past his lips.

He groaned, the sound vibrating through his mouth, his chest, through me, then grabbed my hips and yanked me against him. I rolled my thumb over him once, then slid a fingernail down his length.

Cursing, he pulled away. My hand came out of his pants. We were both breathing heavily, staring at each other in the silver-shrouded night. I inched sideways, blocking the door.

He reached down, pulling the black T-shirt up, up, up, revealing stomach, then ribs, then chest, his biceps flexing and releasing, the muscles in his belly rippling like water. I was suddenly parched.

I led him to the bed and with a slight shove of my palm against his chest, he went down.

I pressed my mouth to the hard ridge just above his navel, then drew my tongue across his abs and scored his ribs with my teeth. He tasted like the ocean—both salt and the sea—I wanted to savor so much more.

He tugged on my clothes. "I need to feel your skin against mine."

I yanked my shirt, then my bra, off and tossed them away before pressing an openmouthed kiss to the curve of his waist, then suckling hard enough to leave a mark.

His long, beautiful, yet slightly rough fingers ran over my shoulders, my back, then loosened my hair. I mouthed him through the denim, using my teeth at the tip of his erection. He grasped me by the elbows and hauled me up his body, latching onto my mouth, then grinding our hips together until I was rubbing against him as if there weren't four layers of clothing in the way.

He tried to unbutton my jeans; I fumbled with his. Both of us were shaking.

"Screw it." I rolled away so that I could deal with my own fastenings. He did the same. It was a race. Whoever finished first got to be on top.

I lost. I didn't mind. Especially when he covered me with his body and filled me so completely with a single thrust I began to come even before he began to move.

I cried out his name, clenching around him, and he buried his face between my breasts, pulling me more tightly against him, slowing down, drawing it out, until I was poised halfway in between, perched on a second edge. My hips moved of their own accord, taking him more deeply, feeling the tingle start harder, stronger, this time as his lips drew my nipple into his mouth once, twice, the rhythm syncopated—hips, lips, hips, lips.

He nipped me, and I exploded, gasping for breath as he spilled himself into me, body and soul.

When the tremors died, I held on with my legs, my arms. "Stay with me," I whispered. "Stay in me." I didn't want to break the connection. Not yet. Maybe not ever.

He did as I asked, and we kissed languidly, touched gently. I tangled my fingers in his hair, stroking my thumb over his feather as I tumbled toward sleep. He slid away, but I felt him close, our legs tangled, the scent of his skin all over mine.

I awoke in that strange hour between night and day, no moon, no sun, when everything is frighteningly still and just a little creepy.

The rain had stopped, though trickles of water continued to trace the window. The air felt close and hot. At first I thought he was gone. That he'd crept out of bed, gotten dressed, and disappeared, and I sprang up with a gasp. Then I saw him.

He sat on the side of the bed, head in his hands, hair spilling over his wrists, covering his face. He was breathing as if he'd run ten miles in the heat. His back shone slick with sweat, and he was shaking.

"Nightmare?" I asked.

He didn't answer.

I put my palm against his tattoo. He jerked as if he hadn't even known I was there.

"Ian? What's wrong?"

His shoulders raised and lowered several times before he spoke. "I see her sometimes when I wake up, hovering, laughing. Not the woman who loved me so much, but the thing that hated me."

"I'm sorry." I didn't know what that was like. To love someone, to have them love me, to lose them so horribly. I'd lost people, sure, Grandmother, Dad, but it was nothing compared to this. I wasn't sure what to say.

"She's dead," he said.

"I know. The Anada' duntaski killed her."

"No." He turned his head, and his eyes met mine. "I did."

31

Y OU CAN'T KEEP blaming yourself. The Anada' duntaski took her life."

"The first time."

I began to understand why his eyes were always haunted, why they probably always would be.

"The instant I realized the truth, I—" His voice broke.

"You don't have to say it."

He'd cut off her head. He'd made sure she hurt no one else, and even though he knew the body that he'd destroyed had not held the woman he'd loved, what he'd done still tormented him.

"When the body dies and the demon comes," he whispered, "does the soul go to Heaven? She didn't want to become what she did, so why do they say the soul of a vampire is damned?"

He was agonizing over something he could never know the truth of. At least not in this life. What was I supposed to say but the only platitude I had?

"You had to do it. They left you no choice."

"That doesn't make the doing of it any easier." He touched my face. "You love the people in this town very much."

I frowned. "So?"

"I'm going to have to kill one of them."

I straightened, and his hand fell away. I glanced out the window. Dawn hadn't even begun to lighten the horizon, but when it did, we'd go back out and keep searching for the Raven Mocker.

"Or I will," I said.

"Can you? Can you look at the Raven Mocker, perhaps see the face of someone you care about, and do what needs to be done?"

"Yes."

"What if it's Claire, Malachi, Cal, Jordan? What if it's me?"

"You?" I blinked at him. "It isn't."

"It could be anyone, Grace. Anyone at all. Once, it was my wife." He touched my knee. "Let me finish this."

"No." I met his eyes, determined. "We'll do it together. The power of two is greater than the power of one."

His head sank between his shoulders. "I don't know if I can bear it, Grace, if you die because of me."

"Why would I die because of you?"

"If I can't figure this out. If I can't find a way to destroy the witch—"

I put my fingers against his lips. "You will. We will. Good versus evil. Us against them. We can do it, Ian. I know we can."

He just shook his head.

"Come here." I lay back and pulled him with me, flipping the covers over us both. "Hold me awhile," I said.

But it was me who held him for what remained of the night.

⦿⦿⦿

I must have dozed, because I came awake with a start when someone knocked on the door. Ian wasn't in bed and for a second I panicked, thinking he'd gone witch-hunting without me. Then I heard water running in the bathroom and relaxed.

I dug my brand-new robe out of a shopping bag and answered the door. Cal stood on the other side, and I got an extreme case of déjà vu.

I nearly asked him how he'd found me, then remembered Jordan.

"Hey, Cal," I greeted. "What's Chuck Norris up to this morning?"

"There's been another death," he said, without sugarcoating it. "Just outside of town. The Browns'."

"But—" I stopped myself before I could blurt that we'd left a protective buzzard feather at the Browns'. Perhaps this death was just a death. I kept hoping.

"Henry or Harriet?" I asked.

"Neither. Their niece was visiting from Chicago."

"Was she sick?"

He shook his head. "She'd come to help them pack and move north to live with their children. According to Harriet, the kid was healthy as a horse and strong as an ox."

Simile city. Sounded like Harriet.

"Then they went to wake her for breakfast this morning and—" He spread his hands. "Dead in her bed."

"Anything strange?"

"Besides a healthy eighteen-year-old woman dying in her sleep?"

"Yeah, besides that."

Cal cut me a glance, but he knew his job. He'd asked questions.

"Strange shrieking in the night, attributed to that weird increase in ravens we've had reported. I think we need to get the DNR in here to blast a few. That noise could scare the life out of a person unfamiliar with mountain living."

"You're saying the Browns' niece got scared to death?" I laughed a little, as if it were a joke, even though I knew damn well it wasn't.

His eyebrows lowered until they nearly met in the middle. "She did look weird, Grace. I pulled the sheet over her face. I couldn't stand to see her."

My hopes that this was an unaided death fizzled. The Raven Mocker was sticking to the new pattern—taking young, healthy people rather than old or ill ones.

"Did you call Doc?"

"I waited until he was on scene before I came here."

I relaxed a little. Doc would know what to do without my having to tell him.

"You could have called me," I said. "You didn't have to track me down."

"This isn't the kind of thing that should be told over the radio or even the phone. What the hell's going on around here, Grace? You've got Doc doing autopsies on citizens who died by natural causes. You're exhuming bodies and doing autopsies on them. We've got people dying for no reason all over the place. Maybe we should call the FBI."

"There isn't a serial killer, Cal. It's—"

"A virus." Ian stood in the bathroom doorway, a towel around his neck, chest bare, pants zipped but unbuttoned.

Cal didn't appreciate the view as much as I did. He scowled first at Ian, then at me. I felt like I'd been caught in the backseat of Daddy's truck with a boy. Not that I ever had been, but I could imagine.

"Is that true?" Cal asked.

"So Doc says." Or would.

"I've had some experience with this." Ian bent and retrieved his shirt from the floor. "Grace called the CDC. Doc's working with them. We need to let the experts do their jobs."

"And in the meantime, people die?"

"I'm afraid so. It's the nature of this beast."

I blinked at the dual meaning to the word but managed to keep my expression concerned when Cal turned to me. "Is it contagious? Is there something in the water? The air?"

"We don't know, Cal."

"Should we evacuate?"

"It's too late for that. If it is contagious, we'd be spreading it across the country."

His face creased in frustration. "How close is Doc to figuring this out?"

"Very close," Ian answered. "Any day now."

God, I hoped so.

"Okay." Cal cracked his big knuckles, something he did when he didn't feel totally in control of things. "What can I do?"

"Keep it quiet," I said. "Don't even tell Jordan. We can't afford a panic."

"Right."

"And if you could continue to handle things at the

office for a few more days, that would free me up to help Doc."

Boy, the more I lied, the easier it got.

"Of course. You can count on me."

I could, which only made me feel like scum for keeping the truth from him. When he left, I sat on the bed with a sigh.

"You couldn't tell him," Ian said, and I glanced up in surprise at how easily he'd read my mind.

The agony he'd revealed during the night was evident in the shadows beneath his eyes, but other than that, he seemed all right—rested, strong, ready to do his job.

Ian smiled. "What you're thinking is all over your face. Your deputy's a good guy, and you wanted to share everything."

"But I can't. He's a good guy who wouldn't understand. Either he'd lock us up for crazy people or his head would spin round and round until it exploded from the stress. I couldn't do that to him."

"You made the right decision. He can take care of the real-world issues, which will leave you free to help me with the out-of-this-world troubles." He paused. "What brought him here? What made him think you need the FBI, which, by the way, would be a waste of a phone call."

"Because?"

"Stuff like this would be routed to the *Jäger-Suchers,* and since you already called them . . ."

"Waste of a phone call. Got it. But don't people become a little suspicious when they call the FBI and get a *Jäger-Sucher*?"

"Not when they get the agent who's also a *Jäger-Sucher.*"

I sighed. "There's an FBI agent who works for Edward?"

"There are agents of Edward all over the place. Saves time."

"Sometimes I think he's as scary as the creatures he's hunting."

"He is," Ian said shortly. "Now, getting back to your deputy—"

"He came to report another death."

"Who?"

"The niece of some residents."

Ian nodded, face intent as he absorbed the information.

"It was at a house we visited." His gaze shot to mine. "One where we'd left a buzzard feather."

"So either the buzzard feather doesn't work against Raven Mockers or it doesn't work against this particular one, which appears to be growing stronger and changing the rules however the hell it wants to."

"I hate it when that happens," I muttered.

Ian coughed. I wasn't sure if he was stifling a laugh, a sob, or maybe both.

"I know of one other method to repel the witch," he continued. "But it's more elaborate. Not as easy to cart around and distribute as a feather." He got down on the ground and pulled his shoes out from under the bed. "I'll need to find some sticks, a sharp knife, pick up my notebook for the spell."

Something tickled in my memory. I tilted my head, waiting for it to tumble free.

"Aren't you going to get dressed?" Ian stood in front of me. "Not that I don't like this robe and what's under it." He untied the sash. "Or rather not under it."

"Shh," I said, and held up my hand.

Ian had the sense to go quiet.

"Sharpened sticks. Set at the corners of a house. Point facing skyward."

"Right." He smiled as if we were sharing a secret. "What we call old tobacco, a sacred blend used only for rituals, smoked just after dusk. Walk around the house, puffing the smoke in every direction, repeating the incantation. When the witch approaches, the stick will shoot into the air and come back down, fatally wounding the creature, be it in human or animal form. How did you know that?"

"I saw it."

His smile faded. "Where?"

"Quatie's."

32

"IF SHE KNEW how to repel a Raven Mocker, then she knows there *is* a Raven Mocker."

Ian held on to the dashboard as I took the winding roads to Quatie's place faster than I should have.

"That doesn't mean she knows who it is," I pointed out.

"No. But we can ask."

And maybe we'd get lucky. Although I had to think that if Quatie knew the identity of the evil, shape-shifting witch, she would have told me.

"This is so weird," I said. "Quatie isn't a medicine woman. She doesn't know any of this stuff."

"Some of *this stuff* is common knowledge."

"Well, I didn't know it."

"Grace, I'm sorry to say so, but you don't know much. What was your great-grandmother teaching you all those years?"

I tightened my lips to keep from being defensive. My great-grandmother had tried and I had refused, for the most part, to listen. So we'd made do with what we were both comfortable with.

"She spent time with me," I said. "Talked to me. Walked with me. Showed me her things. Told me about my mother. I didn't have many women in my life." Except for Claire and Joyce, but as much as I loved them, they weren't different, like me.

"She didn't tell you about your heritage?"

"She spoke of the clans, specifically our clan. She showed me a few spells, taught me how to go to the water. She wanted to teach me the medicine, but I kind of got freaked out."

"Why?"

"She was . . ." I glanced at him, then back at the road. "Well, she did some things I couldn't explain."

"Like what?"

I'd never told anyone about this, because I'd known no one would believe me. There were times I'd convinced myself I'd imagined it, that I'd dreamed of Grandmother performing impossible feats, and as time passed I'd come to believe those feats had actually happened. But this was Ian, the man who could change his eyes to an eagle's and back again. He'd believe me.

"She was an old woman, but she never walked like one. She had this gait that reminded me of—" I glanced at him and lifted a shoulder. "A big cat."

His lips curved as he nodded for me to continue.

"Once when we were out walking in the mountains, she tripped over a stone in the path. Instead of falling and breaking a hip, she did some fancy tuck and roll. She bounced back to her feet like a five-year-old. Wasn't a mark on her."

"Spry."

"Very. Another time she saw some root or herb she

needed. She got so excited she leaped onto a boulder. That rock had to have been seven feet high."

In my mind's eye I saw her flying up, up, up, and landing on top. My brain added *Six Million Dollar Man* sound effects.

I smiled now at the memory, but back then I'd insisted we go home, and I hadn't returned for two weeks. Though I knew E-li-si had wanted to talk about it, I'd pretended nothing ever happened.

"She could walk me into the ground any day of the week," I continued. "One Saturday I showed up early and she wasn't there. I waited on the porch and saw her running up the driveway. I'm not slow, but I never would have caught her. I don't think a U.S. track-and-field star could have caught her."

Ian just nodded solemnly, waiting for me to finish.

"But the most interesting thing of all was when we ran into a bear after dusk one night. Usually bears run the other way, but this one had cubs. They ran right up to us. I didn't think, I put my hand on one, and the mother came bellowing out of the trees. Grandma put herself in front of me and—"

"What?" Ian murmured.

"She snarled." I heard again the sound she'd made—feral and furious. It had stopped that bear cold.

"Like a panther?" he asked.

I'd never heard a panther before that day, but after—I'd gone to the library, the Internet. I'd searched and searched until I found a recording; then I'd known the truth.

"Yes," I said. "She snarled like a panther, and the bear and her cubs ran away."

"What did your great-grandmother say about it?"

"Nothing."

"Nothing? She didn't teach you—?"

"I didn't want to hear about it, and by the time I did, she was gone."

"Grace." He shook his head, disappointed.

"I was a kid. My father constantly told me that he'd put an end to my visiting her if I started to act weird. I needed to see her; I couldn't take that chance, so I pretended nothing magical happened, and she let me."

"She could access her other nature like I can. That's a gift not everyone has."

"I certainly don't." My hands clenched on the steering wheel as I turned into Quatie's long, rutted drive.

And I never would, because I'd been too cowardly to fight for what was important, and now it was gone forever.

"Not necessarily," Ian said. "How do you explain the animosity between Elise and you if there isn't a little canine-versus-feline involved?"

"Maybe we just don't like each other. She is kind of a pain."

"And you're not?"

"Hey!"

"You have to admit your social skills could use some work."

I wasn't going to admit anything, even if he was right.

"E-li-si told me we were connected to the panther in a way no one else could ever be."

"She was right."

"But she died without teaching me what to do."

"There might still be a way, if you're interested."

I bounced into Quatie's yard and turned off the motor. "Would your spell work for me?"

My voice shook. I wasn't sure if I wanted it to or not. The thought of losing control of myself, of becoming something else, even partially, scared me.

"No," he said.

I caught my breath in relief, even as my stomach dipped in disappointment.

"I haven't translated all of Rose's papers yet. But if I were your great-grandmother, I'd have left the secret there. You could choose to use it or not, but if she didn't write it down, it's gone forever."

I wondered momentarily if that secret was the reason she'd come over from the Darkening Land. I hadn't seen the wolf in several days, which made me think whatever message she'd brought had been delivered. I just wished I knew for certain what the message had been.

"I didn't know her," Ian continued, "but I can't imagine she'd want such a huge part of your heritage to disappear."

I couldn't, either, but I put aside that problem as the door to Quatie's cabin opened and someone stepped out.

Not Quatie but a much, much younger woman. The great-great-granddaughter whose existence I'd doubted had arrived.

She was maybe an inch taller than Quatie, thinner, though not thin. Anyone lugging around D cups could not lay claim to that. But her waist was trim, and the legs revealed by her knee-length multi-colored skirt were shaped like a runner's.

The voluptuous curves of her body and the way she held herself, as if she knew how to use them, reminded me sharply of Katrine—most likely because I'd seen her last night outside of Ian's clinic. There really was very little that was similar between the two women beyond a huge rack—and even that wasn't the same, since Katrine's was bought and paid for, and this one appeared to be a gift, or perhaps a curse, from God.

Her hair fell long and straight to the middle of her back, framing a wide, attractive face that spoke of very few white ancestors and a whole lot of Cherokee. The type of face one didn't see often around here anymore.

I got out of the car. "Hello. I'm Grace McDaniel."

The woman shaded her eyes against the bright morning sun. "Grace. Grandmother's spoken of you so often I feel like I know you."

I couldn't say the same for her. I hadn't even known Quatie had children until she'd mentioned this relative.

"Is Quatie here?" I asked.

"No. She went—" The young woman waved a hand toward the trees, then shrugged. "You know how she is."

I did. Even though I'd asked her not to wander, I'd known she wouldn't listen. At least there was someone here now who would go searching for the old woman immediately if she didn't come back.

"I'm Dr. Walker." Ian stepped forward, waiting pointedly for her to introduce herself.

I silently thanked him for that. I hadn't wanted to admit to the girl that Quatie had never mentioned her until this week. I'd had enough instances of that in my childhood, when I'd met acquaintances of my father's who'd been very familiar with the names of his sons but had no inkling he had a daughter at all.

She smiled at Ian the way all women must. "I'm Adsila."

" 'Blossom,' " Ian translated.

"Yes."

She did resemble a blossom, all fresh and new. But

she also looked like Quatie around the eyes and the mouth, which made me warm to her right away.

Adsila came down the steps and crossed the grass, holding out her hand. Ian took it and shook, but when he tried to release her, she held on. He glanced into her eyes, startled.

"I have to thank you for helping my grandmother."

"Not a problem. I enjoyed meeting her." He tugged again; she didn't let go. My eyes narrowed. He couldn't be tugging too hard.

"You must be very good," she murmured, her voice low, almost suggestive. "At everything you do."

I wanted to shout, *Hey, I'm right here!* but she obviously didn't care. I was certain this kind of thing happened to Ian all the time. Combine his face, that body, and a medical degree . . . Well, he was kind of asking for it.

"I do my best."

Her smile was definitely suggestive. "I bet your best is amazing."

Ian coughed, or maybe he choked. My warm, friendly feeling cooled. She might just be grateful because he'd helped Quatie feel better; I know I was. But if Adsila thought she was going to show him her gratitude the way that I'd been showing my gratitude . . .

I cleared my throat. They both glanced in my direction, and Ian succeeded in retrieving his hand. Adsila smiled, shrugged as if to say, *You can't blame a girl for trying,* and stepped back.

"I've been having trouble with my neck," she said. "Maybe you could take a look at it?"

"I—uh. Of course."

"Not now," I blurted.

Adsila laughed, the sound bubbly and sweet. Why

couldn't she cackle like an old hen? "Of course not. I'll walk into town sometime this week and come to your clinic."

"That would be fine."

Ian flicked a finger toward the sticks now positioned at the four corners of the house, reminding me why we'd come.

"Do you know what those are for?" I asked.

"Granny Q. said they were for protection. I'm not sure against what."

Ian and I exchanged a glance.

"Is there something wrong, Sheriff? Something I should be worried about?"

I hesitated, but Ian gave a slight shake of his head. Telling Quatie's great-great-granddaughter about a shape-shifting witch would only convince her we were nuts and make her ignore anything else we might say in the future. Quatie had protected the place in the best way she could, the way we would have if she hadn't done it first. They were safer than anyone in this town at the moment, even us.

"Could you have Quatie call—" I stopped. No phone. "I don't suppose you brought a cell phone?"

"She hates them. I know better."

"Do you mind if we wait?" I asked.

Adsila opened her mouth, but Ian spoke first. "We should get back," he said. "I need to finish translating your great-grandmother's papers."

I really wanted to know what Quatie did about the Raven Mocker, but we had sticks to whittle, people to protect.

"Maybe you could bring her to town?"

"No car." Adsila spread her hands. "Sorry."

She *had* said she was going to walk in to see Ian.

"How'd you get here?" I asked.

"My father dropped me off. He had to be in Atlanta for a conference. He'll pick me up on the way back. I figured I could either walk or hitch into Lake Bluff if I needed to." She smiled at Ian.

I couldn't fathom that a young girl would choose to spend any time in the mountains with an old woman and no cell phone, electricity, or Internet connection—although I had. Not that there'd been too many cell phones or Internet connections back then.

"Could you tell her I'll visit again late this afternoon?" I asked. "Make sure she doesn't wander off?"

"I'll do my best," Adsila said.

Ian and I headed for the car. I reached my side first and glanced over to find Adsila staring at Ian's backside. She met my eyes, smirked, then shrugged before disappearing into the house.

Ian opened his door, noticed the direction of my gaze, and paused. "What's the matter?"

"Besides her hitting on you two seconds after we met, she was ogling your ass just now."

He looked at the cabin, then back at me. "I'm a little old for her."

"Ten years? That's nothing."

As he leaned on the top of the truck, his biceps flexed against the sleeves of his black T-shirt, and I did a little ogling of my own. He was so damn pretty.

"I have no interest in anyone but you."

I dragged my gaze from his muscles to his face. He was serious.

"When this is done, if we're both still standing, we're going to have a long, long talk about the future," he said.

With that he got into the vehicle, and I was left to

ponder his words and fight a growing fear. Because he'd said "if" and reminded me that one or both of us could die.

I wasn't afraid of dying, even before the wolf that could be my great-grandmother had come trotting through my life, solidifying my belief in the great beyond. But Ian's words revealed a new wrinkle.

I was downright terrified that he might.

33

I KEPT THAT fear to myself. Ian couldn't stop searching for the Raven Mocker any more than I could.

Driving around the last curve before we reached Lake Bluff, I cast an absent glance toward the trailer park nestled in the shade of a hill. Then I hit the brakes so hard, we skidded on the gravel as I turned into the drive.

"Grace, what the—?" Ian stopped when he saw what I had.

A squad car parked next to a dingy, tiny trailer, a crowd gathering. Cal earnestly speaking to several of the people.

"You think . . . ?" I asked.

"Let's find out."

Together we got out of the truck.

"Who saw her last?" Cal asked as we approached.

"She went to town to see—" The man, whom I identified as Jarvis Trillion, a regular at both the Watering Hole and my jail after he'd been at the Watering Hole, suddenly looked up and pointed. "Him. She went to see that newfangled, fairy doctor."

"Fairy?" Ian murmured, both confused and a little pissed.

"Well, you do wear a feather in your hair," I said. "In certain circles, like this one, you're just asking for it."

Ian's hand lifted, brushing the eagle feather, and Jarvis sneered, "What'd you do with Katrine, asswipe?"

Cal cleared his throat. "No need for that, Jarvis."

Jarvis scowled and muttered, but he knew better than to screw with Cal. Cal ate guys like him for a midnight snack. Or was that Chuck Norris?

I motioned for my deputy to join us away from the others. "Why didn't you call me?" I asked.

"You told me to handle things. That you'd be working with Doc." He scowled at Ian, who stared back non-committally.

"I didn't mean that you shouldn't call me if another dead body showed up."

"Dead?" Cal returned his gaze to me. "Who's dead?"

"Katrine?"

"Where'd you get that?"

"You're here."

"And that leads you to think she's dead? Sheesh, Grace, talk about ghoulish."

"Well, we have had a bit of a problem with dead citizens lately."

He tilted his head. "I guess you're right."

"So?"

"Katrine's missing. Didn't show up to open the Watering Hole this morning, and the regulars got antsy. Came out to roust her." He lifted one shoulder, then lowered it. "She had the only set of keys. When she wasn't here, they called me."

"You checked her trailer?"

"No sign of her. Nothing knocked over. No blood. No note. Her suitcase is in the closet, and so are her clothes, but her car's gone." His gaze switched to Ian and cooled. "Jarvis said she went to see you."

"He was with me, Cal. You know that."

"I know he was there this morning. I don't know anything about last night. He could have killed her, dumped the body, then come to you for an alibi."

"He didn't."

"You got proof of that?"

"He had dinner with me and Claire and Mal. You want to, you can call the mayor for verification."

"And after dinner?"

"I checked into Fosters'. Jordan will confirm that, and he's been with me every minute since."

"That just figgers." Jarvis had crept close enough to hear the end of our conversation. "Two Injuns *stickin'* together."

He made an obscene hand gesture by circling his thumb and forefinger, then pushing his other forefinger through the hole several times fast.

"Is this guy for real?" Ian asked.

Jarvis had been at the head of Dad's list of potential cross burners, though Dad had never been able to prove it. My arresting the man for drunk and disorderly five times a month had not endeared me to him, either.

"Oh yeah," I said. "He's a real Indian lover."

"Bitch," he spit.

Ian's fist caught Jarvis on the jaw. He went down hard. The crowd began to murmur and shift. I recognized quite a few other cross-burning types in the mix. This could get ugly fast.

"Cal," I said.

"I know." He moved in front of me. "Everyone just settle." He rested his hand on his gun and the murmurs faded. I could have done the same, but with these guys that would have only made them crazier. They'd barely been able to tolerate an Indian sheriff; now that the Indian was also a woman, I had all I could do to keep them from foaming at the mouth every time they saw me.

I turned to Jarvis, who shook his head as if he'd been dunked a few times under the water.

I shot Ian an exasperated look. "That was unnecessary."

"No, it was definitely necessary."

"I'm gonna sue your ass!" Jarvis yelled. "I'm gonna kick it, too." He tried to get up but fell on *his* ass with a thud.

Ian moved so fast I didn't have a chance to stop him. Cal tensed, ready to grab him if he needed to. But all Ian did was lean over Jarvis and whisper.

The other man went pale, staring at Ian, transfixed. Then Jarvis slapped his hands over his face and screamed, "His eyes! His eyes!"

Ian straightened and strolled back to us so calm, I half-expected him to start whistling.

"What did you do?" I asked, but I knew, even before he winked.

The crowd murmured some more, this time staring at Jarvis as if he were crazy. Cal did, too. "You been drinking already, Jarvis? You'd better get on to bed."

Cal motioned to two of Jarvis's cronies, and they hauled him away.

"Move along," Cal told the others. "We'll handle things."

Though they mumbled and grumbled, the crowd dispersed, some to the trailers parked in a zigzagging row that disappeared into the trees, others to their pickup trucks. Maybe I should sell mine.

Cal returned. "You say you were with him every minute. You didn't sleep all night?"

"Of course I did. But Jordan was at the desk. I'm sure she would have seen Ian leave."

"There's a back door."

I tightened my lips. Even though Cal was handy in a crisis, right now he was getting on my nerves. "I saw Katrine hanging around outside Ian's clinic last night. We drove past and straight to the Fosters'. She could have gone anywhere. She's probably holed up with—" I stopped.

She could be with anyone, but it didn't seem like a good idea to say so until we knew what had happened. This could end badly, and I didn't want to have spoken ill of the dead.

But I doubted Katrine was a victim of the Raven Mocker. The witch tended to go after people in their own beds, although that didn't mean it had to. Still, if Katrine were dead by Cherokee witch, this would be the first time we had no body and the first time, as far as we knew, that the Raven Mocker had killed so many times in one night. The violence was escalating.

"Start searching for her," I said. "I'm sure she'll turn up."

I only hoped she turned up alive.

"I gave Katrine a buzzard feather, too," Ian said as we drove away.

"When?"

"When I gave her the jar of vitamin solution. I've

been giving a feather to every person who comes into the clinic." He shrugged. "Figured it couldn't hurt."

"It didn't help, either. Where do you think she is?"

"Like you said, she could be anywhere. But for her to have been a victim of the Raven Mocker breaks the pattern again."

He'd noticed that, too. It was so nice to work with someone I didn't have to explain my every thought to. Cal was so literal sometimes he made me want to bang my head against a wall.

"Not that the pattern can't be broken," Ian continued. "We've already seen that. I just wonder why."

Considering the first suspect in Katrine's disappearance had been Ian, I had an idea. If I hadn't been with him, *I'd* have wondered if he were responsible. Which might just be what the Raven Mocker was after. Divide and conquer. Get the man who knew the score and was trying to find a way to even it thrown into jail, and leave the woman who didn't know much alone and floundering.

However, if the Raven Mocker realized we were on to him-her-it, why hadn't the creature just ripped our hearts out of our chests? It would be easier.

My phone rang. I glanced at the caller ID. *Claire.*

"Any news?" she asked.

"You know there was another death?"

"Yes. Same as the others?"

"I assume so, though I haven't heard from Doc yet."

She sighed. "Why is it that since you and I took over, weird stuff keeps happening?"

"Yeah, why is that?"

"You think that weird stuff happened before, but our dads were better at keeping it quiet?"

"Doubtful. More likely our dads figured out a logical solution and rationalized away all the scary stuff."

"I doubt rationalizing did any good. Someone would have had to kill something."

"Maybe last summer wasn't the first time Edward came to town."

"Hadn't thought of that." Claire paused. "Listen, can you come over here?"

"I'm a little busy with a shape-shifting witch and its epidemic of death."

"It'll only take a minute; there are a few things we have to discuss about festival security. Life does go on, Grace. We're going to have hundreds of visitors pouring into Lake Bluff real soon."

We had to have this situation cleared up before then. Last year's Full Moon Festival had brought the town back from the brink of financial ruin. But this year's could destroy us if tourists began to turn up without their hearts.

"Where are you?" I asked.

"The basement of town hall."

"I hate it down there." The place was downright eerie.

"Girl."

"Oh, that always works."

She went silent, remembering the times my dad had used the same insult, which really shouldn't have been an insult.

"Sorry."

"Forget it." I glanced at Ian. "I'll need to bring someone along." I wasn't letting him out of my sight.

"You two are attached at the hip, huh?"

"Pretty much."

"Good. I like him." She hung up.

I found it interesting that Claire liked Ian. She wasn't a man hater, but she wasn't much of a fan, either. She'd had some trouble in the past, and only Malachi had been able to reach through the wall she'd erected between herself and the world. Maybe having a son had helped. It was hard to condemn all males when you had such an adorable specimen at hand.

"I should go to my place and translate the rest of your great-grandmother's papers," Ian said. "We need to know everything she did."

"Fine." I picked up my phone. "I'll tell Claire I can't make it."

"You don't have to. You do your thing; I'll do mine. We'll meet later."

"I don't think that's a good idea."

"It's daytime." He put his hand on my thigh. "The Raven Mocker can't hurt you in the sun."

"I wasn't worried about me."

His eyebrows shot up. "Me?" He paused as if to think about that. "I've never had anyone worry about me before." His fingers tightened; then he slid them higher, stroking the inside of my leg until I shuddered. "I think I like it."

"I don't." He removed his hand, but I caught it and brought it back. "That I like. It's the worrying I don't."

His fingers continued to stroke. I drove down Center Street with his hand between my legs. No one could see, which only made what he was doing all the more exciting.

"You don't have to worry," he said. "As you've told me several times, I can take care of myself. Going after evil spirits is my job, and I'm pretty good at it."

"I don't like being separated. Two are stronger than one, remember?"

"We've got a lot to do and not much time to do it in. Separating in the daytime makes sense."

I parked in front of the clinic. "I know."

Ian got out of the truck, then leaned back in through the open window. "Come back as soon as you're done. Maybe I'll know something by then. We can start pounding sticks into the four corners of houses. Tell people they're squirrel repellents or something."

With a quick grin and then a wave, he disappeared inside. Seconds later he reappeared on the second floor, moving toward his office. My body still hummed from the touch of his. I exited the vehicle. This wouldn't take long.

He'd left the front door open, so I locked it behind me, checked the back door and locked it, too, then climbed the stairs. He turned, surprised, when I came in the room, but when he saw my face, he dropped the papers onto the desk and drew the shade over the window.

I unbuttoned and unzipped my uniform, tossed the bra, lost the gun belt, shoes, underwear, and socks. By the time I was done, so was he. From the appearance of his body, he was as aroused as I was; naked, we met in the center of the room.

Our lips crushed together. I wrapped my legs around his waist, and he walked forward until my back met the wall, then drove home.

I clung to him so my head didn't bang drywall. He was rough; I didn't mind. I'd been on the edge since his finger had first inched from my thigh to my clitoris as I drove through town. He'd been asking for this, begging for it without words, and now I was, too.

The slap of flesh against flesh was loud in the silent room. Our breath harsh, our movements harsher, I began to convulse, to clench around him. He plunged into me once and went still.

"Ian." I arched, pressing against him, and saw stars behind my closed eyelids.

"Grace," he answered. "Look at me."

I opened my eyes, and his were right there, that odd combination of brown, green, and gray. He stared at me with a curious expression, as if seeing me for the very first time.

"Ah, hell," he muttered, then pressed his forehead against mine and laughed.

"What's so funny?"

The shift from rough, intense passion to easy, gentle humor confused me. My body still hovered at the edge of orgasm, and I wanted to go there with him.

"I've gone and fallen in love with you." He rubbed his forehead back and forth, his hair sifting over my cheeks like a waterfall. "Didn't see that coming."

I shoved at his shoulder. "You what?"

He began to move, slowly, surely, softly—in and out as he rained kisses all over my face. My hands clenched on his shoulders, and I rested my head against the wall, limp, oblivious, forgotten.

He tensed, pulsing within me, and I began to pulse, too, the sensation seemingly so much deeper now than it had ever been before. As the tremors faded he gathered me close and whispered, "I'm sorry."

34

WHEN I CAME back to myself and heard what he'd said, I punched him in the shoulder. "What the hell's wrong with you? You don't make a girl come like that and then apologize."

I left out the part about him loving me. I wasn't sure what to say about that.

He kissed my hair and let me go, gathering my clothes and pressing them into my hands without meeting my eyes.

"Ian?" I grabbed his arm. "What is it?"

"They'll come after you now."

I snorted. "Let them try."

"They will. To get back at me. Just like they came after her."

"We've had this talk. I'm not Susan. Whatever comes after me is asking for a very thorough ass kicking. Maybe I should learn how to roundhouse kick."

"What?" His forehead creased. "Why?"

"Jack be nimble. Jack be quick. Jack still can't dodge Chuck Norris's roundhouse kick."

"Are you okay?"

I guess that had been kind of random. "Never mind."

I hadn't realized how those jokes had seeped into my head. Maybe I should make Jordan stop. Then again, I wasn't sure I wanted to start a day in the office without one. What fun would that be?

"What if they make you evil, too?" Ian drew his shirt over his head.

I picked up my shoes. "Then you'll kill me."

He dropped his pants. "No!"

"Yes." I picked them up and handed them to him. "I'll understand, and if the worst happens, I'll want you to."

He just shook his head, looking miserable.

"Let's make a promise. If I'm stupid enough to get infected with the evil virus, you kill me." I held out my hand; he stared at it in horror. "And I'll do the same for you."

His eyes lifted; I met them without flinching. "You would, wouldn't you?" he asked.

"If it comes to that."

Instead of shaking my hand, he pulled me into his arms. "Thank you."

"God, you're weird." My words were muffled against his chest. "Now let me go. I've gotta clean up and get to town hall."

He held on for a few more seconds, then kissed me—gentle and sweet. My stomach turned over.

Aw, hell. I loved him, too.

But now was not the time to tell him. He was already

wigged-out enough. Later, when we'd killed this thing, had a victory under our belts, then I'd let him know. Then we'd decide what, if anything, we'd do about it.

I went down the hall to the bathroom, where I washed up and got dressed, thinking all the while.

What *would* we do about it?

Could I spend my life with a man who was fighting things that existed merely to kill him and anyone else who got in their path? Eventually Ian's luck would run out. Could I go into a relationship knowing he'd leave me, just like everyone else I'd loved in my life had left?

I wanted a family, but I wanted the whole package— husband, kids, a real home. With Ian, I could never have those things in the way that I'd dreamed. But now that I loved him, would having them with anyone else be any closer to that dream?

I'd always wanted to find a man who stayed, but Ian wouldn't, couldn't.

"Hell," I said again.

Before I left, I went in search of Ian and found him at his desk, already engrossed in my great-grandmother's papers. I slid my arms around him and kissed his neck. Absently he patted my arm.

"I'll be back soon," I whispered.

"Mmm."

Why did I find his distraction cute? Whenever my father ignored me, patted me, murmured, or muttered, I'd wanted to lash out with words or kick him in the shin. As a child, I often had. Which might just explain why he'd always done his best to avoid me.

I stepped out of the clinic into the bright sun and heavy heat of a Georgia afternoon. Leaving my pickup where it was, I turned toward town hall and froze at the sight of the wolf on the sidewalk.

I couldn't see the cement through her body. The light summer wind ruffled the beast's fur. The thing appeared pretty corporeal to me. I started to worry that this one was actually a wolf when a pair of tourists walked right through it.

The wolf growled. The couple paused, looked down, frowned, and the woman shivered. "Goose walked over my grave," she said.

I knew what that was like.

They smiled and nodded in my direction but didn't mention seeing any wolf or hearing the disembodied growling. I waited until they were out of earshot before I asked, "What now?"

The wolf promptly turned north, ran a few paces, then stopped and looked back, tongue lolling.

"Trouble again?" I glanced at the clinic. "Ian is trouble? Or is trouble coming? Maybe from the north?"

The animal shimmered and disappeared.

"I hate messenger wolves," I muttered, scuffing my shoe against the cement. "They're too damn vague."

I continued north to town hall, entering the cavernous confines and heading directly to the basement.

When we were kids, Claire had always avoided this place. As I descended the dark, dank cement staircase, I understood why. Back then, the lower level had probably been full of cobwebs and mice.

Someone had cleaned up recently. The only cobwebs occupied a high corner near a ceiling full of old pipes. I listened for the scrambling of rodents, but all I heard was a distant humming.

This area had once been used for storage and maintenance items, but the old cardboard boxes and rusted filing cabinets had disappeared; the dirty brooms, buckets, and mops had all been replaced with shiny new ones.

The lighting was new, too. Fluorescent rectangles glowed above the twisting, turning corridors. I followed the hum toward an old storm cellar with access to the street, since town hall served as the tornado shelter for all of downtown Lake Bluff. There I found Claire in what appeared to be a second office. Desk, tables, telephone, fax.

"What's the deal?" I asked.

She stopped humming and spun around. "Hey. Joyce and I use this place to get work done when it's too nuts upstairs."

"First time the tornado siren goes off, your secret's going to be out."

Her smile faded. "Then we'll have to move." She glanced around. "Too bad, because all the electrical connections are here."

"Yeah, bummer," I said, anxious to get this done and return to Ian. "What was so important I had to come into Dracula's Dungeon?"

As soon as I said the words, I gave a mental cringe. What used to be a joke was now, in the light of Ian's information about his wife, too real to make fun of.

"I cleaned down here," Claire said. "Didn't you notice?"

"Yes. Lovely. Nice job. Get to the point."

"Sheesh, you certainly got up on the wrong side of the bed."

"Being woken up by my deputy with news of another murder usually does that."

"Sorry." Claire rubbed her forehead. "You're right. Let me put these away." She leaned over the table and gathered together the pictures lying there. "I was trying to identify some of these for the show."

Claire had decided to put together an exhibition of

old photographs Joyce had unearthed in the bowels of town hall. The display would open during the Full Moon Festival next month.

"There's one here of your great-grandmother." She pulled a sheet out of the stack. "She's really young. Probably younger than we are now." Claire shoved the photo across the table.

I'd never seen E-li-si like this. I'd been born long after her hair had grayed and her shoulders had stooped. In this grainy black-and-white image she stood tall, slim, and straight, her dark eyes full of mischief, her full, high cheekbones so much like mine, her lips curved as she smiled into the camera.

"That's her, right?" Claire asked.

"Yes." I touched my finger to Grandma's face.

Outside, the wolf began to howl, and I snatched my finger back. "Did you hear that?"

"What?" Claire met my eyes. "You okay?"

Why did everyone keep asking me that?

"Peachy," I answered, returning my gaze to Grandmother.

"I don't know who she's with." Claire tapped the photo. "Do you?"

My phone began to ring, and I held up one hand as I pulled it from my belt, then glanced at the caller ID. *Ian.*

"Hold on," I said to Claire.

The static was so bad I was surprised I'd even received the call down here. "Grace? Can you hear me?"

"Barely. What is it?"

"The sticks. I thought they were meant to keep a witch away."

Snap. Crackle. The sound seemed to explode in my brain.

"The word was 'spirits,' " he said. "Keep away spirits."

"What does that mean? Ghosts?"

Crrrrraack!

"Ian?"

He said something that I couldn't understand.

"Say again."

While I waited for the line to clear, I moved closer to the table, to Claire and the photo of my great-grandmother. My gaze went to the other person in the picture and I stilled.

I knew that face.

I picked up the print, turned it over, but I don't know what I expected to find on the opposite side. "Where'd you get this?"

"In one of the old cabinets with all the others."

"Is this a trick photo?"

"How do you mean?"

"A combination of one image and another."

"No. Why?"

I stared at the woman who stood slightly behind and partially obscured by my great-grandmother. However, I clearly saw her face.

It was Adsila.

But in this picture my great-grandmother was perhaps twenty-five. Adsila's grandmother was a baby. Adsila wouldn't be born yet for over half a century. So how could she be standing next to my great-grandmother in an antique photograph?

All sorts of things fluttered through my head along with the static still coming from the phone.

Time travel. Aliens. Ghosts.

Then, as I continued to look at Adsila's face, all the pieces came together. "Ian—"

"Hold on," he said at the same time. "There's some-one here."

Suddenly I could hear him quite clearly, his foot-steps on the bare floor, thumping down the steps, open-ing the door.

"Adsila. Hi."

Shit.

"Ian!" I shouted, and Claire jumped. The pile of pho-tos in her hand scattered across the floor.

"Too late, Gracie," a voice whispered over the phone.

I dropped everything and ran.

35

THROUGH THE CORRIDORS, up the stairs, out the front door, and into the light.

Down the street to the clinic, up to the second floor, through every room.

He was gone, as were my great-grandmother's papers. How had Adsila managed that so fast?

I glanced out the window and understood. Where my truck had been was a great big empty. I reached for my cell, but I'd dropped it in the basement, so I went to Ian's phone, but it was dead.

"Nice touch, Adsila." Or should I say "Quatie"?

Someone pounded up the steps and my hand went to my gun, but it was only Claire. She bent at the waist and tried to catch her breath. I snatched her cell phone out of her hand and dialed Cal. "I need everyone on the lookout for my pickup truck," I said the instant he answered.

"Stolen?"

"Yes."

"Any idea who?"

"A young Cherokee woman—five-five or -six, a hundred and twenty-five pounds, long black hair, brown eyes. Her name's Adsila. She'll be traveling with Ian."

Cal cursed. "I knew he couldn't be trusted."

"She kidnapped him."

"Oh."

"Yeah. Get moving."

I disconnected, then pocketed Claire's phone. "I need a car."

Without a word, she reached into her khaki slacks and handed me her keys. "Who's Adsila?"

"Quatie's great-great-granddaughter, or at least that's what she said. But I think she's Quatie, grown younger through the supernatural means of the Raven Mocker."

"And you figured this out how?"

"The picture. The woman next to Grandmother must be Quatie. They were the only full-blood Cherokee women in town then and now. But I met the person in the photo, and her name's Adsila." I started for the stairs and Claire followed. " 'Adsila' means 'blossom' in Cherokee."

"Makes sense," Claire said. "The blossom of youth. The sprout from which the flower grows. Clever."

"I'll be sure and tell her so right before I kill her."

Claire gave me an uneasy glance, but she didn't argue. "How did she grow younger?"

"The legend of the Raven Mocker says the witch steals the lives of the dying, appearing as a crone from the weight of all the years it's stolen. But our Raven Mocker began to kill young people, who had a lot of time left."

"She got younger because she stole more time."

"That's my theory." I remembered the odd flash I'd had when I'd first met Adsila, thinking that her body reminded me of Katrine's, then Katrine turned up missing. I had a bad feeling we were going to find her somewhere minus her cold, cold heart.

"Why did she kidnap Ian?" Claire asked as we exited the clinic and headed at a fast clip toward town hall and her car.

"We must have tipped her off that we were on to her when we went to talk to Quatie about the sticks."

"You went to talk to Quatie about sticks," Claire repeated. "What a fascinating life you lead."

"Crap." I stopped so fast Claire smacked into me from behind. Several passersby looked at me oddly and skirted around us. "We didn't suspect Quatie of being the Raven Mocker because she'd placed sharpened sticks at the four corners of her house, which we thought repelled witches. A spell," I explained at Claire's frown. "But on the phone just now, Ian said the sticks are meant to repel spirits."

"What was Quatie trying to keep away?"

"The messenger wolf." I snapped my fingers. "Which kept trying to tell me she was trouble, and I wasn't getting it."

"What's Quatie going to do with Ian?"

My eyes met Claire's. "I think she's going to kill him."

◯◯◯

It wasn't easy getting out of the parking lot without Claire. She'd insisted on going with me.

The only way to leave her behind was to say, "Oh, Malachi's here."

Then, when she turned, I jumped in her car—actually

her dad's old Ford Focus—locked the doors, and drove off. I'd rather have her mad at me than dead.

Claire's phone rang as I left the parking lot. The caller ID read: *Town Hall.* I ignored it. Claire would only yell at me, and I wasn't in the mood.

Though I doubted Quatie would be stupid enough to go back to her cabin, I checked the place anyway.

Empty, as I'd expected, with no evidence of two people living there, either. Sure there were two sets of clothing, but since Adsila couldn't fit into Quatie's things and vice versa, that was understandable.

But all the clothes, old woman's and sweet young thing's, hung in one closet. Despite there being two bedrooms, only one showed signs of use. There was a single coffee cup, cereal bowl, spoon in the sink, and there wasn't a suitcase, backpack, or overnight bag to be had. Maybe Quatie had taken it with her, but I doubted it.

I ransacked the drawers, the garbage, tore every book off every shelf and shook them out, upended knickknacks trying to find some clue to where she'd taken him, but there was nothing.

I stepped onto the porch and contemplated the sun falling down. I didn't have much time. She'd stolen Ian in the daylight, but she'd kill him in the dark. I knew it as surely as I knew I'd never get over him.

But why had she stolen him now? If she knew we were on to her, that we were working together to end her reign of death, why hadn't she killed us both instead of giving us time to figure out her true identity?

"Grandmother, where are you when I need you?" I whispered.

The wolf didn't come. The last time I'd seen her, the thing had disappeared. Had she gone away forever?

How could I bring her back? I needed Ian, in more ways than one.

I let my eyes wander the tree line, hoping the wolf would appear; then my gaze caught on the sharpened sticks still buried in the ground at the four corners of the cabin, and the light dawned. Even if she *could* hear me, she couldn't come to this place.

I ran down the steps and into the woods, calling for her, but still she didn't arrive. I was at a loss until I saw the glimmer of water nearby. I sprinted for it, losing my clothes as I went. By the time I reached the creek, I was naked, so I jumped right in.

Sun sparkled on the water. I sank in to my neck and recited the only chant I knew. "I stand beneath the moon and feel the power. I will possess the lightning and drink of the rain. The thunder is your song and mine."

Holding my breath, I waited. But nothing came.

I smacked the top of the water. The words said in English were worthless, but I didn't know them in Cherokee.

Frustration clawed at me. I began to jabber every Cherokee word I knew.

"Năkwĭsĭs. A ni sa ho ni. A ni tsi s kwa. A ni wo di."

Nothing.

Finally I closed my eyes and shouted, "E-li-si!" I repeated the word seven times, and when I opened my eyes, the wolf stood on the bank of the creek, proving once and for all that the messenger was my great-grandmother.

"Rule of seven," I murmured. I should have known. Every Cherokee ritual involved the sacred number seven.

I climbed out of the water and used my uniform top to dry myself, which left me looking like an entrant in a wet-blouse contest, but I didn't care.

Once dressed, I followed the wolf to the cabin. She wouldn't go near the house but stayed at the edge of the trees. Considering those sharpened sticks were supposed to shoot into the air and kill her if she came too close, that was understandable.

"Which way?" I asked.

The wolf stared north. I stepped in that direction, and she growled, then glanced toward the car. *Woof*.

"I need to drive?"

I didn't wait for an answer—which would only be *woof*—but climbed in and followed Grandmother down the drive to the highway.

Last summer, when we'd had our own wolf problem, I'd done some research. Wolves can run 40 miles per hour. They've been known to travel a hundred miles in a single day. They can chase a herd for five or six miles, then accelerate.

According to my speedometer, at 55 miles per hour Grandma was one fast wolf. Of course she wasn't a real wolf, but I was still impressed.

I hoped we didn't have far to go. The sun seemed to be falling faster than usual. I knew that wasn't true, but I was afraid. Afraid I'd find Ian, but too late. Afraid I'd never find him at all.

My hands clenched on the steering wheel as another thought occurred to me. What if I found him changed into something evil just like Susan had been? I didn't think he could become a Raven Mocker—didn't we need a Thunder Moon for that?—but if Quatie was a witch and she was becoming more and more powerful, who knows what she might be able to accomplish?

Would I be able to kill him as I'd promised? I didn't want to make that choice.

Ian had been forced to kill the body of the woman

he loved, even though he knew the spirit that inhabited it was no longer human. I was struck anew by his courage. Certainly he'd lived with the guilt, thrown himself into his job, probably taken chances that he shouldn't have ever since, but he'd done what had to be done and it had not been easy.

The sun went behind a cloud, throwing shadows across the road, and I panicked, pressing down on the accelerator, trying to get wherever we were going faster. My bumper would have sent the wolf sprawling, if she'd had a butt to bump. As it was, the metal just passed through her tail and she shot me a snarl over her shoulder, so I eased off the gas.

I had to find Ian before Quatie did her worst. If she ate his heart, would she gain his power, too? Considering what she'd gained so far, I had to think so.

Perhaps she'd stolen him more for his magic than his knowledge. To possess the heart of an A ni wo di, a paint clan sorcerer, would make her infinitely more dangerous. If she accomplished it, I had no doubt we were all doomed.

I came around a corner and suddenly knew where we were going.

"Blood Mountain," I whispered.

And the wolf disappeared.

36

THE PEAK OF Blood Mountain loomed over me. Though the sun still shone, the shadow thrown by the massive summit made me shiver. I knew without a doubt that this was where Quatie had brought Ian, even before I saw the flash of red in the trees.

I slammed on the brakes and swung around, unsurprised to find my truck abandoned a few yards down a dirt track. I got out of Claire's car, approaching my own cautiously, gun drawn, but no one was there.

I'd learned how to track at my father's heels. He'd been the best and now I was. Though the past few days of heat and sun had dried the rain from the last storm, I could still find traces of a trail headed upward.

Blood Mountain might not be the highest peak, but it wasn't low, either. Most estimates put the elevation at 4,458 feet. There was no water at the top; countless people had fallen prey to dehydration climbing this mountain.

I hadn't brought a canteen, but it didn't matter. The

sun was falling; I wouldn't reach the top before night-fall, which meant I'd be lucky to reach Ian before the witch killed him. Dehydration was going to be the least of my worries.

As much as I wanted to, I couldn't run. I had to be alert for signs that Ian and the witch were still on the trail or that they might have left it.

About halfway up, I found just that. A tiny scuff of a shoe at the edge of the dirt, then broken twigs and leaves and indentations in the softer ground beneath the canopy of trees. They were headed parallel to the ridge instead of up.

I tried to think about what I'd do when I found them. I had silver bullets in my gun, but I wasn't sure they'd be of any use. I should shoot Quatie in Adsila form—witches could die, couldn't they?—but I wasn't certain I'd be able to. As Adsila, or Quatie, she was a person. As Quatie, she was a person I loved. But if I waited for her to become the Raven Mocker, then she would be damn hard to kill, damn hard to see, too.

The heat made my already-damp shirt damper. Bugs flew into my eyes, stuck to my sweaty face, and all the time I was conscious of the sun tumbling down.

The shadows lengthened. In the distance, thunder rumbled. The scent of rain rode in on the breeze.

I caught sight of a roof ahead and approached cautiously, scooting from tree to tree, just in case Quatie was watching.

The tiny log cabin in the clearing had seen better days. The porch was mostly kindling. The roof had a hole so big I could see it from here, and the windows were nothing more than shards of glass.

I pulled my gun from its holster and hurried across the open space to the rear of the structure. I made it without an outcry or hail of bullets. Maybe they weren't even here.

Peeking into the window, I jerked quickly back. Someone lay on the bed.

Since the shadows of the unlit cabin had combined with the increasing darkness of the coming storm, I couldn't determine if the lump was Ian, Quatie, or someone else entirely.

I slid along the wall, checked the corner, then did the same down the side and the front, until I was at the door. Taking a deep breath, I gave it a shove and went in low.

Nothing moved. No one spoke. Was the body on the bed another corpse?

I inched forward, gun in position, then I tugged the thin blanket with my free hand.

"Ian!"

Someone had beaten the crap out of him. The same someone, I was sure, who'd tied him up. My hand clenched on the edge of the cover until my knuckles went white; then I felt for a pulse, letting out a long, relieved breath when I found one.

He was unconscious. From the amount of blood on his face, he had a head injury. I only hoped it wasn't a serious one.

"Ian," I tried again, got no response. I looked around for water to throw in his face or at least wet his lips. I was out of luck there, too.

As much as I'd like to, I couldn't carry him down the mountain. I checked Claire's cell phone. No service. I hadn't really expected any.

I patted his face, gently, because of the blood. I had no idea where it had come from—head, nose, cheeks, or chin. I didn't want him to awaken in pain.

My eyes burned with tears and before I knew what I meant to do, I leaned over and kissed his big fat lip.

Beneath mine, his mouth moved. I reared back, my own eyes widening when his opened.

"Grace?" His voice was thick, hoarse, confused.

"I'm here."

"How?"

"My father didn't leave me out in the mountains when I was four for nothing."

"He what?" Ian jerked upward, then moaned and fell back.

"Hey, relax. I just meant I know how to find my way around, how to follow someone. She didn't stand a chance."

"It's Adsila."

"I know. She's Quatie."

His face screwed up in confusion, then straightened out as he hissed in pain.

"Killing young, healthy people made her younger and healthier," I explained. "I saw a picture of Quatie when she was about my age. Spitting image of Adsila."

"Interesting."

"Yeah, great stuff," I said impatiently. "Where is she?"

"I don't know. She said she'd be back when the sun died and the thunder was born."

I glanced out the door. The shadows had lengthened, and the storm had begun to swirl old dead leaves across the stubbly grass. "Soon."

He nodded, then cursed.

"What did she do to you?"

"Tied me up and beat me bloody," he said, as if what had happened were nothing more than a normal day's activities. I had to wonder what his life had been like in Oklahoma.

"Why now?" I asked. "She knew I had Grandmother's papers."

"She also knew you couldn't read them until I showed up; then she lit your house on fire."

"How? She could barely walk."

"She could fly."

I recalled the blaze of sparks in the sky as I'd driven from Quatie's place to my own. I guess flying instead of limping, growing younger instead of dying, was some kind of rationalization for why Quatie had decided being evil was better than being herself.

"So she flew to my house and used the sparks flying out of her butt to flame my roof?"

"Or a match."

I guess it didn't really matter how she'd done it. "But the joke was on her because you'd already taken the papers."

"Then we foolishly let her know we still had them."

Whoops.

"Even though she didn't think I knew how to kill her," I said, "it would make sense, in an evil villain sort of way, to kill me, just in case."

"She was fond of you, at least until the Raven Mocker took over completely. The more lives she ate, the less Quatie she became."

"Then why didn't she tear out *your* heart before now?"

"She needed more power. I might not be strong enough to end her, but I had enough juice to keep her from ending me—until today anyway."

"Then why are you still alive?"

Realization spread over his battered face. "Dammit. I'm the bait, Grace. You've got to go. Now. Before she comes back."

"Like hell." I set to work picking at the knotted rope around his ankles.

"She read your great-grandmother's papers. She knows that the only way to kill her is for a sorcerer of greater power to see her in raven form."

"I thought it was great power, and it didn't work. You couldn't see her, even with your eagle eyes."

"The writing's faded. The word was 'greater,' not 'great.'"

"I don't see what that has to do with me."

"I couldn't see her because my power is from the eagle—a great war bird, but a bird just the same. I'm of equal power."

"Okay, still not getting how I can help."

"You're a panther, Grace. Much greater power than a raven."

"I'm not a panther."

"You could be. Remember what you told me about your great-grandmother and the bear? She could access the panther."

"Just because she could doesn't mean I can. I don't know anything about that, Ian."

"She left the spell in her papers. All you have to do is believe." I snorted. "And say the words."

"I have a better idea." The ropes fell away from his ankles. "Let's get the hell out of here."

I reached for the ties that bound his hands, and lightning flashed overhead so brightly I could still see it when I closed my eyes. The thunder that followed shook the mountain. When it faded, another sound drifted in on the wind.

The caw of a raven, the beat of supernatural wings.

"Forget the hands. You can run without them." I

yanked him to his feet, but when I headed for the door, he didn't follow. "Ian, let's go."

He was staring up at the hole in the roof, head tilted, listening. "It's too late, even if I'd planned to run," he lowered his gaze to mine, "which I didn't. I came to kill this witch, and I'm not leaving until she's dead."

"You came because she dragged you here and beat you bloody," I muttered. "And if we stay she's going to send us to the Darkening Land, then feast on the rest of my town."

"Not if you do what I say."

My heart pounded so loudly I couldn't hear the beat of approaching wings anymore, but I felt it. The Raven Mocker was riding in on the storm.

Nervously I kept picking at the knots holding Ian's hands together. "What do I do?"

"The spell's simple. Words and belief. I'll say the Cherokee; you repeat."

"I won't understand what I'm saying."

"Right." I gave an impatient tug on the rope, and it fell away. "Thanks. What we'll be saying is this: 'I feel the power of my past. I walk the path of my people. Give me the knowledge, the strength, the magic of the panther.' Got it?"

I nodded, then flinched as the horrible shrieking commenced from above.

"Repeat after me," he shouted.

He held my gaze as we said the words. I had a hard time concentrating as the wind swirled through the windows, the door, the roof, sweeping past my cheeks like the beat of invisible raven's wings.

The shrieking increased. I wanted to put my hands

over my ears. Then suddenly my chest began to ache as if someone, or something, had punched my solar plexus.

The witch was here.

"Do you see it?" Ian asked.

I shook my head, and the ache turned to sharp, shiny needles of pain. I fell to my knees; I could hear nothing but the thunder from the sky that pounded in my ears like the beat of my dying heart.

A thud drew my attention. Ian lay on his back, eyes wide, face contorted. He groped at his chest. Beneath his palms, beneath the tatters of his shirt, his skin rippled and pulsed as something fought to break free.

"No," I managed. "Take me."

Laughter swirled around the room—both human and birdlike—mocking my foolishness. The Raven Mocker was going to take us both.

My chest on fire, my head threatening to explode from lack of oxygen, I reached for Ian's hand. I was surprised when his squeezed mine.

"Say the words," he whispered. "Believe the magic."

I tilted my face to the night, felt the rain on my fiery skin. I shouted the words in Cherokee into the raging night. I knew what every single one of them meant.

A hum began in the air, electricity all around. Behind my closed eyelids I saw my great-grandmother. I remembered how she'd leaped onto a boulder, how she'd growled at that bear. I knew she'd had magic, and I wanted to be magic, too. I would do anything to keep the witch from hurting the one I loved.

Ian cried out in agony; a snarl came from my lips. Feral fury, the need to defend my mate, a prowling wildness erupted within, and I opened my eyes.

The Raven Mocker hovered in front of me—a huge bird with a wingspan that brushed the walls of the cabin, red glowing eyes in a black beaked face; its shriek shook the mountain. The creature looked nothing like Quatie, not that a resemblance would have stopped me from doing what I had to do.

"Die," I said in a voice that hovered between woman and beast.

Sparks blazed from the wings; lightning flashed above, seeming to spill a celestial glow in a column from the clouds to the earth; thunder rumbled, first loudly, then softer and softer until it blended in with the sound of the rain.

The Raven Mocker screamed one last time before crumpling to the ground, and the pain in my chest eased.

Ian struggled to sit up. I scooted closer, put my arm around him, and together we watched as the raven became Adsila, then her face took on the countenance of everyone she'd killed, ending with Katrine. I wondered if we'd ever find her body.

Last, she became Quatie again and I experienced a moment of sadness for the loss of the woman she'd once been; then she slowly turned to dust and blew away on the remnants of the storm.

"You did it," Ian said. I turned, and he brushed his fingertips along my cheekbones, his expression one of wonder. "You have the power of a panther."

I didn't feel any different, although when I glanced through the open door I could see a lot farther than normal in the total darkness of the mountain beneath a cloud-filled sky. I could hear tiny, furry things rustling in the bushes; I could smell them, too, and my stomach contracted in hunger. I had to fight the urge to run into that darkness and hunt those scrumptious creatures.

"How do I put myself back?" I asked, a little weirded out by the temptation to chase and to kill.

"Close your eyes and say, '*Ahnigi'a*.' "

"Which means?"

" 'Leave.' "

I did as he said, and when I opened my eyes again, I couldn't see past the threshold or hear much beyond the whirl of the wind.

"You were amazing," Ian said, and kissed me.

I clung. I'd nearly lost him. Hell, I'd nearly lost me. The remnants of what I'd done made me shaky, but I also felt stronger, better, more myself than I'd felt in my whole life.

"Ow." Ian's hand went to his damaged mouth.

"Sorry."

"*I* kissed *you*. I thought we were dead, Grace."

"You and me both."

"What changed? The first time you said the spell nothing happened."

I looked away, uncertain if I should tell him what I knew. That he was my soul mate, my future, my everything. I wasn't certain I could survive if he left me, too. Not after this.

"I remembered my great-grandmother, how she'd protected me, and—" I stopped, uncertain.

"You did the same."

I shrugged. "Yeah."

"You took care of not only yourself but me, too."

"That's my job."

"Was it?" he asked. "Just your job?"

I hesitated, still afraid to reveal my heart, afraid to have it broken again, this time for good. His job was dangerous; it was only a matter of time until something evil ended him. I wasn't sure I could survive that.

"We should get back." I refused to meet his eyes. "Claire's probably called the Marines by now."

Woof.

I glanced toward the door. Great. The messenger wolf was back.

"What is it?" Ian followed my gaze.

I wasn't sure. The witch was dead; what else did Grandmother have to tell me?

She threw back her head and howled, long, loud, lonely, and I understood her as clearly as if she'd spoken. Better to have some time with Ian than none at all. No matter what happened, at least we'd have love. We'd both nearly lost our lives tonight, and we needed to—

"Seize the day," I said.

"Excuse me?"

"I love you."

"I love you back. What brought that on?"

I glanced at the wolf, but she was gone. I must be headed down the right path.

I returned my gaze to Ian. "Hard to say."

He lifted a brow, but he didn't press for more of an answer than that.

"*Carpe diem,* huh?" Ian brushed loose hair out of my face and smiled. "Seize the day?" I nodded, and he ran his thumb over my lips. "How about we *carpe noctem,* too?"

I grabbed the tip of his thumb between my teeth, then suckled it until his brown eyes flickered topaz. "Would that be 'seize the night'?"

"Yes," he said, and began to unbutton my uniform. "Just be careful of the lip."

37

I WAS RIGHT about Claire calling the Marines.

Or at least one Marine—Cal—who'd brought every cop in town. Luckily, they weren't as good at tracking as I was, and by the time they'd found us, Ian and I were dressed and making our way down the mountain.

We'd gotten our story straight—a garbled tale of jealousy and obsession, starring Adsila. She'd wanted Ian; she'd taken him. I'd taken him back, and she'd taken off. Cal would be occupied trying to find her for days. By the time he realized she was nowhere to be found, there'd be something new to worry about.

Quatie's disappearance could be laid at Adsila's door as well. She'd wanted the land; she'd buried her great-great-grandmother in the forest somewhere. We'd never find Quatie, either. Only Ian and I—and Claire, Mal, and Doc—would know why.

Doc met us at the cars. "Everything all right?" he asked, eyes searching mine.

"Dandy," I said, and he nodded once in understanding. His gaze said he'd expect a complete report when we had time alone. I'd be happy to oblige.

"Claire wants you to come straight to her house," Cal said when Doc had patched Ian up the best he could.

Ian refused to go to the hospital. "I've got better cures at my clinic than any hospital could ever hope for."

Remembering my black eye and how quickly it had faded, I shrugged and drove him home.

"I'll just run to Claire's and fill her in," I said.

"Come back soon." He kissed me, gingerly because of the lip.

"Put some of that gunk on your mouth," I called as he went inside.

Claire ran onto the porch as soon as I pulled up. She didn't wait for me to reach her but flew down the steps and threw herself at me.

"Hey, people will say we're in love," I quipped as she hugged me so tightly I had to fight for breath.

Claire let me go. "Don't ever do that again."

"No problem," I agreed, though I knew if I had to do it over, I'd do exactly the same thing. If we had any other supernatural problems—and considering our track record, I had to think we might—I'd do whatever I had to do to keep the people I loved safe.

I followed Claire inside. The house was quiet; it was just the two of us.

She tossed me a beer; I drank half in one gulp. Then I filled her in on everything that had happened.

"You can make your eyes go panther?" she asked.

"Yeah. It was—" I'd been about to say *weird,* but I changed it to, "Pretty cool."

"Let me see."

"Now?"

"Why not?"

I shrugged. *Yeah, why not?*

I closed my eyes and chanted the spell in Cherokee, felt the power, the magic, the belief, flow through me, and when I opened my eyes again, Claire narrowed hers. "Don't tell Elise or Edward."

"Don't worry," I said, then murmured, "*Ahnigi'a,*" and felt the magic fade. "Elise would want to take me apart and see what made me . . . well, me. Edward would just want to shoot me."

"They're slightly predictable in their reactions to shape-shifters."

"I didn't shape-shift."

"But you might. Considering this was the first time you tried it . . ." She took a sip of her own beer. "There's no telling what you could do with a little practice."

I hadn't thought of that. I wasn't sure I wanted to, despite any childhood dreams to the contrary. There's a difference between seeing like a panther and actually being one.

We worked out our strategy for what we'd say to the people of Lake Bluff to explain all the autopsies and the exhumations. Doc had already laid the groundwork for the virus excuse. Now we'd claim *false alarm* and everyone could go back to their lives. If the medical examiner, the sheriff, and the mayor all agreed, and the news was good, I didn't think we'd have too many people pressing the issue.

I'd learned in my years as an elected official that most citizens didn't want to know the truth.

"We'd better call Elise," Claire said. "Tell her what happened so she can check the Raven Mocker off her list. You know how anal she is."

"You do it. Now that I've actually accessed my inner panther, I doubt she and I will ever get along."

"You weren't ever going to get along anyway," Claire said, and dialed.

I drank the rest of my beer as I waited for Claire to speak. When she didn't, I lowered the can. The expression on her face made me stand. "What is it?"

"No one's answering."

Someone always answered the *Jäger-Sucher* hotline. *Always*. Although the last time I'd called, the place had sounded frantic.

Claire hung up and tried again. She listened, shook her head, and disconnected. "I'll try tomorrow."

I suddenly felt antsy. I wanted to see Ian. Now.

"I'd better go." I set my empty can on the counter. Claire followed me to the door and hugged me again. I let her. Last summer when she'd nearly died by werewolf, it had taken me a while to get over it.

As I walked to the clinic, the sky cleared and a lopsided moon spilled silver across the rooftops. God, I loved this town.

The front door stood ajar. Shaking my head at Ian's absentmindedness, I slipped in. I followed his voice upstairs to his office where he stood at the window, talking on the phone.

He'd showered and now wore loose cotton pants and nothing else. His hair was wet; the eagle feather lay on the desk next to a jar of balm. Even from the doorway, I could see the bruises on his back and across his ribs. I got angry all over again.

"I think at one time Quatie read about the Raven Mocker in Rose Scott's papers." He paused. "No, she didn't say that, but it makes sense. She read the spell, and when her body began to break down she remembered and performed it."

For several seconds he listened to whoever was on the other end of the line.

"You're sure they're all missing?" Ian cursed. "Okay. Right. I'll be there in the morning." He hung up but didn't turn around. "You heard?"

I nodded, then realized he couldn't see and cleared my throat. "You're leaving me?"

He spun around. "No. Of course not."

"But—"

"Grace," he said softly. "Just because I have to leave doesn't mean I'm leaving you. Didn't you ever wonder why I opened a clinic in this town when I've never stayed more than the time it took me to kill something in any other?"

"Why?"

"I'm tired of wandering. I need a home."

"You're coming back?"

He crossed the room and pulled me against him. "Have so many people left that you don't know they sometimes come back?" I nodded. "I'll come back."

"Unless something kills you."

"I've been doing this for years. Not a scratch on me."

I stared pointedly at his beaten face. He shrugged. "Until tonight."

I walked to the desk, picked up the balm, and screwed off the top; then I spread it gently over his skin just as he'd once done for me.

His gaze remained on mine. "I'd never ask you to quit being a cop. It's part of who you are. But I wish you could—"

I stopped spreading the goo. "What?"

"Come with me."

I considered it. I'd be good at chasing monsters. I'd save more people helping Ian than I did protecting Lake Bluff from the tourists—although there'd been more than tourists here lately. Still—

"I can't."

He smiled and kissed the inside of my wrist. "I know. Lake Bluff is where you belong. It's where I belong now, too. Even if we hadn't found each other . . ." His voice trailed off, and he glanced out the window at the distant hills of blue. "I'd come back here just for them."

I linked my fingers with his. I hadn't known him long, but the bonds we shared—the mountains, our heritage, what we knew about the world that so few others did—gave us a history that went much deeper than mere days.

"When you say you want a home, does that include a family?"

"Don't they go together?"

"Not for everyone."

"For me and for you, too. The way you look at Noah, Grace—" He smiled, and everything I wanted was in his eyes. "I never thought I'd be able to love again. I couldn't take the chance that I'd get someone else killed. But tonight—you were unbelievable—your power, your strength, your courage. I know you'll be safe, and our children, too, because of who you are and what you can do."

Later, much later, when we were all wrapped up together on his bed, I thought to ask, "Who's missing?"

"The *Jäger-Suchers*."

I remembered Elise's phone ringing and ringing and felt a trickle of dread. "All of them?"

"Yes."

"That's impossible."

"So are werewolves, vampires, and witches."

"Very funny." Except I didn't feel at all like laughing.

Without the *Jäger-Suchers* to keep the call of the monsters down to a dull roar, the human race was in big trouble.

"What are you going to do?" I asked.

"Search for them, and take up the slack."

"You're going to be gone for a while."

He shifted so he could see my face. "Probably."

"Okay." I kissed him. "I'll be right here when you get back."

EPİLOGUE

F ROM THE *National Enquirer*

Werewolves Attack Small Town in Northern Maine

> *Under seige during a terrible blizzard, the residents of Harper's Landing watched their numbers dwindle as the number of werewolves increased.*
>
> *They were saved when an old man with a heavy German accent walked out of the storm carrying guns and silver ammunition. Within days, every werewolf was dead, and the old gentleman disappeared as mysteriously as he'd arrived.*

"Edward," I murmured. I knew he was too tough to die.

I read a lot of stories like those over the next few years. The *Jäger-Suchers* had gone into hiding, popping up here and there, usually in the annals of magazines and newspapers catering to the bizarre. Sometimes I recognized Edward's signature. Sometimes the stories mentioned a gorgeous blonde or a shaggy white wolf and I knew Elise was still alive, too. Other tales told of people I didn't know, but I could recognize the handiwork of a *Jäger-Sucher* anywhere. When there were a lot of ashes left behind, it was kind of obvious.

No one ever got close enough to them to find out just what in hell was going on, why they'd disappeared, how they'd managed to continue their work, but they did.

And because of the *Jäger-Suchers*, the human race not only survived; we thrived.

Read on for an excerpt from
Lori Handeland's upcoming book

ANY GIVEN DOOMSDAY

When I awoke from the coma, more had changed than the weather. I distinctly recalled going to Ruthie's house on a clear spring day. The door had been open—very un-Ruthie-like—as was the blood all over the walls.

Post coma—the windows of the hospital room revealed swirling snow. I experienced a moment of panic—thinking I'd lost nearly a year—then remembered where I lived.

In southern Wisconsin, April sunshine often brought May blizzards.

Something moved in the room, and I turned my head. A blinding flash of pain made me close my eyes, and what I saw when I did made me open them again.

"Whoa," I muttered. "That's new."

I'd always been psychic, but I'd never had a vision. If that's what the horrific scene I'd just flashed on had been.

No. Couldn't be. I'd seen monsters. Tooth and claw,

lots of blood and death—and I'd seen it at Ruthie's place.

Ruthie was an ancient black woman who ran a group home on the south side of Milwaukee amid an explosion of ranch houses built in the 1950s. Nice yards. Good schools. A lot of last names that ended in "ski."

Back in the old days, Ruthie had been the only African-American within thirty miles. She hadn't cared. Amazingly no one else had either. Ruthie was like that.

People who would have walked across the street to avoid a . . . well, let's not say the word, took to Ruthie like a long lost auntie.

Nowadays a few more colors had popped up amid the Caucasians, though the majority of the names still ended in "ski."

"Nightmare," I mumbled, my tongue dry and thick. Who knows what meds they'd been giving me? There was no such thing as monsters—unless you counted those who preyed on the weak and the innocent, which, of course, I did.

I tried to remember what had happened when I'd gone through that open door, seen the blood, and started screaming Ruthie's name, but couldn't, and trying only exhausted me so much I slipped back into the soft, dark place where safety beckoned.

Funny, I hadn't needed a safe place since before I'd come to Ruthie's.

Ruthie was a no-nonsense throwback to a time when parents ruled with love and an iron fist. Once Ruthie took you in, she never gave you up. She understood that part of the problem for throwaway kids was the being thrown away. She was the only mother I'd ever known—or at least the only one I allowed myself to remember.

When I awoke again, Laurel and Hardy had drawn two chairs up to my bedside.

Their names were really Hammond and Landsdown, but one was tall and thin, kind of dopey-looking, the other was shorter, fatter, even dopier. They were homicide detectives and about three thousand times smarter than they appeared.

I was used to cops. I'd been one once. What I wasn't used to was having them stare at me in a hospital room.

Usually they called; I came. Very discreetly of course. No cop in his right mind wanted the public or the media to find out he'd hired a psychic.

While on the force, my far-too-accurate hunches had made the other officers nervous. No one had wanted to work with me, and eventually I'd given up working. But I'd been good enough at finding things—mostly people, some of them even alive—that the police asked me to "advise" them a time or two. Word got around and voila—I had my own little business.

Psychic consultant. I preferred the term private detective. So much so that I got my license and hung up a sign.

Elizabeth Phoenix—Dick for Hire.

The sign didn't actually say that; I only wished that it did. Can you imagine the business I'd get just from the walk-ins?

"What do you want?" I reached for the bed controls to raise my head and shoulders. If there were anything seriously wrong with me, the doctors wouldn't have let these guys darken my door.

As soon as I was upright, my mind flashed on what had happened to put me here. Suddenly I remembered everything, or almost everything.

"Who in hell hit me?" I demanded.

Hammond's eyes widened. "Hit you? When?"

"I went to Ruthie's. The door was open and I—" My breath caught. The smell. The blood. The bone-chilling silence.

The significance of these two being homicide detectives reached me at last. So I wasn't firing on all cylinders; I blame the coma.

"She's dead, isn't she?"

"Yes," Landsdown said simply.

I wanted to cry, but I wasn't sure how. People like me have the crying beaten out of them pretty early.

They waited a respectable amount of time for me to shed a tear, and when I didn't, they moved on.

"What did you see?" Hammond asked.

I took a deep breath, closed my eyes, and experienced again the flashes of tooth and claw, the strange, nightmarish beings that couldn't be real. What had they been putting in my IV?

I shook my head, opened my eyes, and met Hammond's steady gaze. "Ruthie on the kitchen floor."

Lying in a puddle of sunshine and blood. She'd always loved the sun, really hated blood.

"I went to her," I continued. "Checked for a pulse."

Then her eyes had opened, and she'd grabbed me in a surprisingly strong grip for a dying old lady.

"Did she have one?" Landsdown pressed.

They seemed to follow the tag-team method of questioning—first one, then the other, no good cop–bad cop for these guys. They were almost interchangeable.

"Yes," I answered.

"Did she speak?" That was Hammond.

"She said, 'I knew you'd come.' "

"Why would she know that?"

I hesitated. Why had she? I'd gone there on a whim, beset with an irresistible urge to see her.

"I have no idea," I said, then frowned. "What about the kids?"

Ruthie's was always filled to capacity, which meant there were at least eight children living in that house along with her.

"They're fine," Landsdown assured me. "All at school. Didn't see a thing."

I let out the breath I was holding. "Good. Where are they now?"

"Back in the system."

I winced, but there wasn't anything I could do about it. Even if I were capable of mothering eight problem kids, the state would never let me.

"You think someone hit you?" Hammond asked.

"Someone did. Ruthie grabbed my hand, and then wham! Next thing I knew I woke up here."

The two of them exchanged glances.

"What?"

Landsdown nodded and Hammond spoke. "According to the doctor, there wasn't a mark on you. No head trauma. No gunshot or knife wound. No drugs in your system."

"But—" I lifted my hand to my head, trailing tubes and sensors. I didn't feel any bumps either. "How long have I been out?"

"Four days."

I glanced at the window where snow still swirled. I'd been right about the weather. Still springtime in Wisconsin. Gotta love it.

"Someone hit me," I insisted stubbornly.

"Maybe you fainted."

I glared at Landsdown. I did not faint at the sight of blood like a swooning maiden.

"If no one conked me on the head," I pointed out, "then why was I in a coma for four days?"

Hammond shrugged. "No one knows."

The two detectives shuffled their scuffed shoes and twitched their necks as if their ties were too tight. Considering that the offending pieces of clothing appeared to have been loosened hours ago, perhaps when they'd slept in those suits, I didn't need a psychic flash to understand they wanted to ask me something, and then again they didn't.

"We need a favor." Hammond actually tried to smile. He must need a favor bad.

"Mmm," I said noncommittally.

Without even a "do you mind?", Hammond tossed something at me, and I caught it. The instant I did, I murmured, "Jimmy."

"Jesus," Landsdown muttered. "How do you *do* that?"

I wish I knew. Because if I did, maybe I could quit doing it. Though my gift or my curse—depending on the day and my mood—was how I made a fairly decent living, *not* being psychic was a big goal in my life.

If wishing could have made the flashes of intuition disappear, they'd have been gone shortly after I was able to voice what I'd been seeing all my life. That was when everything pretty much went to hell.

"Where is he?" Landsdown demanded.

"What?" I shook the cobwebs from my mind, peered at the baseball cap gripped desperately in my fingers. The Yankees. I hated the Yankees. Doesn't everyone?

"Do you see where he is?" Hammond murmured.

My heart picked up in panic. These guys were homicide. However, if they wanted me to tell them where

Jimmy was, he couldn't be dead. Or at least I hoped not. I might have kicked him out of my bed a long, long time ago, but I'd had a much tougher time kicking Jimmy Sanducci out of my heart.

"No." I tossed the cap into Landsdown's ample lap. "What do you want with him?"

They exchanged glances again. The two of them were like an old married couple, which is what most long-time partners were. They squabbled, made up, shared jokes, and spoke without having to speak. My partner and I had never been that close. Even before he'd called me a freak and tried to have me fired.

"You know Sanducci?" Landsdown asked.

"You know damn well I do."

They might be annoying, but they were thorough. They knew about Jimmy and me—at least what was fit to print in the records of Social Services.

"When was the last time you saw him?"

I didn't bother to be nice. I rarely did—especially when the conversation involved Jimmy Sanducci.

"I believe it was right after I told him not to let the door hit him in his incredible ass on his way out of my life."

Hammond coughed, but his lips quivered as he tried not to laugh.

"You had a relationship with Mr. Sanducci?" Landsdown asked.

"No."

What Jimmy and I had once had could by no stretch of the imagination be called a relationship. Jimmy didn't know the meaning of the word. In truth, neither did I. I shouldn't be angry with him, but I was.

"Why are you looking for him?"

Hammond met my eyes. "Why do you think?"

For several beats I still didn't get it. When I did, I straightened so fast, Hammond stumbled back from the bed. Smart man.

"Jimmy wouldn't hurt anyone."

"He wasn't so particular about hurting people when he was a kid."

My eyes narrowed. Juvenile records were sealed. They couldn't know about Jimmy and—

I cut that thought off before it could drift through my mind and show on my face. But obviously not fast enough.

"You know Sanducci is capable of murder," Landsdown said triumphantly.

I did. But I wasn't going to tell them that.

"He'd never hurt Ruthie. Never."

Hammond shrugged. He didn't seem convinced.

"Why are you so sure he did it?"

"Smoking gun."

"Gun?" That definitely didn't sound like Jimmy.

"Figure of speech," Hammond said. "Knife."

I winced. *That* sounded more like Jimmy.

"He fled the scene."

"You're gonna need more than that."

"Fingerprints on the knife, hell, every old place."

"Too dumb for Sanducci."

Landsdown lifted a brow. "Why would a photographer be so savvy about evidence?"

Jimmy was a globe-trotting portrait wizard. Annie Leibovitz with a penis. An artiste of epic proportions. Everyone who was anyone wanted their picture taken by the great Sanducci.

"Any moron knows better than to touch everything," I said.

"Maybe he was pissed. Maybe he'd just found out Ruthie was going to leave you all that she had."

I frowned. "Ruthie doesn't have anything."

"According to the neighbors, they were shouting at each other. Then Ruthie's dead; Sanducci's running. Open and shut."

Not so much. Jimmy never yelled. Unless it was at me.

"So do you know where he is?" Landsdown pressed.

"Give her the hat again," Hammond ordered.

I held up my hand. "It doesn't work like that. You can't tell me what you want to know, then expect an answer. I'm not a crystal ball."

"What are you?"

Though Landsdown's voice was neutral, his face gave him away. He thought I was a freak of nature, if not a con artist.

"I've never been quite sure of that myself," I murmured. "I get flashes sometimes when I touch things, or people."

"But not always?" Hammond asked.

"No."

"And not now." Landsdown sighed. "Let's go."

I didn't bother to say good-bye, just listened to the door shut behind them. Then, seconds later, listened as another opened behind me.

"Why didn't you tell them?"

The voice came out of the darkness, flowing over me like a warm summer wind, making me remember things I'd spent years trying to forget.

"You knew I wouldn't, Jimmy. Otherwise you never would have come here."

Look for

"MOMMY FOR RENT"

By Lori Handeland

A novella in *Mothers of the Year*, an anthology
from Harlequin Superromance—April 2008